Don't Call Me
CUPCAKE

Center Point
Large Print

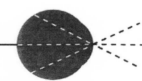

**This Large Print Book carries the
Seal of Approval of N.A.V.H.**

Don't Call Me CUPCAKE

The Holloway Girls

TARA SHEETS

Center Point Large Print
Thorndike, Maine

This Center Point Large Print edition
is published in the year 2018 by arrangement with
Kensington Publishing Corp.

The text of this Large Print edition is unabridged.
In other aspects, this book may vary
from the original edition.
Printed in the United States of America
on permanent paper.
Set in 16-point Times New Roman type.

ISBN: 978-1-68324-823-1

Library of Congress Cataloging-in-Publication Data

Names: Sheets, Tara, 1973- author.
Title: Don't call me cupcake / Tara Sheets.
Description: Large print edition. | Thorndike, Maine :
    Center Point Large Print, 2018.
Identifiers: LCCN 2018009823 | ISBN 9781683248231
    (hardcover : alk. paper)
Subjects: LCSH: Large type books. | GSAFD: Love stories
Classification: LCC PS3619.H45136 D66 2018 | DDC 813/.6—dc23
LC record available at https://lccn.loc.gov/2018009823

To my mother Rita,
who always encouraged me to
write fearlessly and to follow my heart.

Don't Call Me
CUPCAKE

Chapter One

The storm on Pine Cove Island was about to make history. Thunder rumbled in the distance and the sky darkened to a charcoal gray. Clouds loomed over the sleepy island town, casting shadows against the rocky shore. For Emma Holloway, this just wasn't acceptable.

She stood in her kitchen, eyeing a mixing bowl with the single-minded focus of an ER surgeon as she whipped lemon frosting into soft peaks.

A loud clap of thunder made her jump, and she quickly scooped out a dollop of frosting and tasted it. The sharp, clean zest of lemon burst on her tongue, but it needed more vanilla to balance it out. She checked the ancient cookbook. "Close. But not quite there yet."

Lightning flashed, making the old two-story Victorian house creak. A door slammed upstairs.

"I know, I know," she called out. "I'm working as fast as I can."

Another door slammed and Emma sighed. The house was chastising her. In the seven generations her family had lived on Pine Cove Island, the house had been a part of their lives, and just like the quirky, unusual Holloways, the house had a mind of its own. It wasn't always feisty. Most of the time, it was as warm and inviting as a cozy sweater. Doors would open for her when her arms were laden with grocery bags, and if there was a cold snap, the heater would go up a notch to chase away the winter chill.

No one in the family knew exactly how the house had become enchanted; they just accepted it as part of the Holloway family gifts. Emma shook her head and added a splash of vanilla to the frosting. *Gifts*. That's how her grandmother had lovingly explained it, but Emma could think of a few other names for the Holloway family abilities. If her mother hadn't had the "gift" of wanderlust, maybe she'd have stuck around to watch Emma grow up. Maybe Emma wouldn't be so alone, now that her grandmother was gone. She swallowed the lump in her throat and mixed faster.

Thunder struck again, and this time a hard, steady rain began pelting the windows. She spun the whisk one last time and quickly spread the frosting over the vanilla cupcakes on the counter. They smelled divine, like a warm summer day. *Perfect*.

She placed the tray of frosted cakes on the counter near the window. Heavy sheets of rain cast a dreamy quality to the gardens that lined the path to the old house. It was a typical Pacific Northwest spring morning, and any other time Emma would have already been working in her bakery down by the waterfront, but today, she couldn't leave the house defenseless.

"Okay, house. I think this will do it." She raised a cupcake to her lips and took a bite. Delicious. It was like sugared sunshine, and she smiled as the rain began to ease. Her body thrummed with warmth and she licked frosting from her fingertips, waiting.

The stairs creaked and the old house seemed to sigh. Emma sighed, too. With three holes in the attic roof, the last thing she needed was a torrential downpour. She had climbed up to the attic last week to try patching the leaks herself, but her magic skills in the bakery did not translate over to carpentry. What she really needed was decent weather until she could afford to hire a roofing contractor. With property taxes coming due soon, it was all she could do to come up with the money for either.

Emma watched out the kitchen window as the rain slowed to a steady drizzle, eventually settling into a soft mist. A few moments later, sunlight burst through the fog, and the clouds were swept away on a sudden breeze. The sky returned to a bright, clear blue and the trees swayed softly, their leaves sparkling with raindrops. Somewhere outside, a bird began to sing and Emma slapped powdered sugar off her hands. *Done and done.*

"There you have it," she told the old house. "We live another day."

The house settled in what sounded to Emma like a *hmph*. She knew her kitchen charm wouldn't last forever. A few days, at most. Mother Nature always had her way in the end, and it was never a good idea to use magic to mess with the weather. The next time the storm came around, it would be even worse. But she'd have to worry about that consequence later. At least now, she had bought some time to figure out how to get her roof patched.

Emma crossed her arms, hugging herself. By many standards the old house was falling apart, but she refused to think of it that way. Aside from her quirky cousin, the Holloway house was the only family she had left. Somehow, some way, she was going to protect and keep it.

Fairy Cakes was located near the wharf on Pine Cove Island's waterfront. Emma skirted a puddle on the sidewalk, balancing the box of lemon cupcakes as she nudged open the turquoise door to her shop. It was quiet inside, but that was to be expected for early spring. By summer it would be bustling with tourists from Seattle and British Columbia.

As always, the shop smelled heavenly. Today it smelled like toasted marshmallow buttercream frosting, and—*yes!*—freshly brewed coffee. "I brought a new batch," Emma called.

"Good, because you're going to need the extras." Her cousin Juliette stood up from behind the pastry case, licking frosting off her finger.

"I've already eaten like, three of them. Seriously, if I worked here every day, I wouldn't be able to fit through that door."

Emma rolled her eyes. Juliette was one year older than her, and at twenty-six, her cousin was utterly, stupendously gorgeous. She was curvy in all the right places, and had that milky, porcelain complexion Emma had always envied growing up. "Jules, you look like you just floated off the pages of a Victoria's Secret ad. The only thing missing is a pair of wings. You have nothing to worry about."

Her cousin grinned. "See, that's why I love you so much. You're so very smart." She gave Emma's shoulder an affectionate nudge and took the box of cupcakes, inhaling. "Mmm, lemony. What are they called?"

Emma took out a scalloped tray, placing it on the counter. "They're called 'Summer Sunshine.'"

"Ha! I knew it. I *so* knew this weather was your doing. I mean, this morning there was a storm rolling in, and the forecast for the week was rain, rain, and more rain. And now we've got blue skies and even a rainbow. What gives?"

Emma leaned against the sink and balled a dishrag in her hands. "There's another hole in the roof."

Juliette nodded solemnly. "A fine reason to do a little sweet charming, then. How's the house?"

13

"Grumpy." Emma grabbed a flouncy black-and-white apron, cinching it around her waist.

A gift from Juliette, the apron had rows of frothy lace and looked a bit too much like a French maid costume for Emma's taste. But with business so slow, she didn't have to worry about appearances. The only customers coming through the door were the town regulars, anyway. Everyone on Pine Cove Island knew one another. It was both a blessing and a curse. "I have to get someone to fix the roof, but I can't seem to find anyone who wants to work for cupcakes."

Juliette swung a colorful bag over her shoulder. "*I* work for cupcakes."

It was true. Her cousin practically did. Emma could barely afford to pay her for the few hours she took over the shop each week. Juliette was busy enough working at Romeo's florist shop, and selling her handmade bath products to local vendors. She didn't really need the extra work. It made Emma all the more grateful. "Seriously, Jules, I don't know what I'd do without you."

"Well, since we're the last two Holloways left, you'll never have to find out. You're stuck with me." She planted a kiss on Emma's cheek. "Hey, I'm going out dancing tonight with the girls from Dazzle. You should come."

Emma thought of their two friends who worked at the local hair salon. They were always ready to paint the town red. Or a glittery shade of hot pink. "No, I don't have the energy for that right now."

"Come on, Em, it's Friday. You've been stuck here too much and you need a break. You should come out." Juliette shimmied her hips and smiled mischievously. "Shake things up for a change."

"I don't want to shake things up. I don't need change." What she needed was a truckload of money, dumped directly into her dwindling bank account.

Juliette groaned, grabbing Emma by the shoulders and shaking her dramatically. "Everyone needs change! It's good for the soul."

"My soul is fine. It just needs to finish baking. Now get out of here." Emma laughed in spite of herself.

"All right, I'm off. Everyone in my garden will be in fine form today with all this sunshine. I can't miss it."

Emma waved good-bye and began stacking the cupcakes. By "everyone," she knew Juliette meant her garden plants. That was her cousin's gift. She could make roses grow in the middle of winter, and her garden was always brilliant, with a profusion of flowers that had even the best green thumbs shaking their heads in awe.

The dragonfly wind chimes tinkled over the front door as Emma placed the last cupcake on the tray. She glanced up, then froze.

A man stood just over the threshold, surveying

her tiny shop. He didn't see her at first, so she had several heartbeats to recover. He was striking: tall and broad shouldered, with sun-bronzed skin and dark hair. He wore a navy sweater over dark denim jeans, but despite the simplicity of his clothing, Emma could tell they were expensive. Cashmere maybe, and designer denim. Not the kind of relaxed, slightly outdated attire that most of the locals wore. A tourist, then. Figured. Someone like him didn't belong in her world.

He turned, his leaf green eyes sweeping over her. A dark brow rose for just a moment.

Emma suddenly remembered her French maid apron. *Crap.* Her cheeks grew hot and she cleared her throat, giving him a perfunctory nod. "Good morning." Totally professional. All business. She set the tray of cupcakes on a display stand.

He approached the pastry case slowly. "Those look amazing."

His voice was deep and smooth, reminding her of dark chocolate mixed with honey. Sweet, but with a subtle bite that made a person want to savor it on the tongue, so it would last longer. She shivered. *What the heck? Get your head in the game, Holloway.* Pretty boys like him were not a good idea. She had about a million past experiences to prove it.

He gestured to the cupcakes in the case. "What do you recommend?"

Ahh. Emma studied him for a moment. This was her favorite part of her talent—learning a little about what people needed. "Well, what do you usually like?"

He shrugged and gave her a crooked grin that sent a tiny ripple of warmth over her skin. "I like anything sweet, so I'm a pretty easy target in a place like this."

Emma felt her knees go weak. This guy was some serious kryptonite. *Focus, Holloway.* "Well, what brings you to the island?"

"How do you know I don't live here?"

It was laughable, really. As if he thought for one second that he blended in. She had lived on Pine Cove Island almost her entire life, and a man like this could never be a native. He looked like some business tycoon on holiday, or a marauding pirate from one of her romance novels. Someone who'd breeze in on a whim and then move on to his summer home in Spain or his high-rise penthouse in New York.

"Trust me, I'm good at reading people," she said. "Are you here on business or pleasure?"

"Business, as a matter of fact."

Emma noted the slight shadows under his eyes, and the way he stretched his neck as though to work out some stiffness there. For a moment he stared down at the pastry case as if he were a million miles away.

He seemed to catch himself, then glanced up.

"Big day today. Lots of negotiations to handle." His smile was suddenly so warm and genuine that Emma felt as if sunlight bloomed inside her chest. On impulse, she made a decision. "*Success is what you need, then.*"

"Sure," he laughed. "That would be great."

She lifted a pair of silver tongs and pulled out a chocolate cupcake with salted caramel frosting. "This one is called 'Sweet Success.' It will grant you luck in what you want most." She smiled brilliantly, wishing him all the luck in the world on his next marauding adventure.

Wide green eyes studied her for a moment. There was laughter in his gaze, but his expression remained all seriousness. "In that case, I'll take three."

Chapter Two

Emma watched the dark stranger leave her shop, his profile strong in the morning sunshine. Jeez, if ever there was a man who could embody all her secret fantasies, it was that guy. She dragged her gaze away as he walked down the street toward the waterfront. *So long, pirate king.*

"Well then," a chirpy voice called from the front door. Mrs. Mooney, owner of the curiosity shop next door, stood beaming on the threshold. "I've got a new shipment of Venus flytraps today. The kids love them, and I brought one for your front window."

Emma murmured her thanks. A Venus flytrap? Not her first choice for a cheerful window plant, but Mrs. Mooney seemed so pleased with herself. Her white hair was fashioned in its usual shellacked pouf, and her blue eyeliner was just a little too thick and a bit crooked. Emma suspected Mrs. Mooney's eyesight was going, but it certainly didn't stop her from seeing everything that happened on Pine Cove Island. If there was one person who knew the latest gossip and kept a sharp eye on everything, it was Moira Mooney.

The older woman bustled in, setting the small plant on a table near the window. "What have you got whipped up today? I could really use something for Bonbon. He's been chasing squirrels again, and I think he bruised his paw."

Emma arranged her features into what she hoped was a look of polite sympathy. Bonbon was Mrs. Mooney's ridiculously spoiled toy poodle.

Mrs. Mooney sidled up to the counter and stared down. "Well, there's the chocolate one, but that's poison for dogs."

"Mmm," Emma agreed. She had learned long ago that "mmm" was an all-purpose answer that seemed to appease Mrs. Mooney. There were only three other options for Bonbon in the case. "How about 'Summer Sunshine'? Would Bonbon like to feel warm and cozy?"

"He's plenty cozy in his new doggy sweater. What else have you got?"

"Well, here's 'Raspberry Kiss,' " Emma said. "But I don't imagine Bonbon needs a boost of confidence in the looks department."

Mrs. Mooney snorted. "My Bonbon is the most beautiful dog on the island, and he knows it."

Emma didn't doubt it. But she did have to wonder if Bonbon minded having his toenails painted fuchsia. "I think this would be just the thing." She reached in and pulled out a pale lilac–frosted cupcake. "This is 'Lavender Bliss.' It is intended to bring about peaceful moments and good feelings."

Mrs. Mooney nodded firmly. "That's perfect for my baby. Thank you, dear."

Emma couldn't help but feel a wave of gratitude for the older woman. Mrs. Mooney had been a friend of Emma's grandmother, and she never doubted Emma's gift. Her grandmother had been kind to Mrs. Mooney over the years, never missing a chance to remind Emma that true friends came in all different packages— sometimes even the nosy, quirky ones. Mrs. Mooney had always been a believer, which wasn't very common. There were only a few people on the island who truly believed in the Holloway magic. Almost everyone else, including tourists, treated Emma's cupcake charms as a whimsical marketing gimmick. Oh, they still bought her baked goods with a wink and a good-natured smile. But they felt the same way toward her cupcakes as they would about finding a four-leaf clover, or making a wish on dandelion fluff. Fairy Cakes baked goods were just like their namesake: make-believe. And if a person happened to feel good after eating a "Be Well" cupcake, they usually shook their heads and told themselves it would have happened anyway.

That was the odd thing about people. They were surrounded by magic all the time, but they just couldn't see it.

Mrs. Mooney leaned in, her voice vibrating with the gossip she was about to spill. "Have you heard the news? You know the old property on the waterfront?"

Emma knew it well. She could see its front door from her own shop window. It had once been a seafood restaurant, before it went out of business when the economy fell. Since then it had remained empty, and nobody had taken it because the rent was so high. "What about it?"

Mrs. Mooney lowered her voice to a fierce whisper. "It's been purchased! I saw the new owner just yesterday."

"Mmm." Emma wiped the counter and eyed the clock on the wall. If prattling on forever was an Olympic sport, Mrs. Mooney would win the gold. "Well, it's good to know we'll have another restaurant again."

"But no, that's what I'm trying to tell you." Mrs. Mooney fluttered her hands dramatically. "It's not nice at all, my dear. At least not for *you*. The new shop is going to be a fancy restaurant with French pastries and a bakery with cakes and everything."

Emma stopped wiping the counter and stared at the older woman, a sinking feeling taking root in the pit of her stomach. "What do you mean, cakes?" It was the last thing she expected to hear. In all the years she had lived on the island, restaurants and coffeehouses had come and gone, but Fairy Cakes had always been there. Her grandmother had owned it, then left it to Emma when she had shown her affinity for sweet charms.

Surely, the new place wouldn't overshadow her establishment. *Surely.* But a small knot of fear curled its way through her rib cage. Summer was coming, and she needed all the tourist trade she could get. Would the new place ruin her? She clenched her fingers on the edge of the counter as Mrs. Mooney chattered on about the handsome new shop owner, French pastries, and Bonbon.

If Emma didn't make enough money to pay the property taxes on her house, she could lose it, and she had lost so much already. The tight grief she kept locked away spiked through her, making her knees weak. First her grandmother dying, and then losing all her savings to her scheming ex-fiancé. She rubbed a hand over her eyes to chase away those awful memories. The house and shop was all Emma had left.

"Oh, and there he is now!" Mrs. Mooney burbled excitedly. "His name is Hunter Kane." She pointed out the window to the far end of the street. A tall, striking figure of a man stood in a navy sweater and dark denim jeans. He was staring at the vacant waterfront shop, eating a chocolate cupcake from a pink-and-white polka dot box.

No.

It couldn't be. And yet, as Emma watched the wind ruffle his glossy dark hair, she knew she had made a huge mistake.

Hot anger flooded through her and she took

a deep breath. He *knew*. He had to have known her business would be affected by his fancy new restaurant and bakery, and yet he never once mentioned who he was. She balled her hands into fists, barely hearing Mrs. Mooney's prattle. It was all too familiar, really. A handsome face, a casual attitude. And underneath it all, he was harboring secrets that would ruin her.

The nerve. The sheer nerve of a man like that was enough to make her want to kick something. Just because he looked like some movie-star god didn't mean he could just waltz into town, upsetting the lives of lowly mortals because it suited him. Emma hated men who lied, and the only thing she hated more than a lying man was a beautiful lying man.

Without another thought, she marched to the front of the shop and jerked open the door, leaving a bewildered Mrs. Mooney mid-sentence.

"Where are you going, dear?" Mrs. Mooney called.

"Watch the shop for me for just a second, will you?" She slammed the door behind her and narrowed her eyes at her target. "I have to go talk to a rat."

Chapter Three

Hunter Kane savored the last morsel of chocolate, wondering how he could have eaten all three cupcakes and still want more. Chocolate wasn't even really his favorite, but the way that woman in the shop had looked up at him with her smoky gray eyes, he probably would have eaten stale bread and moldy cheese with an idiot grin on his face.

He stared out at the ocean, wondering how he was going to survive in a place like this. After months of weighing choices, he had finally made the decision he couldn't put off any longer. Buying property on Pine Cove Island was the first step in his newest business plans. It was remote, and nothing like Seattle, which was exactly what he wanted to clear his head. But it was close enough to the city to visit while he was getting the business going, which was exactly what he needed.

Hunter let out a harsh breath as the all-too-familiar feeling washed over him. Regret. There were too many memories in Seattle, and most of them too exhausting to think about. He hunched his shoulders as a bracing wind blew in off the shore. He just had to stay focused. This new plan would be a fresh start. He'd throw himself into his work and do what he did best: build something new and watch it thrive. Things were going to get better. They had to.

"You." A woman's voice called behind him, and he turned to see the cupcake girl marching toward him. She was still wearing that black-and-white frilly apron. With her blond ringlets flying around her delicate face and flinty sparks in her gray eyes, Hunter felt like he was about to be attacked by a sexy Goldilocks.

He searched behind him as she approached, to make sure she wasn't talking to someone else. "Me?"

She stopped in front of him, a little out of breath from her march down the street. Her chest lifted and fell intriguingly over the white apron lace, but her rosebud mouth was pursed tightly and Hunter took a step back. He had seen that look on women before. Goldilocks was not happy.

"Yes, you," she said through gritted teeth. "You lied to me. You're not a tourist."

"Uh." Hunter glanced around for a moment. "I'm not?"

"No, you're not." She stepped in close, grabbing the pastry box out of his hand. She peered inside and glared up at him in accusation. "And of course. You had to go and eat all three of them, didn't you?"

He blinked. "But, I paid for them, remember?"

"That's not the point. You. Ate. Them."

"Yes," he said carefully. Maybe Goldilocks

liked to spike her morning porridge. "They were delicious?"

"Ugh." She stomped her foot and he tried not to smile. She was irritated, yes, but so damn adorable. Even if she was a little bit odd.

"You shouldn't have eaten them because you weren't being honest with me. You're not just a tourist passing through. You're the new owner of *that*." She pointed to the empty waterfront building that would soon be his café.

"Yes." He held out his hand and gave her his best smile. "I'm Hunter Kane."

She frowned back at him, ignoring his hand. "I know who you are. And you should have told me that before I gave you those cupcakes."

"Why?"

"Because I own Fairy Cakes, and now your business is going to take away all my customers." She looked so upset that Hunter felt a twinge of pity for her, even though she was being ridiculous. Competition was the name of the game in any industry, and restaurant ownership was no exception. "Look, I'm sorry you feel that way, but it's just business. And why would my eating your chocolate cupcakes be a problem anyway? It's not like I'm going to steal the recipe or something."

"Ha," she scoffed. "As if you ever could. My cupcakes are special, and everyone on this island knows it."

27

"Oh . . . kay." He still wasn't quite sure what she was getting at.

"And now you've gone and eaten them." She threw her hands up in the air.

Hunter frowned down at her. "Well, excuse me, ma'am. I thought that was the whole point of buying them."

She jammed her hands onto her hips. "First of all, I'm twenty-five years old. Don't call me 'ma'am.' Save it for old ladies with lapdogs."

"Fine, Cupcake." He shouldn't have said it. He knew it. But something about her righteous indignation made him want to tease her. She gasped, her eyes narrowing on him like an angry feline. He was so dead.

"You . . ." She shook her head, sending blond ringlets into her eyes. Hunter had the sudden urge to reach out and brush them away, but thought better of it. He had tried petting a feral cat once when he was a boy. Not a good idea.

"Don't call me 'Cupcake.' Ever. In fact, don't speak to me again. I would never have sold you my 'Sweet Success' cupcakes if I had known who you really were."

Hunter opened his mouth to reply, then shut it. The little beauty was nuts, plain and simple. He tried again. "Look, I'm sorry, okay? How about if I just wish you success, too? Then we're even."

"No." She was already backing away, folding the pink box in her hands. Were those tears in her eyes? "You don't get it. Guys like you never understand the important stuff."

Hunter watched her turn and charge back up the street, her frilly apron bouncing with each step. *Guys like him?*

What the hell had just happened? The last time he saw her in the shop, she had been all warmth and kindness. Her smile, with that intriguing dimple on one cheek, had almost made him feel . . . something. Different, maybe. Different than he'd felt in months, and that should have been a good thing, but it wasn't.

Hunter shook his head. It *definitely* wasn't. The last thing he needed was to get sidetracked by a pair of silver siren eyes.

Up the street, she yanked open the door to her shop with one withering glance back in his direction, then disappeared inside.

He turned back to his waterfront building, frowning. These island locals were crazy. If Pine Cove Island wasn't such a hot spot for tourists in the summer, he'd have looked somewhere else to expand his business. The people here seemed to have a few screws loose.

Just yesterday, some old man had stood outside his restaurant as the contractors hauled in the new dining furniture. He saluted them all, then proceeded to scatter an entire bag of breadcrumbs all over the dock near the front entrance. Seagulls had instantly swarmed the walkway and the contractors had had to wade through a bunch of squawking birds. "It's for good luck!" the old man had cackled.

Hunter scoffed at the memory as he walked into his building. The people were whacked, yes, but it didn't matter. His expansion project was going to be the best thing that ever happened to this town, and if he played his cards right, it would benefit him in a very lucrative way. The locals might balk at his plans, but again, it didn't matter. He'd drag them into this century whether they liked it or not.

Inside, the contractors were already laying the new carpet in the dining area, and the industrial kitchen appliances had just arrived the day before. Even with the dust created by the renovations, the place was immaculate. Hunter had made sure to hire the same crew that had worked on his other restaurants in Seattle. As a real estate investor in upscale properties, he insisted on having only the best contractors. They were meticulous in their work and didn't cut corners. It was costing him an arm and a leg to bring them over here, but the end result would be worth it.

The place was big, with floor-to-ceiling windows along the perimeter overlooking the ocean. Once the new light fixtures came, everything would begin falling into place. Hunter had spared no expense, working with his designer to choose the best colored glass sconces and hanging lamps from a renowned art gallery in Seattle. With the dark mahogany wood and warm-hued leather booths along the back, the place would be edgy, but comforting and inviting. The name they had chosen, Haven, suited the space perfectly.

The lead floor contractor looked up from where the men were installing the carpet and nodded in greeting. "Mr. Kane."

"It's looking good," Hunter called. "My designer said the light fixtures are on their way. They should be here today."

"We'll get moving on that as soon as they come in."

Hunter settled into a booth near the front reception area where he kept his laptop. It served as a makeshift desk/ office, but he'd have to find a better arrangement soon. After scanning e-mails, he sat back and rubbed his face. Of course, there had been no messages from his ex, Melinda. There hadn't been for a few months now, but he still expected it and always felt a flood of relief when there wasn't. After what she did, there really wasn't anything left to say.

Oh, she had sent a few e-mails when he broke things off. And every one of those messages had been textbook Melinda; straight to the point, no-nonsense, cynical. *You're being unreasonable, Hunter. You can't hold what I did against me. I thought we were on the same page. You've changed.*

31

Maybe he had changed, but she had played a big part in that. A sharp stab of anger twisted in his gut, then faded quickly. He wasn't mad at her anymore. Not really. He was mad at himself. They should have been more careful. He shouldn't have been so careless. He should have been better at articulating his feelings.

His phone rang and he shoved all thoughts of his ex-girlfriend aside. He had business to attend to, and nothing was going to sidetrack him this time. Least of all a woman.

Chapter Four

"I'm telling you, Jules, he's a liar and a shmuck." Emma grabbed another nail and continued hammering a crooked plank into the attic ceiling, pounding the hammer as she emphasized, "Total. Jerk."

She swiped sweat from her brow and scowled at the ridiculous patch job. They had been in the attic for the last half hour and she knew her handiwork was a total joke. But until she could afford to hire someone to do it right, it was better than nothing.

"He was casing my shop yesterday, acting like a passing tourist. God, I can't believe I sold him those cupcakes. I mean, I basically offered him glorious success. On a plate." She threw the hammer onto the attic floor, sending dust motes flying. "Jerk!"

"But a handsome one, you have to admit," Juliette said dreamily. She was perched on an old antique trunk, her impossibly long legs drawn up at the knees under a flowing white gypsy skirt. "I saw him talking to Mrs. Mooney yesterday down by the wharf. The way that old lady was leaning into him, you could tell he was charming her. He kept saying 'yes, ma'am' and 'no, ma'am.' All super polite. And Mrs. Mooney giggled!"

I'll just bet. Emma slapped dust off her faded blue jeans. "He's not that good-looking," she lied. "Besides, I don't care what he looks like, as long as he leaves. I have to get him out of here before the summer festival, or I won't ever make the money I need." After two days of pondering the problem, it was all Emma could come up with. "He needs to go, or I'm ruined."

Juliette raised her brows. "And how do you propose to do that?"

"I have to think of something." But what? If only her affinity for baking sweet charms could somehow force Hunter to leave. But Emma knew that wasn't her gift—negativity had no place in it. She could hope for temporary good weather for the house and it usually happened. She could wish to inspire sweet dreams, or confidence, or comfort in others. But her magic didn't work directly on herself, and wishing bad things didn't work. Her gift was one born from light, her grandmother had explained. Ill intentions did not factor in.

"We could lure raccoons into his kitchen," Juliette said with a gleam in her eye. "Ooh! I could sprinkle that itching powder I have on all his restaurant chairs."

Emma frowned. Juliette was always game for something on the darker side of mischievous, but Emma didn't want to do anything that would make other people ill. "No, it has to be just him.

If only there was a way to make him go away and never come back."

Juliette sighed. "He's like a garden pest."

" 'Pest' "—Emma began gathering up her tools—"is putting it lightly."

"No, I mean he's like those bugs that kept damaging my roses and vegetables. They were ruining my life. But then I doused the entire perimeter of my home, including the gardens, with that herbal spell I mixed up, remember? I did it on the full moon last July, and they've never been back since." She waved a hand as if swatting at a bug, and then suddenly her face lost all expression. She leapt off the trunk and stared at Emma with wide, eager eyes.

"What?" Emma watched her cousin with a twinge of alarm. That look on Juliette's face was never a good sign.

"We could do it, you know," Juliette whispered excitedly. "We could make a spell together. You and me."

Emma put her hands up. "No way, Jules. Remember the last time we tried to combine our gifts? It never works out. Been there, done that." She cringed, remembering their ninth-grade fiasco. They had tried to turn Juliette's hair red, because her high school crush had decided he loved redheads. Emma had mixed up red velvet cupcake batter for attraction, and Juliette had added blood-red rose petals with herbs from her garden for "drop-dead-gorgeous hair." For one week, Juliette's skin was lobster red and the hair on her eyebrows "dropped dead" and fell out.

Juliette scoffed. "Come on, Em, we were just kids back then. I have complete control over my garden now, you know that. My plants and herbs love me. People come from all around to get my garden potions, and they work. All of them work exactly as they're supposed to."

"It's too risky." The last thing Emma wanted was to deal with some magical disaster, especially when she had so many other things to worry about.

"No, it's not. We would be really, really careful. And besides, even if something goes wrong, he would deserve it anyway. Right? It's a win-win situation. Admit it."

Emma considered her cousin's proposal. Could it work? They were just trying to get Hunter to leave, nothing more. And even if it backfired, it would most likely backfire on him, so who cared? If his eyebrows fell out, or his skin turned a little red, then it would be an added bonus. She'd enjoy watching him squirm. Besides, it wasn't like anything truly bad could happen to him. The Holloway women's magic was too pure to cause any real harm.

Still, so much could go wrong. Anytime they tried to manipulate magic for selfish reasons, things went awry. It just wasn't done. Her grandmother had always warned them to be careful. Making sweet charms or garden spells to help people came as easily to Emma and Juliette as breathing. But really strong magic, the kind with ulterior motives that weren't for the direct benefit of others? That was something else entirely, and magic like that always demanded a price. The real question was, what would the price be?

"I don't know," Emma said.

Juliette began pacing, excited now with her new idea. "I could mix up the spell I used for the garden pests, and you could bake it into a special cupcake with ingredients to complement it. What would you use?"

Emma considered the recipes in the ancient cookbook she kept in the kitchen downstairs. "I don't know, something with coconut, maybe. Something to make him yearn for the tropics. He'd definitely have to get out of here if he wanted warm, tropical weather."

Juliette clapped her hands in excitement. "Oh, let's do it, Em. I've been dying to combine our gifts now that we've mastered them. It would be so much fun." "Fun" was a relative term. Juliette's idea of fun was often completely different from Emma's. But she had to admit it had its allure. The idea of Hunter Kane leaving town forever was more than appealing. It was necessary to her life.

"Maybe," Emma said. "Let me think about it."

"Well, don't think too long. Summer solstice is just around the corner, and that's when the spell will be most likely to work. Full moons don't just hang around, waiting for you to be ready, you know. If we're going to do it, we have to get moving."

No, Emma thought grimly. *He* had to get moving.

The following afternoon, Emma took a bite of her sandwich and watched snowy gulls swoop and dive over the waves. She leaned her elbows on the picnic table and sighed in contentment. Really, was there anything more delicious than an O'Malley's turkey and brie sandwich on toasted sourdough, enjoyed while sitting in her favorite lunch spot overlooking the water? No.

She kicked her shoes off and spread her toes in the soft spring grass. The midday sun was warm against her skin, but the breeze off the water tempered it to perfection. For exactly thirty minutes every day, she hung the OUT TO LUNCH sign on her front door and made her way to her secret spot. It was flanked by huge lilac bushes she had helped Juliette plant when they were little girls. Even at nine years old, her cousin's ability to make things grow was an amazing thing to behold. Emma still remembered helping Juliette dig holes for the lilac plants, giggling as

Juliette told the earthworms to move aside, then laughing when they actually did.

Over the years, it had become Emma's special retreat. A place for quiet reflection, where no problem seemed insurmountable. The picnic table was partly hidden from the main path and most people overlooked it, which made it the perfect hideaway. She took another bite and closed her eyes.

"I want that," a deep voice boomed.

Emma glanced up, mid-chew, to see Hunter Kane sauntering up the path toward her. Her perfect moment took an instant nosedive.

Hands on hips, expression fierce, Hunter looked even more like the marauding pirate than she remembered. There was a savage determination in his eyes she hadn't seen before, and he was staring straight at her . . . sandwich?

She looked down at it, then back at him as he approached.

"I want it," he repeated. "And you should know by now, I always get what I want." A muscle ticked in his jaw and his face seemed colder, the sharp angles more pronounced.

Emma swallowed fast and sat up straighter. This guy was a real piece of work. Who the hell did he think he was? First he weaseled his way into her shop, getting her to give him "Sweet Success," and now he demanded her lunch?

"No," she shot back. "Get your own."

He scowled and shook his head. It was as if her words didn't even register. Figured. A guy who looked and acted like him probably didn't understand the meaning of the word "no." His gaze shifted to just beyond her left ear. Oh, now he was pretending he didn't see her?

"That answer is unacceptable," he said.

Oh, re-hee-heally? Emma narrowed her eyes, then took a big, deliberate bite of her sandwich. She smiled evilly as she chewed. Two minutes ago, she wouldn't have thought it possible for her sandwich to taste any better, but now it did. Nothing like a little side of How's-It-Feel-To-Want, Mr. Kane? to add to the delicious medley of flavors.

"Dammit, Jerry," he barked. "I don't care what the locals are used to. I want my place done right."

Emma swallowed, finally noticing the Bluetooth earpiece he wore. He was now glaring into the bushes, completely engrossed in a conversation with someone else. So he was on the phone. He hadn't been talking to her at all.

She yanked the cap off her flavored water and drank. Stupid Bluetooth earpieces. She hated those things. It was always so embarrassing when someone was yapping away, smiling and laughing, and you smiled and answered, and then they looked at you like you were a big dork for thinking they were talking to you.

He was pacing now, back and forth over the grass. Clearly, she was too insignificant to acknowledge. The fact that he was intruding on her peaceful spot and blocking her lovely view of the ocean wasn't even a blip on his radar. In that moment, Hunter didn't even see her. For some reason, that bothered her even more.

"He better damn well do it," Hunter said, voice raised. "I want the Chihuly glass fixtures we specified. No. It doesn't have to fit in with the rest of the wharf's style." He pinched the bridge of his nose. "If you saw the way things looked out here, you wouldn't even ask me that. My place is going to look good, Jerry. I have standards. Tell him I'm not changing my mind about the glass. You can offer him a bonus if he delivers by the end of next week, but that's it."

There was a pause on the other end of the line, and then Hunter said, "Of course he'll jump. It's always about the money."

Emma shook her head in disgust. For big-city people like him, it was.

He bent down and picked up a stick, gripping it in his fist. "Nothing's set in stone. Everyone has a price."

He glared at the ground, the sky, the ocean. Whatever the person on the other end of his call was saying, he didn't like it. He paced over to the lilac bushes. "Then the designer is clueless, like everyone else on this rock. Are you sure he's

41

from the Seattle firm? Because he'd fit right in here."

Angry heat prickled up the back of Emma's neck. So, that's how he felt about Pine Cove Island. What a hypocrite. He believed the town and its people were beneath him, but he had no problem setting up shop so he could reap a steady income off it. Everything about him smacked of disrespect.

"Just tell him I'm not changing my mind. If he doesn't want to comply, then he's fired." Hunter gave the lilac bush a brutal swipe with the stick. A spray of purple petals and leaves scattered across the grass. He did it again.

"Hey!" Emma said angrily. "Stop that."

Hunter whipped his head around, startled. It was as though he noticed her for the first time. He turned back to the bushes, scowling. "Just get it done." He swiped at the lilacs one more time and ended the call.

Emma jerked up and marched over to him. She grabbed the stick from his hand. "You're ruining the flowers." *And my peaceful lunch. And my life.*

He gave her a look that told her she belonged in Camp Clueless with the rest of the island locals. "It's just a tree, lady. I think it'll survive."

Oh, he did *not* just call her "lady." That was almost worse than "ma'am." "You won't survive," she seethed, "if you don't get out of here."

"So it's threats, now?" he said in dry amusement. "Last time you almost took my head off for eating those cupcakes. Now what are you going to do? Pelt me to death with your sandwich for talking on the phone?"

It sounded like a great idea. Too bad she still wanted to eat it. "You're being disruptive and obnoxious," she said through clenched teeth. "And this is my lunch spot. You're intruding."

He stared around the tiny alcove and scoffed. "Oh, is this *your* spot? I must have missed the plaque with your name on it." He walked over to the picnic table and glanced down. "Nope, no engraved nameplate there."

He was pissed off from the phone call, and even though Emma knew his anger was misdirected at her, it didn't stop her from wanting to shank him with the stick.

"You know," he mused, "I kind of like this place. It's secluded, and there's even a table. Maybe I'll take my business calls here from now on."

She inhaled sharply. "Don't even think about it."

"Try and stop me, Cupcake." He strode off down the path without looking back.

Emma let her breath out in one angry *whoosh*. She tossed the stick to the ground. That was it. He was *so* going down. For the thousandth time in the past twenty-four hours, she tried to think of a way to fix the mess she was in. It was bad enough that his business was going to ruin her. The fact that he had just acted like a total jerk made her even more determined to get him *gone*. She hated everything he represented. Big-city callousness. Arrogance. No regard for Pine Cove Island's community.

She plunked herself back on the picnic bench and began wrapping up her lunch. Anger trumped hunger and she just didn't want it anymore. He'd insulted them all by calling them clueless, and he thought the waterfront businesses weren't good enough for his vision. Sure, the shops were a bit shabby around the edges, but that's because they had been around for decades. The waterfront provided a steady living for most of the merchants and their families, but it wasn't exactly the latest Disneyland attraction. The people did what they could each year to spruce things up for the summer crowd, and it had always been okay.

Now he stormed in, bringing his big-city pomp and circumstance with him. He ruined everything. Juliette's idea of combining their magic to make a "Go Away" cupcake was beginning to fit in with the reckless way Emma was feeling about him. She wasn't reckless, by nature. She had always followed the rules her grandmother taught her. In fact, her grandmother used to tease her about following all the recipes exactly, and not experimenting with her own personal style.

"It's okay to try new flavors, honey," her grandmother had said. "Every Holloway brings their own special gifts, and part of the joy in having kitchen magic is finding ways to tweak recipes and make them your own."

But Emma had preferred to stay true to each recipe, down to the last teaspoon. She didn't want to make mistakes. She needed everything to be "just so." Maybe it was because she had spent the first few years of her life flitting all over the world with her mother, before she was finally dumped on her grandmother's doorstep for good.

Emma sighed. If only her grandmother were here to help her now. That woman could charm even the surliest of customers, and she never met a problem she couldn't fix. Emma used to watch her grandmother change a recipe on a whim, altering it just a tiny bit to suit the person who needed it most. But Emma never did that. It was too risky. She liked organization and order. She liked knowing that everything had a place. And Hunter Kane had no place in her world. He needed to leave. Maybe combining magic with Juliette was the only answer.

Chapter Five

The next evening, Hunter made his way through the crowded chamber of commerce meeting hall, eyeing the long table of potluck dishes set out on festive red tablecloths. People actually cooked things for this? There were homemade pasta salads and mysterious casseroles sprinkled with . . . cornflakes. *God.* Platters of unevenly cut vegetables with dip. Plates of cookies, some singed around the edges from being left too long in the oven. It was an unorganized mishmash of food. No rhyme or reason to any of it.

The only notable dish was a three-tiered, china serving platter near the center of the table. Delicate pink cupcakes topped with edible flowers dusted in crystalized sugar were artfully arranged on each tier. They were exquisite, and nothing like the other dishes. Hunter had a pretty good idea who might have brought them. He casually scanned the room for the mysterious baker.

He couldn't remember the last time he had attended a potluck. As a finance investor and owner of upscale restaurant properties, parties like this just weren't common. Not now, and certainly not when he was a kid. His parents would have been insulted. They'd have called it gauche and blue-collar. Even after their divorce, they'd have still agreed on that. In his mother's opinion, if a party wasn't catered by the best, it wasn't worth having.

But laughter and music filled the air, and although Hunter generally shied away from large social parties, there was an easygoing warmth about the crowd that couldn't be denied. It was odd. Like everyone had known one another a long time. Like they were family. He had expected the chamber of commerce gathering to be more subdued and formal. Maybe he shouldn't have worn the suit.

"There you are, Mr. Kane," said a stocky man who had to be in his eighties. Sam Norton, the commerce committee chairman, had the jovial, ruddy complexion of a man who was no stranger to a strong glass of scotch. He had long since lost most of his hair, but his comb-over was still going strong. All fourteen strands of it.

Hunter held out his hand. "Mr. Norton."

"Call me Sam, everyone does." He gestured to Hunter's suit, grinning. "Look at you all gussied up. Here, we only dress like that if we're going to a wedding or a funeral. But you do look mighty dapper. I'd wager there'll be a wedding in your future soon, if the ladies here have any say in it." Sam hooted with laughter and took a swig of his drink.

Hunter nodded in resignation. Next time, he'd skip the suit. Maybe he'd burn it, just to be safe.

"Look here," Sam said, leaning closer. "I've been wanting to ask about your new restaurant and café. Any plans to serve steak dishes? Gary Sawyer's butcher shop is one street over from you and he has the best sirloin prices in town. You two should talk." He held his glass of bourbon up to Hunter in salute and winked, downing the rest of it.

An upbeat song came on over the large speakers set up at the far end of the hall, and several people laughed and grabbed partners to dance. Hunter glanced up at the entrance and Sam's words suddenly faded into the background.

Goldilocks stood near the door. She was in a lively conversation, laughing at something another woman said. Her golden ringlets hung loose tonight, and she wore a knockout black dress that stopped at her knees, hugging her in all the right places. And there were so many right places. Hunter swallowed hard. Damn, she was gorgeous. It was really too bad she had taken such a dislike to him. Not that he needed to be entangled with a woman, God only knew. But still, it was tough to be on the receiving end of someone that alluring when they only wanted to shoot daggers at you.

She had been so angry at him yesterday when

he intruded on her private lunch spot. Granted, he'd been barking orders at Jerry on the phone, but he'd been waiting on that Chihuly glass order for weeks, and he was so frustrated when Jerry said their designer wanted to change things at the last minute. Still, it wasn't an excuse to be rude to her. If he could go back and do it over, he would.

Sam nudged him with his empty glass. "I see you've noticed Ms. Holloway. As sweet as her cupcakes, that girl." He leaned forward and said with a hiccup, "The Holloways are special, you know."

"Are they?" Anyone could see by looking at her that she was special. It wasn't just that she was beautiful, although objectively speaking, no one could argue that. It was something else. She glowed with a warmth and vitality that made others around her fade in comparison.

"Yes, yes," Sam said, nodding. "They've always been special. Most people don't believe it." He tapped his temple with one gnarled finger. "But I know better. I knew her mother and grandmother. The Holloway women. They have *talents*."

Hunter glanced back at Emma. If rocking a little black dress was a talent, then she had it in spades.

"Magical talents." Sam hiccupped again. "You know, spells and the like."

Hunter stared at him in surprise. The man was

deeper in his cups than he realized. "I see." But he really didn't see. What was Sam getting at? Visions of the old shows *Bewitched* and *I Dream of Jeannie* floated through his mind. He could just imagine her in some sexy sixties getup, and his mouth kicked into a wicked grin. "Are you saying she's a witch?"

Sam pursed his lips and frowned into his empty cup. "Well, not exactly. At least not the kind who do bad things."

"What a shame." He could think of a few naughty things he might like to—

"Eh?"

Hunter cleared his throat. "What's her name?"

"Emma. Emma Holloway. She has a way with charms, that one. Her grandmother had kitchen magic, rest her soul, and Emma takes after her with the baking. All the Holloway women have some kind of gift. Just born that way."

Hunter's curiosity peaked. A family of beautiful, magical women sounded like something out of a storybook. Impossible. But if anyone could make you believe in fairy tales, it was Goldilocks over there. "Are there many of them?"

Sam looked surprised. "Well, no. Not anymore. Aside from her cousin, Juliette, Emma is all that's left. Her grandmother died a while ago and now Emma takes care of the Holloway house and runs the cupcake shop by herself."

Hunter blinked at the vision before him. She

was the incarnation of warmth and light, from her genuine smile to the way she touched people when she talked. He had never seen a woman who radiated that much kindness. It seemed wrong, somehow, that she would be so alone. No wonder she was so distraught about his new restaurant opening up. That shop was her legacy; all she had left.

He shifted uncomfortably as the upbeat tempo changed to a softer, slow song.

Sam grabbed him by the elbow. "Come, let me introduce you."

Before Hunter could respond, Sam hollered across the crowd, "Emma! There's someone I'd like you to meet."

She glanced up, her smile faltering. For a moment she looked as though she wanted to bolt, then thought better of it. Lifting her chin, she stood her ground as they approached.

"Emma Holloway, meet Hunter Kane," Sam said jovially.

She crossed her arms. "We've met."

"Wonderful." Sam seemed oblivious to the sudden tension in the air. "I'd wager the two of you have a lot to talk about. Hunter's building the new restaurant, you know. Say, have you tried one of her cupcakes yet?"

"I have," Hunter said carefully. He still remembered how angry she had been when she found out he actually ate them.

51

"Oh, splendid! Which one did you give him, Emma? It's very important, you understand." Sam nudged Hunter with his elbow. "Was it 'Sweet Dreams'?" He wiggled his eyebrows at Emma. "Or 'Raspberry Kiss'?"

A shadow passed across Emma's face. "I gave him 'Sweet Success.'" She looked suddenly tired and resigned. It was a terrible thing to see on such a vivacious face, and Hunter wanted to make it go away.

Sam let out a booming laugh and slapped him on the back. "You couldn't ask for a better welcome to Pine Cove Island than that. 'Sweet Success,' indeed. How perfect. Especially since you two will be sharing the contract for the summer festival kickoff."

Hunter watched the color drain from Emma's face as Sam mumbled something about refills and teetered off in search of another drink.

Emma felt like a fish that had just been yanked out of the water and tossed into a frying pan. Hunter eyed her with what seemed like genuine concern, except how could it be? He was single-handedly ruining her business, and her life.

She forced her voice to sound casual. "Did Sam just say we would be working the summer festival together?"

"Yes, Haven will have its grand opening on the day of the festival."

Haven. Even the name of his restaurant sounded egotistical.

"So they decided it would be good for publicity if I was part of the planning," he continued. "The board made a unanimous decision a few days ago. Didn't you get the letter in the mail?"

Emma thought of the small stack of unopened mail she had on her kitchen table. For the past couple of days she had been like an ostrich with its head in the sand. She wouldn't open anything that looked like a bill or an official document. She just needed a break from all the bad news.

"I must have missed it," she said as breezily as she could manage. God, how could it get any worse? She and Hunter, planning and coordinating a full day of catering for hundreds of people.

He shrugged. "They wanted to try something new this year. Said it would be a good idea to have us co-cater the event, since we have somewhat complementary venues. You could sell your cupcakes, and my place would offer French croissants and pastries, espresso, that sort of thing."

A dull ache began spiraling through Emma's head. She needed a glass of water. Make that one-hundred-proof whiskey. She didn't *want* to try something new. The summer festival was one of her largest money-making events of the year.

Sharing the contract with him meant sharing the profits. If she didn't make her sales quota, then she could just kiss her beloved home goodbye.

She suddenly wanted nothing more than to be home in her house, where she could wallow in misery alone. She pasted a grin on her face. There was no way in hell he was going to see her break down.

"Hey, do you want a drink or something?" he asked.

She nodded mechanically. Smile and pretend. "That would be great."

He turned away, weaving through the crowd toward the concessions table. When he was far enough, she whirled and bolted toward the door, not slowing down until she reached her car outside.

The misty night air cooled her overheated cheeks, and she pressed the heels of her hands to her eyes for just a brief moment. What was she going to do? Another obstacle in her path. Ever since Hunter Kane had come to town, her problems seemed increasingly insurmountable. And now this.

She pushed back her frustration and took a deep breath. No, it would be okay; she would figure something out. She had to. If only he would leave and take his fancy new place with him. Juliette's "Go Away" cupcake idea seemed more and more appealing by the second.

Emma rummaged through her purse for her keys.

"I don't think you'll find any drinks in there."

She spun around to see Hunter standing behind her. She hadn't even heard him approach. Typical. Rats were sneaky like that. "I changed my mind. Not thirsty."

"Look, Emma," he said softly. There was that voice again, all smooth melted chocolate and honey. "We seem to have gotten off on the wrong foot here. I don't want that, and I'm sorry I disrupted your lunch yesterday."

Yeah, right. He wasn't sorry. The only reason he was being nice now was because they were being forced to work together and he needed her.

He ran a hand through his hair. "I was dealing with a major issue at work and I wasn't at my best."

Excuses. Excuses.

"But that's no excuse."

Whatever.

He placed a hand on the roof of her car. "Why don't you meet me tomorrow around eleven and we can discuss the details about catering for the summer festival? It's only one month away and I could use your expertise. I hear you did it on your own last year."

So now he wanted her expertise, did he? Well he'd be ice skating in hell before that ever happened. "Yup," Emma said as she slid into her car, "I sure did."

Hunter stood back as she started the engine. "So, tomorrow then?"

"Sounds like a plan." *Your plan. Too bad I won't be a part of it.*

He gave her a slow, devastating smile and she forced herself to look away.

On the highway, she sucked in a deep breath and let it out slowly. The memory of his sexy smile still lingered in her mind. She yanked out her cell phone and dialed Juliette's number. He wouldn't be smiling for long.

"Hello?" Juliette's voice sounded muffled from sleep.

"Let's do it," Emma said in a rush.

"Um, whoever you are, I'm flattered, but I prefer men."

"Not funny," Emma said impatiently. "Come on, Jules, it's me."

"Oh, good," she said through a yawn. "Cuz that would've been an awkward conversation."

"Listen up. Summer solstice, you and I are combining our magic." She gripped the steering wheel tightly. "We're making that cupcake."

Juliette squealed in delight and Emma had to hold the phone away from her ear. She took a deep breath and lifted her chin.

Game on. Hunter Kane was leaving town, and never coming back.

Chapter Six

Hunter groaned and cracked open one eye. He blinked against the floral pillowcase wedged under his face. Where was he? Head pounding, tongue like sandpaper, he groped on the nightstand for water. The plastic bottle bounced off his fingertips and landed on the floor with a hollow *thunk*. Empty. He was in hell.

This had to be one of the worst hangovers he'd ever had. He dragged himself to a sitting position and flinched. The rented room was like a heavyweight punch to the face. Dusty florals and crocheted ruffles were splashed across every surface. The corner table held a vase of fake roses, and the only chair was covered in some kind of lace doily thing. It all needed to die. First chance he got, he was searching for a furnished rental house close to the waterfront. Preferably something not decorated by Norman Bates's mother.

For several minutes, he sat on the edge of the bed and waited for the room to stop spinning. How much did he drink last night? After Emma left the party, he had gone back inside to mingle with Sam Norton and several of Pine Cove Island's business owners. This meant drinks, small talk, and more drinks. By the time Mrs.

Mooney introduced him to a snarling little dog with pink painted toenails, his head was swimming in a lake of Jack Daniel's.

The phone rang and he slammed his hand over the receiver, fumbling for it. Anything to make it stop. "Yes."

"Good morning, Mr. Kane." The lobby receptionist's voice felt like cymbals crashing against his temples. "Ms. Andrews would like to see you in her office when you come down to the lobby."

"Who?" He didn't know any locals well enough for them to call. Not for the first time, he was reminded how cozy everyone on Pine Cove Island was with everyone else's business. The small-town lifestyle was nothing like he was used to. In Seattle, you could be truly anonymous if you wanted. And right now, he really wanted.

"It's Bethany Andrews," the cymbals crashed. "The owner."

Hunter remembered the woman from when he checked in to the B&B. Impressive cleavage, attractive, a little too eager to please.

"She says she wants to discuss island tours with you."

"Not at this hour." What the hell time was it, anyway?

A slight pause. "Ms. Andrews says she'll be available whenever you're ready."

He glanced at the clock on the nightstand and

swore under his breath. It was already ten and he was supposed to meet Emma Holloway at eleven. By nature he was an early riser. He never slept in this late. "Tell Ms. Andrews no, thank you."

He hung up and gripped his skull with both hands. An hour wasn't nearly enough time for this hangover to disappear. He was tempted to cancel, but he had to play his cards right with the locals. Emma wasn't happy about sharing the summer festival contract. If he backed off now, there was no telling how she'd react, and he needed her on his side. Small-town people were quirky and unpredictable, and he had to make a good impression. His future business plans depended on it.

Swallowing hard, he picked up the phone and endured the crashing cymbals one more time. After the receptionist had called Emma's shop to confirm their meeting, Hunter swallowed some Tylenol and dragged himself into the shower.

Forty-five minutes later, he stood in the B&B's shared kitchen downstairs, searching the cupboards for a water glass.

"Good morning, Mr. Kane," someone purred. He had heard that voice before when he checked in. It had to be Ms. Andrews-of-the-Impressive-Cleavage. No one spoke like that for real. Not unless they were on the other end of a questionable 1-900 number.

He turned and wished he hadn't. Bethany

Andrews, owner of the B&B, was wearing a leopard-print top in an unforgiving shade of fluorescent pink. It was so bright that it made the backs of his retinas burn. She had to be in her late twenties, but the spackled-on makeup and overdone hair made her appear older than she was.

"Ms. Andrews," he managed.

She waved a perfectly manicured hand and laughed as if they shared a private joke. "Please, call me Bethany."

Hunter didn't want to call her anything. What he wanted was to go back to bed and sleep for another fifty hours. Once he finished his meeting with Emma Holloway, he was planning to do just that. He filled a water glass and drank.

Bethany watched.

He kept drinking. When he was finished, he set the glass on the counter and asked, "Did you need something?"

She put a hand on her waist and ran it slowly down her hip. "Oh, I just wanted to touch base with you. See how you were liking the place."

"It's fine, thanks."

"That's good." She flicked a lock of hair off her shoulder and beamed up at him.

Even with a roaring hangover, Hunter recognized a lure when he saw one. Bethany Andrews was dangling a carrot right in front of his face. Just the thought of getting involved with someone like her made his head ache even more than it already did. He braced against the counter and leaned away.

"Well, let me know if you need anything." She stepped a little closer but didn't look him in the eye, just ran her hand lightly over the granite counter next to him. Stroking it. "Or if you want someone to show you around, I'd be happy to *do it*."

Hunter swallowed. Subtle as a billy club, this one. He considered what she was offering. She was attractive enough, and obviously willing, which had always been a perfect combination for him. But he knew from experience exactly what was at stake if he jumped into something with a person like her. It would be fast and furious, and maybe even fun. For a while. At one point not long ago, that type of relationship was fine with him. He had reveled in it. But it was always empty. And after everything that had happened this last year in Seattle, Hunter wanted something different. He didn't know exactly what, but it sure as hell wasn't this.

"I've got everything, thanks," he said.

"I'm sure you do." She flicked her eyes briefly to his groin, then back up to his face. "But I've lived here my whole life, so I'm a really good tour guide if you change your mind."

She turned to go and "accidentally" dropped a napkin off the counter. Slowly she bent at the waist to pick it up. The jeans strained over her curvy backside as she rose, smiling over her shoulder. "Think about it."

Hunter refilled the water glass, shaking his head. The woman had mastered her act. That sashay out of the kitchen was Hollywood gold, baby. But for the first time in as long as he could remember, he wasn't buying.

"Okay, he'll be here any minute." Juliette pushed a strand of hair away from Emma's face. The morning rush had finally died down and the shop was empty except for the two of them.

For the past ten minutes, Emma had felt like a prized cow going to slaughter. "Remind me again why I'm doing this." She was wearing a navy sundress and silver sandals. Juliette had insisted she wear her hair down, and Emma felt more like she was dressed for a date rather than a simple business meeting. Just the thought of going on a date with him made her heart do a slow somersault in her chest. She shoved the inexplicable feeling aside. No matter how good-looking he was, no matter how charming, she couldn't forget he was the enemy.

"We're doing this because you need to soften him up. He has to think you two are friends, or he's never going to go for it when you walk up to him on summer solstice with a mysterious cupcake and say, 'Hey, what's up? Eat this.' " Juliette whipped a huge blush brush out of her bag and began swiping it across Emma's cheeks. "Remember the last time you gave him cupcakes?"

"Like I could forget." *Total disaster.*

"You stomped after him and practically bit his head off. He's not going to trust you, Em, and you have to change that. Everything will go much easier in the next few weeks if you just act civil. No, better than civil. Friendly. *Flirty,* even. Besides, with the summer festival contract you now have to share, this will make it easier for you. You can keep an eye on him. You know, keep your enemies close, and all that." Juliette finished and stood back, eyeing Emma critically. "Needs pixie dust."

"Pixie what?"

Juliette took a pot of sparkly pink powder out of her makeup case with a flourish.

"Oh, absolutely not." Emma backed away. "I'm not going to a rave, here, Tinker Bell. It's just a business meeting. No glitter."

Juliette pouted. "It doesn't make you glitter. It imparts a soft, luminescent glow." She dusted some of the iridescent sparkles across her own cheeks. "See?"

With her glowing skin and lavender blouse, Juliette was as radiant as the dawn. Emma smiled. "You're beautiful, Jules."

Juliette spun Emma around to the mirror over the kitchen sink. "Look who's talking."

Emma stared at her reflection in mild surprise. Her usual messy curls were smooth and glossy this morning, and her eyes looked brighter and bigger, thanks to some magic Juliette had done with her eyeshadow brushes. "Not bad," Emma said slowly. "You think he'll believe my act?"

"I think," Juliette said as she tossed her things into her bag, "he'll be marshmallow fluff in your hands. Just remember, you have to be nice."

"Nice," Emma repeated.

"Yeah. And charming." Juliette lowered her voice as if she were imparting some secret wisdom of the ages. "Bat your eyes a lot. And laugh at his jokes. Make him feel all manly and stuff. Guys really go for that, no matter how sophisticated they think they are. Besides, it's only for a few weeks. How hard can it be?"

That was really the question. For the next few weeks, Emma had to feign friendship with the man whose very presence meant doom and gloom for her future. She glanced around her tiny cupcake shop, the shop her grandmother had left to her. It had a shabby chic vibe, with whitewashed tables and chairs, and soft floral tablecloths. It was as much a home to Emma as the beloved Holloway house with its weathered edges and dilapidated roof. She would do anything to keep them, even if it meant befriending the devil.

As if on cue, the front door opened and Hunter

stepped inside. He had a slightly rumpled appearance and a smile that was more of a grimace. With his bloodshot eyes, all he really needed were a pair of horns to finish off the look. But even disheveled, he was darkly, dangerously attractive. Emma sucked in a breath. *Hello, king of the underworld.*

Juliette poked her in the back and hissed, "You're on."

Emma smoothed her hair one last time. *Befriend the devil.* "Good morning."

"Morning." He clutched at his temple with one hand. "Sorry, I had a late night and I'm not feeling that well."

Juliette slung her bag over her shoulder. "Don't worry, Emma can fix you up. She's good with stuff like that. I'm Juliette, by the way. Her cousin."

Hunter murmured a greeting and they shook hands. Juliette sidled behind him toward the door, then fanned herself, mouthing, *So hot.*

Emma ignored her cousin and pasted a smile on her face. Some smiles showed happiness. Others just showed teeth. She'd work on it later. "Come on in and I'll get you some coffee."

Hunter winced as Juliette shut the door. He took the table closest to the coffee maker.

Emma studied him from beneath her lashes as she prepared the espresso machine. His features seemed sharper this morning, the hollows under his cheekbones more pronounced. He was much paler than usual, and his full lips were drawn tight. Even though he had managed to make their meeting on time, it was clear he felt terrible.

A knee-jerk wave of sympathy hit her, but she shut it down fast. This man was the enemy. He *should* feel terrible. He was going to ruin everything because she had been too stupid to see him for what he was. If only she hadn't given him those magic cupcakes. But he had seemed so charming and genuine, and she had wanted to help him.

She grit her teeth and banged the portafilter a little louder than was necessary. When would she ever learn? Her ex-fiancé, Rodney, had seemed charming and genuine, too. Emma had been devastated the day he stole all her savings and ran off with another woman. She forced back the painful memories and took a deep breath. Things were different now. She knew how to take care of herself, and whom to trust. No matter what happened, she was never going to be manipulated again. Making the "Go Away" cupcake on the summer solstice with Juliette was going to fix everything. She just needed to stay focused and stick to the plan.

Emma began making a double shot of espresso. "So what did you drink last night?"

Hunter rubbed the back of his neck. "Just punch, mostly."

"Not Mrs. Mooney's Hawaiian Punch Surprise?"

"Yeah, maybe."

Emma tried not to laugh. Served him right. "That stuff will knock anyone flat."

"What does she put in it?"

"You mean, what doesn't she?" Emma grabbed a small espresso cup from the shelf above the machine. "If Jack Daniel's and Jim Beam threw a frat party on the beach, and then Captain Morgan crashed it? That would be her punch. Just a big wild party full of Jell-O shots and Goldschläger confetti."

Hunter grimaced. "I wondered about those little sparkly things."

She handed him the espresso and pulled a fluffy white cupcake out of the case. The crisp scent of peppermint and ginger floated between them. She placed it in front of him, but he was already shaking his head.

"Have just one bite."

He held up a hand. "God, no. I'm not even sure I can handle coffee right now."

"I promise it will make you feel better."

"Look, I already took a swim in that fruit punch last night. The last thing I need right now is more sugar."

Emma pushed the china plate a couple of inches closer to him. "Just trust me." She batted her eyes. Juliette would be so proud.

He eyed her solemnly. "Maybe later."

Emma crossed her arms and fixed him with a hard stare. According to Juliette, the eye-batting thing was a slam dunk. He was a stubborn devil. "Look, if we're supposed to be working together for the next few weeks, then there's something you need to know about me. There are a lot of things I'm not good at. Organized sports, for one. Pretty much any sport. You're doomed if you've got me on your team. And don't ever ask me to give you a jump if your battery's dead because cars— actually most machines in general—are a complete mystery to me. I also can't hang a picture straight if my life depended on it, but I know what I'm doing when it comes to baking. If you're going to be a local here, you need to accept that. Now"— she picked up the cupcake and held it out—"just one bite." She batted her lashes a couple of times for good measure, then lifted her chin and brought out the big guns. "I *dare* you."

With obvious effort, he sat up straighter and squared his shoulders. She had him now. Didn't it just figure? A guy like him wouldn't take a challenge lying down. Too much pride.

His face was ashen, but Emma had to hand it to him. The devil was going for it. He pressed his mouth into a thin line and took the cupcake, stared her straight in the eye, and took a huge bite, chewing forcefully. She watched as his green eyes widened and he blinked, then swallowed. He took another bite. Chewed. Swallowed. Already his complexion seemed less gray.

Emma nodded. "See?"

Hunter stared at the cupcake in amazement. "What's in this?"

"I call it 'Be Well.' It's very popular on New Year's Day."

He lifted the espresso cup and took a sip. "Whatever you put in that thing, it's a miracle cure."

She shrugged and went to pour herself a cup of coffee. "It's just what I do."

"I like it." He leaned forward, bracing his elbows on the bistro table. Emma ignored the way his shirt strained across his broad, muscular shoulders.

He shot her a lazy smile.

She ignored that, too, taking the seat opposite him. He was so tall he dwarfed the little round table, and their knees knocked together for a moment. She scooted back. *Focus, Holloway!*

Sipping her coffee, she let the rich, earthy flavors ground her. "So, Mr. Kane—"

"Hunter."

She took another gulp of coffee. "What do you want to know about the summer festival preparations?"

"I understand you've been the head of the operation for the past several years."

"Three. My grandmother and I used to run

it together before she"—Emma swallowed—
"passed away. For the last year and a half, I've
been in charge."

"I'm sorry," he said.

Emma bristled. "I think I've managed just
fine."

"No." He shook his head.

How the hell would he know? "For your
information—"

"No, I meant I'm sorry about your grandmother.
That must have been hard."

"Oh." He seemed pretty sincere. Crud. "Thanks.
She was important to the community. Always
helping people." Emma cleared her throat and
added, "It was difficult." Understatement of the
century. But what else could she say? That losing
her grandmother had been like losing a piece of
her own heart? That the one person in the world
who truly knew her and loved her, faults and all,
had gone and left a gaping hole inside her that
she feared she'd never be able to fill?

The silence stretched out for too long. This was
getting weird. She needed to stick to business.
"So we basically have a list of festival vendors
that gets updated every January. Once we review
and approve the applicants, we help map out
where the booths are staged. We also do a routine
cleanup around the wharf area a couple weeks or
so before the festival. The town committee has
an annual budget they designate to fund it."

He listened intently, his arms crossed as he leaned back in the tiny bistro chair. Emma could almost imagine him at the head of a conference table in some high-rise office. He just looked comfortable in charge.

"What system do you use to keep track of vendor applicants?" he asked.

"We just keep files. It's usually the same vendors every year."

"But what program are you using to file the information? QuickBooks, I'd imagine."

Uh-oh. That would be a big fat nopey-nopesters. "We don't use QuickBooks."

"Something more manual then? Excel spread-sheets are fine. Just send me what you have so I can familiarize myself with the different vendors. It might be the easiest way for me to acclimate."

Emma thought of the stack of file boxes she kept in her office at home. At the moment, they served as a makeshift table for a vase of roses from Juliette's garden. The only "spreadsheet" was the tablecloth draped over them. "Um, why don't I just bring the files in sometime next week and you can take a look?"

He dismissed the idea with a wave of his hand. "E-mail would be much easier, and more efficient. You don't have to send me anything confidential. Just a database of names and types of businesses would help."

Database? Crap. Emma took a deep breath and let it out fast. "We don't use databases and Excel spreadsheets here. I took the job over from my eighty-year-old grandmother."

His expression was blank. Emma forged ahead. "She wasn't big on QuickBooks or computers, okay?"

Hunter blinked. "But . . . surely you use a computer?"

"Of course I use a computer. I just didn't have a whole lot of time between taking care of her and running the business to change anything. And now that she's gone, I'm still working things out."

He looked as if he couldn't quite comprehend what she was saying.

Heat swept up the back of Emma's neck and across her cheeks. He made her feel old-school, and she wasn't. Just because her laptop at home was mostly used for e-reading her favorite novels and browsing Etsy and Pinterest, it didn't mean she was archaic. Besides, who the hell was he? People on the island did things their own way and it worked fine. "Look, I'm sticking to this filing system right now because it works. Do you want to see the lists of vendors, or not?"

A small crease formed between his eyes, but he nodded.

Surprise, city boy. You're dealing with Small Town, USA, now. Get over it.

"How about we, uh, schedule a time to meet and go over them next week? We could meet here. . . ." He glanced at the little round bistro tables, each barely large enough to hold two plates and cups. "Or we could meet somewhere with more room. Do you have an office?"

"A home office, but that's not an option." The house would have a field day with him if she ever let him inside. It was very protective. "We'll figure it out next week, okay? What else do you want to know?"

"I'd like to check out the wharf with you. I've donated some funding to the cleanup project and I want to see what's been done in the past. Maybe we can walk down there sometime today and you can show me."

"Today won't work. I'm here all day and I have to stay late to fulfill a catering contract."

"How about Friday?"

"I can't. I'm helping Juliette with a project after I close the shop." Technically, eating popcorn and watching old reruns of *Buffy the Vampire Slayer* wasn't really a project, but he didn't have to know that.

"Saturday, then?"

"I close at six o'clock."

"Why don't I come by at six-thirty, would that work? There will still be plenty of light to walk the wharf, and we could grab dinner afterward."

Emma considered his request. It sounded easy

enough, but dinner changed things. She stole a glance at him, sitting there in a stray sunbeam. He looked like sin on a stick. Did he really have to keep doing that? She could almost hear Juliette urging her to play nice.

"All right, fine," Emma said.

He nodded and sipped his coffee, watching her over the rim of his cup.

"I have to get back to work now." She scraped her chair back and stood.

Hunter rose and gestured to the remaining crumbs of the "Be Well" cupcake. "Thanks for that. No idea what you put in it, but I do feel a lot better."

"No problem."

"See you Saturday at six-thirty, then?"

"Yup." Emma watched him go. A flutter of nervous anticipation caught her off guard. She felt like a teenager who had just been asked to the prom. *Get a grip, Holloway.*

Hunter shut the door behind him.

It's just a harmless business meeting.

He stepped onto the sidewalk.

Followed by a harmless dinner.

He glanced back and winked.

With the harmless king of the underworld.

Chapter Seven

On Friday night, Emma sat in her living room with her feet propped on a faded ottoman. A candle glowed on the coffee table, filling the air with the scent of vanilla sugar cookies. She snuggled deeper into the overstuffed couch and pulled a patchwork quilt over her lap, settling a bowl of fresh popcorn on top. Yup, this was heaven.

Her home was filled with a jumble of mismatched things, collected over the years by generations of Holloways. Emma knew the shabby-chic/bohemian vibe would never grace the covers of *Stylish Home* magazine, but she didn't care. She loved it anyway.

In the foyer, the house swung the front door open for Juliette.

"It's ridiculous," Emma called out. "I mean, it's just business. Why am I so nervous about meeting him for dinner? What the heck is my problem?" She stuffed popcorn into her mouth as Spike said something in his sexy British accent on TV.

Juliette glided into Emma's living room with a box in her arms. "Your problem is that Hunter Kane is a total hottie, and you're trying to pretend he's not. Just like Buffy tries to pretend Spike isn't mouthwateringly delicious." She glanced at the TV and set the box on the coffee table. "I can't believe you started without me. Here, I brought you a present."

Did the box just make noise? Emma sat up, frowning. "It's not my birthday."

"No, it's your un-birthday. And you need him."

"Him?" Emma leaned forward and lifted the lid. A small, furry ball looked up at her and wagged its crooked tail. He was the color of brown sugar, and about the size of a bag of flour. "Juliette, what is this?"

"A Labradoodle. Katie over at Soaps n' Sundries had a customer who got transferred to New York and couldn't keep him. So when I dropped off this month's batch of bath products, there he was." Juliette made soaps, health tonics, and lotions with organic herbs and essences she distilled from her own garden. It wasn't a booming business, but she'd been selling upscale body products at all the local boutiques and farmer's markets for years.

She lifted the puppy and placed him in Emma's lap. "Isn't he the cutest thing?"

The puppy grinned at Emma, pink tongue lolling.

Emma reached down and stroked the top of his fleecy head. "He's adorable, but he can't stay with me. I'm never home."

"Well, I brought him to my house but Luna is

having a hissy fit, terrorizing him every time he wanders two feet from his box. I always knew she was the most stubborn cat in the world, but now I'm going to have to add 'malicious bully' to the list. So I thought of you, and how you're here in this big house all alone."

Emma stroked his cloudlike fur and he wiggled in approval. "I'm fine being alone. I have been for over a year and a half."

"But you'd be happier with this guy. I just know it."

"I can't leave him here by himself all day. And do you have any idea how many health code violations I'd be breaking with a dog living in my bakery?"

"I have it all worked out. Mrs. Mooney said she'd be happy to let him hang out in her shop next door until you get off work."

"Come on. Can you imagine Bonbon with a puppy around? That dog is mean, on his nicest day." Emma grinned as the puppy discovered a stray piece of popcorn on the couch. His tail wagged so hard, the whole back half of him wagged, too.

"Well, she said Bonbon would love to have a friend. And she also said it's about time you brought a man into your life, even if he's canine."

Emma shot Juliette a look. "Wow, she said that? I'm so lucky to have you two looking out for me."

"Come on, he's an orphan now. Can't you see he needs you?" Juliette was really laying it on thick.

The "orphan" licked Emma's hand and whimpered. He actually whimpered. And that was all it took. She was a total goner. "I guess I can keep him for a little while. . . ."

"I knew it!"

"But, *only* a little while. He's going to need a real home."

Juliette dropped onto the couch and plunked the popcorn bowl in her lap. "It's fate."

"Don't get too excited." Emma set the puppy on the floor and watched him explore the cozy living room. "We'll have to find him a more suitable family. I can try taking him with me to work for a week."

The puppy scampered across the rug, tripping over his feet. "How big is he going to get?"

"I'm not sure," Juliette said. "He's around ten weeks old, but I think he's a miniature."

He didn't look like a miniature. His feet were the size of dessert plates. But he wouldn't be around long enough for it to matter. On Monday, Emma would put an ad in the local paper and ask around town to try to find a place for him. Maybe a nice home with kids and parents—a real family who could love him the way he deserved.

Emma laid a knit throw blanket on the floor to make a bed near her feet. The puppy pounced on it, fascinated by the tassel fringe.

"Did you feed him?" She'd have to get dog food on her next trip to the grocery store. Just enough for the week, anyway. Maybe a treat, or two. And toys. Puppies loved toys.

"Yup, he's all good. Just tired, running from Luna all day. My cat can be a holy terror. I don't know why I put up with her."

Emma sometimes wondered the same thing. Luna was a huge black cat, with lamplight eyes and a very fickle temper. One minute she'd be licking your hand and the next, it was razor-sharp claws to the forearm. Never a dull moment with that one.

Juliette curled her feet underneath her and snuggled deeper into the couch. "So are you ready for your big date tomorrow night?"

On the TV screen, Spike was kissing Buffy up against a wall as the building crumbled down around them. Emma ignored it. "It's not a date. I'm just going to show him the wharf areas to spruce up before the festival. Then he said something about grabbing dinner. But it does freak me out a little, because it sounds so 'datey.' "

"Yeah, it sucks to be you. A gorgeous man wants to take you out and buy you dinner. How will you ever survive it?"

"It's not that. You know as well as I do that he has to leave, or my business is ruined."

"Which is why you will just go out and schmooze him. Make sure he likes you.

79

Meanwhile, I've checked the calendar, and the moon will be full next Monday. We have to get up before the sun rises and go out on the jogging trail at the edge of the forest. You know, the one by Bethany's B&B?"

Emma groaned. Bethany Andrews never liked the Holloways, and made sure both Emma and Juliette knew it. It probably had something to do with Bethany's father having a rumored affair one summer with Emma's mom, on one of the rare occasions her mom returned home. But Bethany's father was a known womanizer, so that shouldn't have been a big surprise.

"Bethany hates us," Emma said. "If she catches us traipsing through the woods near her place, it won't be a good scene."

"She's not going to be up at the crack of dawn, Em. It takes at least an hour to make those beach wave curls, and don't even get me started on her makeup. It takes time to look that plastic. Besides, that trail has the only wild night-blooming jasmine on the island. I'm going to distill it for us to use in the magic 'Go Away' cupcake on summer solstice. Jasmine binds the heart, so I think it would be a good ingredient. It'll help with the yearning."

Emma had given up trying to make a bed for the puppy. He was now curled on her lap again, using the afghan throw as a chew toy. "Can't we just use the jasmine in your garden?"

Juliette shook her head. "Wild is better. Plus, full moon. The ingredients will be much more potent. We have to do it on Monday."

Not for the first time that week, Emma got the feeling she was getting in over her head. She sighed. "Fine. But you'll have to spend the night Sunday because I'm not going to be held responsible if I oversleep."

"Oh, I totally forgot!" Juliette sat up straighter. "I have another surprise for you."

"No more gifts, please. Yours all come with strings attached."

"Not true." Juliette pointed at the puppy. "He only comes with a leash attached. This is even better. I was talking to Molly, and she needs more part-time work because she's trying to save up for some esthetician training thing. Anyway, she said she could help out in your shop on weekends and two days during the week, if you want."

Emma gasped. "Are you serious? That is crazy wonderful!" Molly was one of their good friends who worked at Dazzle, the hair salon near the waterfront. She had helped Emma in the past, so she already knew what to do. Paying an employee for a few hours per week was going to be tough on Emma's finances, but she was in desperate need of the help. "I can only pay her minimum wage, she knows that, right?"

"She doesn't care. Fairy Cakes is just a block

from Dazzle, so it's an easy commute. She's all for it."

Emma felt a wave of gratitude for her cousin. Juliette was always looking out for her. Their mothers were sisters, and Juliette had been Emma's best friend since she was seven years old. When Juliette turned nine, her mom died in a car accident. Even with the gift of healing, she couldn't heal her injuries because Holloway magic didn't work that way. Juliette was left to be raised by her father. He had been a kind, quiet man with a broken heart, who eventually moved away after Juliette turned eighteen. Over the years, Juliette always said that Emma was her rock, but really it was the other way around. Emma didn't know what she would have done without her cousin. To Emma, Juliette was more than family. She was her lifeline.

"Jules, I would totally throw my arms around you right now, but I don't want to startle . . ." She glanced down at the puppy. "What's his name?"

"Doesn't have one. Orphan, remember? I think my client was calling him something stupid like Fifi or Foofoo. One of those dumb names. But he needs a real one. You'll have to think of something."

Suddenly, with a warm puppy in her lap and the prospect of having someone to help in the shop, Emma felt like the days ahead seemed much rosier. Never mind that she had to meet Hunter tomorrow night, and never mind that she had to go gallivanting through Bethany Andrews's backyard on the full moon next week. Maybe things were going to be okay.

She grinned down at the puppy.

He hopped onto the rug, scampered to the edge of the room, and squatted. A puddle formed on the hardwood floor.

Yeah. Things were looking up.

It was well past midnight when Juliette extracted herself from a nest of throw blankets on the couch and headed home.

Emma stood in the kitchen cleaning up as the puppy explored the tiled floor. He was snuffling around a crack in the wood cabinet near the back wall, his tiny tail wagging so hard, it was just a blur. She smiled. "What are you looking for?"

She lifted him up and held him close to her face. He really was the cutest thing. Soon, she'd find him a real family. "Sorry, Charlie. I just swept the floor, so you won't be finding any more stray popcorn."

He cocked his head, pink tongue lolling.

Emma scratched him behind the ears. "Not Charlie, huh? Well, what am I supposed to call you, then?"

The puppy busied himself trying to lick leftover buttered popcorn from her hands. She set him back on the floor and started on the dishes, laying them out to dry near the sink.

A few minutes later, her ancient recipe book tipped over. Emma straightened it and turned away. Behind her, she heard it tip over again. Turning slowly, she found it lying open on the counter.

Occasionally the house got her attention by putting things right under her nose. Sometimes it was helpful, and other times it was just annoying. For a while, Emma kept finding a leaflet for online dating lying around on tabletops or her nightstand. But after the fiasco with her ex-fiancé, Rodney, Emma was not in the market for a new boyfriend. It took weeks before the house finally gave up.

Now she tilted her face to the ceiling and sighed. "It's past midnight, house. If you have something to say, tell me later."

The pages of the ancient recipe book fluttered as if a breeze had swirled into the room. Except of course, there was no breeze, since all the windows were closed.

"What now?" She glanced down at the pages of her worn recipe book. The leather-bound tome had been in her family for more generations than she knew, handed down from one Holloway woman to another, until her grandmother had given it to her. Most of the original recipes were scrawled in faded ink, the words reinforced over the years with her ancestors' handwriting.

Emma never bothered with the truly ancient recipes. The measurements were far too vague for her comfort. Dash of salt. How much was a dash? Lump of butter. What exactly was a lump? Splash of oil. What kind of oil? None of that was clear enough for her, and if she was going to carry on in her grandmother's footsteps, she was going to do it *right*. For that, she needed precise recipes. Exact measurements. Luckily, there were hundreds of recipes for her to try that were easy enough to follow.

All of Emma's grandmother's recipes used precise measurements. Tablespoons. Cups. Things that were accurate. Things that Emma could count on. After her mother left, Emma had grown to rely heavily on the order of things. For a long time she felt as though she were blowing around in the wind, just like her mom, and it always made her feel unsettled. She never wanted to feel out of place ever again. Rules, or in her case, measurements, were very important to her.

When Emma began to embrace her gift in the kitchen, she had pored over the book in fascination. There was something so soothing about the worn edges, the aged leather, the spells that were her birthright. As a little girl, Emma couldn't imagine any other book in the entire world that held as much intrigue and excitement as this. But when she began making spells and trying out the recipes, she wanted to follow them precisely.

Her grandmother had been a kind and patient teacher, sometimes teasing Emma to try to tweak recipes to make them her own. She often tried to get Emma to listen to her instincts and just "go with the flow," but Emma wasn't comfortable with that. She was perfectly fine with the recipes as they were, thank you very much.

Now the book lay open to a very old spell. The words had faded over the years and the edge of the page was singed, as if left too close to the stove. Her grandmother had written into the margin to complete the ingredients. Emma knew the spell very well, because she had been obsessed with it as a child. It was the only spell in the entire book that was supposed to work on Holloway women, too.

The title of the recipe was "Day of Bliss." It was rumored to bring about the most uplifting, happiest of days to everyone, including the Holloway women. The only spell where, for just one blissful day, the Holloway women could benefit, too. It was supposed to be used on wedding days or birthdays, or whenever someone really needed a boost of happiness.

As a little girl, Emma had been fascinated by the concept. She loved the idea that there was a spell that could make everything fall into place as it should, no matter what hardships people faced. Even if it only lasted for *one* day out of the year, it had been marvelous to contemplate. The last time she'd thought about the spell was the last time she'd seen her mother.

Emma stood at the edge of the yard, watching her mother stroll through the garden. The older woman's blond hair was faded with streaks of gray and her skin was tanned from years in the sun, but she was still as beautiful and elusive as always.

She turned toward Emma, the scent of patchouli and far-off places clinging to her like a love song. "Summer's ending."

Emma nodded. At seventeen, she finally understood why her mother had to leave. Her gift of wanderlust wasn't a choice, it was a calling. She'd never be content unless she embraced it.

The wind ruffled her mother's rainbow silk dress, catching it on the breeze and floating it around her body in a soft blur. She was like a watercolor painting left out in the rain; a dissolving medley of colors that would soon fade to nothing. Her voice held a faint echo, as if she was already far away. "I have to go now."

Emma sighed. "I know." For a brief moment, she wished she could use the

"Day of Bliss" spell to make her mother stay a little longer, but some things were impossible to change.

After that, Emma had forgotten about the spell. Now, as she stared down at it, she wanted to laugh. Her grandmother had never liked the "Day of Bliss" recipe. She swore up and down it was useless, and there had never been any notable day of bliss for *her*. In fact, Emma's grandmother had recounted the tale of how she had tried the recipe once as a young woman, and it had brought her nothing but a day of discord and heartbreak. Faint pen lines made an *X* over the page, and her grandmother had written the word "broken" near the title.

"This old recipe is a dud, house. Grams said so herself. It doesn't work."

The pages of the book fluttered again, then settled back on the same recipe. It was the house's way of disagreeing.

She leaned in and peered at the page. It was so old, most of the words were written in formal, flowery script that had faded over time. Emma read the first few ingredients.

Half splash of vanilla.
Three large bird eggs.
Scant cup molasses.

Yeah, no. This recipe wasn't happening anytime soon. Not if she had anything to say about it.

None of the ingredients were exact. And what the heck did it mean by "large bird egg"? Egg of ostrich? Large egg of chicken? Forget it. The last ingredient was added by her grandmother in the margin, near the burnt edge of the page. *One quarter teaspoon of dried lavender.* Now that, she understood, but it still didn't matter.

Emma shut the book firmly and shook her head. She placed it back against the wall and spoke to the air around her. "I'm not making this recipe, house. Grams tried it once and it never worked. But thank you for thinking of me. I know you're just trying to help and I really do appreciate it, but the recipe's a dud. I'm sorry."

She blew a kiss to the air and a soft breeze wafted across her face, as though the house were kissing her back. "I love you, too."

She called to the puppy and turned off the kitchen lights. The book thumped open on the counter again, but she ignored it.

Chapter Eight

On Saturday evening, Emma stared into his soulful eyes and whispered, "If I'm not careful, I could fall in love with you."

The puppy licked her face and wagged his crooked tail. All day he had been with Mrs. Mooney and Bonbon next door. For the most part, he slept in his cozy basket, occasionally venturing out to wander the perimeter of the baby gate area Mrs. Mooney had set up in the back of her shop. Things seemed to be going well, and the biggest surprise of all was that Bonbon didn't hate him. The older dog just ignored him, which was so much better than Emma had expected. It was really too bad she couldn't keep the little guy.

She set him back in the basket and glanced at the clock. Almost six. Hunter would be arriving in thirty minutes. "Thanks again for letting him hang out with you guys tonight."

Mrs. Mooney nodded. "He's a good boy. Not very refined, of course, but that can't be helped. It's the poor breeding. The American Kennel Club doesn't even recognize Labradoodles, don't you know?"

"Mmm."

"But we won't hold it against him." The older woman smiled fondly at the puppy.

"You're so great to help out with him, Mrs. Mooney. I can't thank you enough."

"Well, I'm staying late to do inventory, so we're happy to have him. Aren't we, Bonbon? Yes, we are." Bonbon was reclining on his pink princess bed in the corner. He yawned and looked away. "Have a good time on your date, dear."

"Oh, it's not a date," Emma said a bit too loudly. "We're just getting together to discuss the plans for the festival."

"Of course, dear. Oh, and make sure you lock your shop up good when you leave. Tommy Jenkins reported a burglary in his garage the other night, did you know? Someone stole his watering can. Can you even believe it? Never can tell what hooligans are roaming the streets these days."

By hooligans, Emma wasn't quite sure what Mrs. Mooney meant. Pine Cove Island was just about the quietest, most laid-back town in the world. The only time it ever got rowdy was during the summer when tourist season was in full swing.

Back at Fairy Cakes, Emma poured herself a cup of tea and checked her appearance in the kitchen mirror for the third time. She looked casual in jeans and a simple black top, but her messy bun was like a ratty tumbleweed on top of her head. *Lovely.* She tried to smooth it out, then forced herself to stop. What did it matter? It was just a business meeting, anyway.

"Halloo," a chirpy voice called. Gertie Fraser

pushed through the back door with her usual enormous tote bag. She was the top hair stylist at Dazzle, and one of Juliette's and Emma's closest friends. In her late forties, Gertie had the kind of vivacious energy that always made her seem younger than her age. It was hard to believe she had two sons in college and a firefighting husband in his fifties. With her petite frame and spiky hair dyed varying shades of red, she looked like an autumn wood sprite.

"The girls are right behind me," Gertie said. "We just wanted to pop in before—*whoa*. Have you been drinking?"

Emma frowned. "No."

"Well, you might not be drunk, but your hair definitely is." Gertie gave Emma a quick hug and pulled a stool in front of the mirror, pointing. "Sit."

Emma sat. No one argued with Gertie Fraser when it came to hair. She was a natural at what she did, and she always seemed to know exactly what a person needed.

Gertie dug around in her bag and whipped out a brush, a large-toothed comb, a can of hair mousse, two different bottles of gel, and a small pot of some sort of pomade. Emma half expected her to do the Mary Poppins thing and pull out a large table lamp.

"I can't believe you carry all of that in your purse," Emma said, shaking her head.

Gertie gave her a pained expression. "Have we met?"

"I don't even own that many hair products, let alone carry them wherever I go."

"Which is why you're lucky you have me. Now turn your head so I can fix this"—she waved her hand over Emma's head—"*thing* you've got going on here. What do you call this, bird's-nest chic?"

Emma rolled her eyes as Gertie worked some papaya-scented mousse through her hair. "I was busy all day. And it's not like I'm going anywhere special tonight."

"That's not what Juliette said," Gertie sang back.

"What did I say?" Juliette bustled through the back door followed by Molly Owens, a curvy woman with shoulder-length dark hair.

"You said Emma had a big date tonight."

Emma sighed loudly. "For the last time, you guys, it's not a date. We are just meeting to discuss the summer festival."

"A Saturday night dinner sounds like a date to me." Molly braced an ample hip against the kitchen counter. "And I should know, believe me. I've been in the dating trenches for a while now." At thirty-two, Molly was desperately seeking Mr. Right and had recently gathered the courage to put up a profile on Match.com.

Emma grinned as Gertie worked the comb

through her tangled hair. "How'd your coffee date go yesterday?"

"It was *meh*-kay," Molly said. "He talked about his mom the whole time."

"Sounds like a great guy," Gertie said firmly. Her two sons had done the unthinkable and abandoned their poor mother to attend colleges on the East Coast. She often wrote letters threatening to disown them if they didn't call their mama or come home for regular visits. These letters were usually mailed in boxes with other serious threats like homemade chocolate chip cookies and packages of socks.

"I don't know," Molly sighed. "Blind dates are so disappointing. He just wasn't right for me."

"Why not?" Emma asked.

Molly's gaze slid sideways. "Well . . . Okay, I'm not trying to be mean, or anything? It's just, he kind of looked like a troll, you know? But in a good way," she rushed to add.

Gertie stopped combing Emma's hair. "How is that good?"

Molly held up her thumb and forefinger. "You know those little troll dolls from the sixties? Smiley, with potbellies and spiky hair? That kind. Not the kind who hang out under bridges and stuff."

Gertie's eyes shot wide. "How nice for him."

"It's just a bummer." Molly rummaged in her purse. "Pine Cove Island isn't exactly overflowing with a plethora of eligible men."

"Preach it, sister." Juliette took another sip of tea.

"I know, right? And after I rule out any guy who has the number 69—*please*—or 007 in his online profile name? It's slim pickings, for sure."

"What's wrong with 007?" Gertie asked. "James Bond is cool."

"On paper, maybe. But Bond girls have garbage luck." Molly pulled some lip balm out of her purse. "They think they've met this nice hot guy, and then"—she applied the lip balm rapidly and smacked her lips together—"they wake up dead. Sprayed gold and stuff."

Gertie waved a hand. "That's just in the movies. You shouldn't be so discriminating with the online names. Most guys aren't creative like we are. Walter doesn't have a creative bone in his body, but he's a good husband to me, and a good father to our sons."

"Walter is a firefighter," Juliette said matter-of-factly. "He saves lives and rescues kittens. He basically walks away from explosions in slow motion, so he's cool by default. It wouldn't matter what online name he used."

"I'm just saying that Molly could be missing out," Gertie said. "She shouldn't judge guys based on their screen names."

Molly rolled her eyes. "Fine. Maybe I'll give PussyPleaser35 a chance."

Juliette choked on her tea. "No way."

"Yes way," Molly said. "PussyPleaser35, you guys. I can't make this stuff up."

"Well, it's a relief to know there are at least thirty-five of them out there," Gertie said. "And I think I speak for all women on Pine Cove Island when I ask, is Hunter Kane one of them? Because he certainly looks like he could be."

Emma threw Gertie a look over her shoulder. "You know you're married, right? To that fireman we just talked about?"

"Married, not buried, honey." Gertie caught the tip of her tongue between her teeth, smiling. "And Hunter Kane is some serious eye candy."

"He really is," Molly said wistfully.

"*So* much candy," Juliette agreed.

Gertie misted finishing spray over Emma's hair, scrunching it at the roots. "You're done. Go look in the mirror."

Emma checked her reflection above the kitchen sink. Her hair was smooth and glossy, with soft waves falling around her shoulders. "I love it, Gertie. How do you do it?"

Gertie waved the hairbrush in the air like a magic wand. "You Holloway girls aren't the only ones with special abilities."

"That's for sure," Juliette said. "You look hot, Em. Now you're ready for your *business meeting*."

"And can you please go wild, for a change?"

Molly asked. "I mean, we all know he's the enemy and stuff. We haven't forgotten that, all right? But at least one of us should be having some fun."

"And then you can come back and give us all the slutty details," Gertie said.

"Yes." Juliette nodded. "We want *all* the details, so make sure to take notes."

Emma pointed to the door. "Out." She tried to look stern, but failed.

Juliette gave her a hug and laughed. "You know you love us."

"Come on, ladies. Let's go." Molly adjusted her miniskirt, frowning as she yanked at the waistband. She was always on a diet, even though she was adorably curvy and had been for years. "There's dancing at the Siren tonight and I have to kill some calories. I stuck a French fry in my mouth and pulled the trigger at lunch today. Ended up eating the whole basket."

Gertie tossed the arsenal of hair products back into her tote. "Well, I'm with you girls. Walter's at the fire station tonight, so let's go whoop it up."

They said good-bye and left out the back door just as the dragonfly wind chimes in the front of the shop announced Hunter's arrival. Emma took a deep breath.

Showtime.

Emma gripped her tote bag like a security blanket as they walked toward the wharf. She let her gaze wander over the scenic street, trying her best to appear casual and relaxed. But she wasn't. How could she be? She stole a glance at Hunter, who seemed completely at ease in his white linen shirt and jeans. Who wore white linen, anyway? Nobody, that's who. Unless they were posing for some yacht club magazine ad. It was stupid. He was stupid.

She turned her attention to the trellis of flowers near the pier. Lovely shade of purple, those. She was not in the least bit attracted to his swarthy, sun-kissed face and wind-blown hair, or the woodsy, pine-soap scent of him tonight. It wasn't intriguing at all. Nope.

Near the pier, she stopped and pointed out some of the favorite landmarks. There was the bronze statue of Coco, the ancient, one-eyed harbor seal who had made a home in the waters surrounding the pier. She showed him the paved alcove where local musicians set up amateur bands, and the gazebo covered in lilacs near the water's edge where weddings took place during the spring and summer. Soft strains of guitar music from the corner pub wafted through the air, and the streetlamps cast puddles of warm light along the edge of the water.

"It's beautiful out here," Hunter mused.

She turned to him. "You say that like it's a surprise."

"It is, a little. Usually you think of these old

places as being kind of backwater, or run-down." He glanced in her direction and added, "But not this place. It's different. It has sort of a . . . timeless feel to it."

"I've always thought so." Emma watched the evening breeze ruffle his glossy hair, and wondered if he was for real. Was he just spinning it to make her like him, or did he really think of the place as being timeless? "The Holloways have lived here for over a hundred years. My grandmother told me they originally came over from Ireland, searching for a more peaceful existence, away from the famines and land wars. They wanted to find a place they could live in harmony, so they went as far west as they could go and eventually settled here. They were fishermen and farmers; important to the island's growing community. The Holloway women became known as healers and bearers of good fortune. They helped people."

Emma stopped at the edge of the grass and glanced at him. "There used to be more of us." The familiar ache of losing her grandmother surged up and she shoved it down again. "But now it's just me and Juliette. Things are a lot different now."

"But you're happy here?" he asked.

"Yes, of course," she said in surprise. "It's home. There's something peaceful about this place that doesn't change, not even when the rest of the world does. It's what I love most about it. You might think all small towns are the same, but this place is special."

His bright green gaze was fixed on her in admiration. "I can see that."

A rush of warmth gathered in the pit of her stomach, and she glanced away before she grinned at him like a fool. It was really hard to stay focused when he looked at her like that.

They strolled along the grassy slope that led down to water's edge. Seagulls called to one another on the wind as the sun began sinking on the horizon.

She pointed to a weathered picket fence that lined the grassy area near a small park. "Every summer before the festival we all get together to paint that fence bright white again. It spruces up the park area. And over there"—she pointed to the rope railing that looped down the pier—"we hang a few flower baskets. Mostly we concentrate on this pier and Front Street. The budget doesn't really allow for any fixing up beyond that."

"This year it will." Hunter studied the street that ran adjacent to his new waterfront café. "I've donated a bit of money so we can really make things shine."

"Shine?" Emma felt a twinge of apprehension. She never was one for change. It made her feel unsettled.

"Yeah, you know"—he spread his arms out—

"all of this. It's going to look like a movie set by the time we're finished."

She didn't like the sound of it. Pine Cove Island wasn't a movie set. Who was he to go changing things? "I'm not sure what you mean by that."

"Well, I think we should repaint all the shop fronts. Some of the signs are so old, they look too dangerous to walk under. They need to be replaced for safety, if nothing else."

Emma felt a prickle of unease. "Maybe the store owners like their old signs. They're vintage."

He frowned, nodding. "That, they are."

She didn't like the way he said it, as if he had judged her town and found it lacking.

"But upgrading signage will affect everyone's businesses in a positive way," he continued. "The public loves nostalgia, as long as it's whitewashed and safe. People want things to look shiny and clean, you know what I mean?"

Emma bristled. Now her town was dirty? "You're very opinionated for someone who just moved here and isn't even familiar with the island culture. What makes you so sure people will agree with your ideas?"

"They already have." He looked so energized, like he was embarking on an exciting new project. "That's what Sam Norton was getting at during the chamber of commerce meeting. They gave me carte blanche to fix up Front Street and the wharf for the festival."

Her stomach churned. "Why would they do something like that?" It was uncharacteristic of the town committee to just hand over that much decision-making to a newcomer.

"It may have something to do with the fact that I've increased this year's cleanup budget by, let's say . . . two hundred percent?"

Emma stumbled over a paving stone near a bench. She grabbed the back of the bench to steady herself. Two hundred percent? He had to be joking. "You donated that much money just to decorate the waterfront for the festival?"

"I think it's a sound investment. I've always wanted to expand onto these smaller islands. This seemed like the perfect place to start. And as you say, there's something special about it." He gave her a slow, melted-caramel smile. It did warm, fluttery things to her insides, but her common sense wasn't having any of it.

"But you're talking about making a lot of changes," she said. "This place has its own special charm. You'll ruin all that if you commercialize everything." Emma sat down on the bench, blinking rapidly. Disturbing visions of the waterfront wafted through her mind, complete with typical chain stores, flashing neon lights, and fast-food restaurants on every corner.

Hunter settled beside her. "I just want the festival to be a success, and I think cleaning up the waterfront and painting the shop

102

fronts, maybe getting a crew out to do better landscaping, will make a difference. I don't plan on drastically changing anything. You want more tourism for the festival, don't you? And for the rest of the summer?"

She thought of her stack of unpaid bills at home in her office and tried to steady her whirlwind emotions. She needed the tourist season to be as big as it could be. If he wanted to throw his money into something that would benefit her, maybe that was a good thing. "What else do you propose?"

He relaxed back on the bench, hooking a foot over one knee. "I was thinking about live music."

"We have live music. The junior college band always plays for the festival."

"Okay, but I was thinking of hiring more seasoned professionals from Seattle. I'd like to have a rotating lineup of musicians. We could set up different venues throughout the wharf." He pointed from one end of the street to the other, his gaze so intent that Emma could almost visualize what he was imagining. "We'll have different bands playing at scheduled times to appeal to a wider audience. Acoustic guitar, jazz, that sort of thing."

Emma considered it. He really seemed genuinely interested. Maybe the town committee was right. Let him make a few changes and do some renovations. What did it matter, as long as she reached her quota of sales? Besides, if things worked out the way they were supposed to, he would soon be gone, anyway. If he wanted to clean up the waterfront with his money for the time being, let him.

She stood up, hugging herself. The sun was still up, but the breeze floating in off the ocean had grown cooler. "We should probably wrap this up. I've got things to do at home."

He rose from the bench and she had to crane her neck to look at him. At five feet four, the top of her head didn't even reach his shoulders. Emma took a step back and tried to ignore the soft flush of warmth that spread through her limbs. No matter how cool she acted, her body was definitely on high alert.

"Are you hungry?" he asked.

"Sure." She was starving. Her stomach had been in knots all day and she hadn't eaten much. If only her cupcake charms worked on herself, she would have eaten something to make her feel calm and confident.

"What's good around here?" He scanned the wharf and Emma tried not to stare. He had such a strong, masculine face and the thickest, longest eyelashes on a guy she had ever seen. So unfair. Against the backdrop of the ocean, he looked more like a rogue pirate than ever.

She pointed to O'Malley's Pub on the corner. "They have good burgers. And seafood, if you're into that." It was close, and the service was quick. Better to get this over with before she started fantasizing about him any further. Really, it was pure stupidity. How was it possible for her to get all dreamy-eyed over someone whose very presence was such a threat to her livelihood?

They crossed the street in silence, and Hunter held the door for her as they entered O'Malley's. When they were seated in a corner booth, Emma scanned the bar crowd.

James Sullivan waved from behind the bar as he mixed a drink. He had the easygoing attitude and self-assurance that seemed a prerequisite for all bartenders. Emma and Juliette had known him growing up, even though he was several years older and, therefore, too busy to pay them much attention. For a while when they were in high school, James seemed to be fascinated by Juliette, but so was every boy between the ages of nine and ninety-nine. Eventually he left for college, and had only recently moved back.

James gave her a questioning look, indicating the back of Hunter's head. Emma shook her own head and mouthed *business*. She was *not* on a date. Let's make that very clear.

Hunter relaxed back in the booth, his face darkly alluring in the low light. He smiled at the waitress as she filled their water glasses. The girl had to be just out of high school, but she blushed furiously and Emma knew exactly why. Hunter's smile was like a loaded weapon. If you happened to be on the receiving end, you had no hope of surviving.

Emma ran her fingers self-consciously through her hair. She knew from experience that the evening humidity was making it frizz. So much for Gertie's hair mousse. She searched for a topic. Anything to break the uneasy silence. "So where are you staying?"

"The bed and breakfast a couple of blocks away."

"The Marina?"

"Yes, I checked in a few days ago."

Poor man. Emma would bet the entire contents of her cash register—which wasn't much, admittedly—that Bethany Andrews already had her crosshairs locked on Hunter. She had seen that woman in action, and most guys didn't know what hit them. Bethany was like Jessica Rabbit coming at you full speed in a Mack truck. No stopping her.

"How do you like it?" she asked, careful to keep her expression neutral.

He shrugged. "I'm hoping to find a house."

"Maybe you should hold off on that. A house is kind of permanent, don't you think?"

He tilted his head, bright green eyes studying her.

"What?"

A slight frown. "I just have this feeling you

don't like me, and I'm trying to figure out why. I can understand your concern about my café, but is that the only reason?"

Emma fidgeted with the napkin in her lap. "No, of course I like you. I mean, I don't *like* like you." *D'oh!* "I barely know you." She gave a nervous laugh. "Look, you're fine. It just seems odd to me that someone like you would consider living here. It doesn't fit."

The young waitress showed up again, all smiles. She had refreshed her lipstick, and barely even glanced in Emma's direction as she placed a small tray of bread and cheese on the table before taking their orders and floating away.

Hunter placed a napkin on his lap and picked up a slice of French bread. "You don't think I fit in here?"

Emma tried not to laugh, but failed. "Oh, come on. It's obvious you don't fit in. I mean, look around you." She gestured to the restaurant crowd, most of whom were swigging beers in old T-shirts and ball caps. A couple of guys were yelling at a Mariners game on TV, and AC/DC's "Back in Black" played on the antique jukebox in the corner.

Hunter sat back, amusement creasing the corners of his eyes. "So my clothes are the problem?"

Your clothes, your sexy smile, your seize-the-world attitude. "I don't know, you just seem more like someone who'd be happier in a big city. I mean, what allure does this place have for someone like you?"

" 'Someone like you.' You keep saying that, as if you have me all figured out."

Emma took a sip of her water, ignoring his piercing gaze. "Well, I know from what you've already said that you're a big real estate investor. I know you're from Seattle and that you plan to expand your business onto the islands. But aside from opening your café, it just seems weird to me that you'd suddenly want to live here."

"Maybe I'm tired of the big city and just want a change of scenery."

Emma didn't miss the weariness in his gaze, and something else. Something sharper. "But why? What are you escaping from?"

Hunter's gaze flicked to the bar, his mouth drawing into a hard line.

She wished she hadn't said it. It was no business of hers. She barely knew him. But it was clear he wasn't happy about something. If she had to assess him right now, she'd probably prescribe one of her "Lavender Bliss" cupcakes. Something to impart peace and contentment. He needed it. She could feel it.

A muscle clenched in his jaw, but his emerald eyes gave nothing away. He was the master of his emotions. "I'm just focused on this new expansion project. What better way to understand the island culture than to live here? Besides, whether you believe me or not, I find this place very—"

A roar erupted at the bar as the Mariners hit a home run on TV. Someone dropped a beer glass and it shattered on the floor.

"—charming," Hunter finished.

Right. He was totally hiding something. But that suited her just fine. He could be all Mr. Secretive if he wanted to be. She thought of Juliette and their plan to gather night-blooming jasmine for the infamous "Go Away" cupcake. Yeah, she had her own secrets.

Emma shrugged. "Whatever you say."

Throughout the rest of dinner, she filled him in on local business traditions, including the Spring Fling dance coming up in a couple of weeks. Every year, the people in town got together for a huge party to celebrate the beginning of summer.

By the time dessert came, she was feeling relaxed and a little fuzzy around the edges from her third glass of wine. The strawberry shortcake with homemade whipped cream was delicious, and befriending the devil was turning out to be a piece of cake.

He was so easy to talk to that she almost forgot she was putting on an act. All she had to do was play nice for a few more weeks, and the magic spell on the summer solstice would take care of everything. A glowing sense of optimism settled over her. Or it could have just been the wine. Either way, she'd take it.

She grinned and ate another bite of shortcake. "You know, whatever your plans are." Were her words a little slurry? Nah. "I bet you'll be long gone before autumn hits."

He took a sip of his beer. "Is that right?"

"Uh-huh. I'm positive. Once the rain comes, there's going to be nothing here you find charming." She sucked whipped cream off the tip of her finger and sat back with a brilliant smile.

He studied her from beneath dark lashes. "Nothing?"

"Nope." Emma shook her head. "It's going to be cold and rainy and gray. And you're going to want something hot and sunny and"—a lock of hair fell over her eyes and she swiped at it—"golden."

Hunter's mouth kicked up at the corner. "I won't argue with that." His voice was low-pitched and a little whiskey-rough around the edges. It made her skin flush and her knees feel all rubbery.

He started to reach out, then stopped. "You have a little bit"—he pointed to the corner of her mouth—"just there."

Her comfortable wine haze evaporated as heat burned across her face. She wiped the back of her hand across her bottom lip. Her hair had to be a frizzing mop, by now. What time was it, anyway?

110

Time to go. And the puppy! She still needed to pick him up.

"Well," she said as brightly as she could. "This was nice, but I really have to get going." She stood up fast and fumbled in her purse for some cash.

"No, allow me." He signaled the waitress and handed her a card. "Are you sure you don't want another drink?"

"No, thanks." Emma settled her bag on her shoulder. "I have to go. He's waiting for me." She thought of the puppy at Mrs. Mooney's. Was he snuggled up in bed by now? He had to be. She never realized how much puppies slept. And he made the funniest noises sometimes when he was sleeping. Dreaming, maybe. Such a sweet thing. Too bad she couldn't keep him.

"Who's 'he'?" Hunter asked.

"He doesn't have a name yet," she said absently. He was probably missing her, poor little guy. Maybe she'd bring his puppy crate into her bedroom tonight.

Hunter gave her a puzzled look. She was so preoccupied, it took her a moment to realize she wasn't making any sense. "Oh, he's my puppy. Well, he's not really mine. I'm just watching him until I can find him a suitable home."

Hunter signed the check and stood. "I'll walk you back."

"No need." Emma waved a hand. It was far

too "datey" for him to walk her back to the shop, anyway. What then? A kiss at the door? Ha! Her face flamed. It was definitely time to go.

"I'm heading in that direction, anyway," Hunter said.

Oh, right. Bethany's Bed & Breakfast. Poor Hunter. He had no idea what he was in for, with that woman. Or maybe he'd go for it. He wouldn't be the first man dazzled by her hubcaps.

Just as they made it to the entrance, Ms. Mack Truck herself rolled through the door.

"Oh my God, hi!" Bethany gushed. She stood inside the threshold in skintight iridescent yoga pants and a matching halter top. Her hair was expertly curled and her perfect makeup looked airbrushed, which kind of ruined the whole "I just did yoga" look. On either side of Bethany, her two friends, Starla and Cherie, beamed like matching headlights.

Emma remembered them well, since they were all popular girls back in high school. For the year that Emma dated Rodney, her ex, they pretended to be nice. But it didn't last long. They were the cattiest women Emma had ever known, and age hadn't changed them much.

"Oh, Hunter, you didn't tell me you knew Emma." Bethany smiled like a piranha, her lululemon scales glistening in the halogen light above the entrance. "We all went to high school together."

"We've been discussing plans for the summer festival," Hunter said.

"Oh, that sounds like a whole lot of boring work for a Saturday night." Bethany laughed. "You should stay and hang out with us."

"Yes, stay." Starla smoothed her sleek black hair. As a recently divorced real estate agent, she looked stylish in slacks and matching jewelry, but she still chewed her gum like it owed her money.

"It'll be super fun." Cherie giggled.

Yep. It was high school all over again.

"You can try the new drink James made us last time," Starla added.

Bethany leaned closer to Hunter. "It's kind of a girly drink, but I have a feeling you'd just love it." She sucked her bottom lip between her teeth and let it out slowly.

Emma had to give Bethany credit. The woman knew how to cast a lure. If Bimbo Basics had been a class back in high school, she'd have aced it without even studying.

Bethany fiddled with the decorative laces on her halter top, drawing attention to her very large, very fake boobs.

Forget acing the test, Emma thought in annoyance. Bethany could've taught the class. "I have to get going," she said. "See you guys later."

To her own—and no doubt, Bethany's—complete shock, Hunter lightly placed his hand on Emma's back. "Sorry, ladies, but we have to go. Maybe next time."

Emma walked briskly down Front Street with Hunter beside her. He followed her out. She couldn't believe it. He followed her out! Olympic-sized cleavage and expert hair flipping, and he turned it all down, just like that.

She glanced at him from beneath her lashes. It made sense, given that he looked the way he did. Being fawned over was probably no big deal. Just another day in the life.

Back at her shop, Emma closed up and brought the puppy outside to meet him. He ran circles around Hunter's legs, tail wagging in pure joy.

"Juliette gave him to me last night," Emma said. "I guess he's going to live at my place for a little while, until I find a family for him."

"Hey, buddy." Hunter dropped down to pet the puppy. The expression on his face was so full of genuine admiration that Emma caught her breath. God, he was gorgeous. And he liked her dog! *And you're being a complete idiot right now,* she reminded herself. *It's not even your dog, remember?*

"You need a name, buddy. What's your name?" He scratched the puppy behind the ears and scooped him up.

Emma tried to ignore the deep sense of pleasure that spiraled through her at the sight of them together. It was like her body was sending out alert signals. Attention: girl parts! Hot guy holding a puppy!

She shoved the feeling aside. "He doesn't have a name yet. I haven't come up with anything."

"I'm sure you'll think of something." Hunter set the puppy back down. "I better get going."

She crossed her arms, hugging herself. "Thanks for dinner. I'll see you next week."

"How's three o'clock on Wednesday?"

Emma nodded. Molly would be working that shift, so she'd have time to show him the files. That was almost four days away. Plenty of time for his hotness factor to fade. No problems there.

He leaned down and ruffled the puppy's fur. "Bye, buddy."

Emma watched as he crossed the street and headed toward the B&B. She heaved a sigh. "What am I going to do about him, buddy?"

The puppy let out a joyful bark and thumped his tail.

She peered down at him. *"Buddy?"*

He wagged his tail so hard, it spun in circles.

"No way. That can't be your name. It's so basic. Like something a little kid would come up with."

Buddy wasn't interested in being sophisticated. He was, however, interested in chasing the tip of his tail.

Emma scooped him up and rubbed her face against his soft fur. "All right, Buddy," she whispered. "You picked it. You live with it."

Chapter Nine

Emma fed Buddy in the kitchen the following evening. "You're still going to get a better name as soon as I find you a family," she promised, patting his head. "Consider it just a placeholder."

She had just posted an ad in the local paper that morning. Even though she adored him, he deserved more. He deserved a place with loving parents and noisy kids who ran wild down the halls and dropped Cheerios under the breakfast table for happy dogs to discover. A place where people gathered and celebrated, where they held on and supported one another and loved one another, no matter what happened. A *real* home.

Behind her, the ancient recipe book thumped open on the counter. She didn't have to turn around to know it had opened to the "Day of Bliss" recipe. Emma sighed and closed the book for the third time that day. "Give it up," she told the house. "I keep telling you, that recipe is broken."

Emma was just about to dive into the piles of unread mail on the entry table, when the house shuddered and a door slammed upstairs.

"My sentiments, exactly," she said, peering at all the overdue bills. How was she ever going to get caught up? There were so many late payments.

Someone knocked on the front door.

The curtains in the kitchen window swirled up and out, like open sails on the wind. Emma glanced up from the bill she was reading. The knock came again, and Emma got the feeling the house wasn't thrilled with the visitor.

She walked into the foyer and tugged open the door, then froze.

Rodney Winters, her ex-fiancé, stood on the front porch.

He was still handsome, but he seemed rougher around the edges than she remembered. His cornflower blue eyes were bloodshot with dark circles, and his blond hair was in need of a trim. The faint scent of cigarettes and whiskey wafted in the air between them.

Buddy ran up and sniffed at his shoes, then turned away and trotted into the living room. He was unimpressed with Rodney. Smart dog.

"Hey, Angel," Rodney said.

The old endearment tasted like ashes on her tongue. Emma couldn't find her voice. The past came crashing back in waves and she struggled against the undertow.

He leaned one hand casually against the doorframe. It reminded her of the first time he paid attention to her in high school, leaning against her locker. He had been the football star running back; the king of the school. All smooth-talking charm and sunshine blond hair. No one was more surprised than Emma when he singled her out during their senior year.

She had been a quiet girl who didn't belong in Rodney's circle. At the time, she couldn't believe her luck. Rodney Winters, the most popular boy in school, liked her. *Her!* For the rest of that year, she basked in the glory of his attention. He represented everything she had ever wanted: a sense of belonging, companionship, acceptance, and what she hoped was love. But not long after graduation, he grew distant. Then he moved away to college in California and forgot about her.

When Emma turned twenty-one, Rodney came home again. He had decided college was too conforming, the teachers too self-absorbed, and he wanted to live life on his own terms. It wasn't until much later that Emma found out it was because those pesky college classes kept getting in the way of the parties, and he was expelled for failing grades.

Still a little in love with him, Emma let him back into her life. Her grandmother's cancer had progressed and Emma needed to feel connected to someone, more than ever. In retrospect, that was the only reason she agreed to marry him when he proposed on her twenty-second birthday. By that time, she had already learned Rodney was far from perfect. He drank a lot. He wasn't always accountable. He could spin any story to suit his needs. But he was familiar, and with her grandmother dying and life feeling so uncertain, Emma needed something familiar.

Shortly after her grandmother died, Emma came home one day to find the canister above the kitchen cupboard empty. It was where she stashed every extra bit of money she had, which added up to a few thousand dollars. Rodney was supposed to contribute to their future savings with his job as a local mechanic, but by then he was giving all his money to Johnnie Walker. Everything in that tin had been Emma's and he took it all, leaving just a scribbled note behind:

E—I'm sorry but I can't marry you. Ever since your grandma got sick, it's like I'm not important anymore. You used to be fun, but I guess people change.
I've got to be free.—R

Later she found out he really meant "free" to see other people. After stealing her money, he had run off to the mainland with some barfly. His abandonment had hurt so much, but the past eighteen months had changed her.

After the initial shock of his betrayal wore off, it was like the whole world cracked open. She could be herself without having to make excuses. She could blast her favorite music anytime she wanted. Eat pancakes for dinner. Go without makeup and not feel self-conscious. She could do whimsical art projects or discuss spells with Juliette or talk out loud to the house without having to endure Rodney's disapproving looks. Oh, he'd heard the rumors about the Holloway family abilities, but he wasn't a real believer. Rodney was all about being the "special" one, and nobody was allowed to eclipse that. Emma didn't even realize how much she had tailored herself to fit into his life, until he was gone.

Now she understood that the truly important people were the ones who accepted her, no matter what. Her grandmother always told her, "Those who matter don't mind, honey. And those who mind, don't matter." Emma had grown up and learned to embrace the life she was given, instead of trying so hard to fit into someone else's. The lustrous glow of Rodney Winters had finally died away.

Her hands trembled but she forced her voice to remain steady. "What are you doing here?"

"I just got back into town and wanted to see you." He shifted a little closer, all easy, masculine grace, until his broad shoulders filled the doorway. "You grew your hair out again," he murmured. "Just how I like it."

He reached out to stroke her hair.

She jerked back. It bothered her that he seemed completely at ease, standing on her doorstep. As if no time had passed. As if they still shared a life together.

Rodney chuckled and hooked a hand into the pocket of his jeans, letting his gaze slide down her body. "You look good."

She crossed her arms tightly around her chest. He had been her first everything. He was the only man on the planet who had ever seen her naked. She didn't like the fact, but there it was. It never ceased to amaze her how you could be so close to someone one moment, and then completely out of their lives the next. Emma knew she could never be one of those people who flitted from one person to another. She put far too much importance on relationships to be so fickle.

"You have no business coming here, Rodney. You left, remember? And you took all my money with you."

He brushed his hair back, arm muscles flexing. It was another "Rodney" move. Her insides coiled with resentment. It used to make her feel giddy when she was a starstruck teenager, but none of it worked on her anymore.

"Well, technically, it was our money, wasn't it?" he asked.

Wow. The urge to kick him was strong. But she was barefoot, and she might chip the polish on her new pedicure. He wasn't worth it. Still, it didn't stop her from fantasizing about it for a second. A nice roundhouse kick to the solar plexus, ending with him flying through the air, just like on *Buffy*. It worked for her.

"It was my money and you know it," she said through clenched teeth. "And now my house is falling apart and I can't even afford to have it repaired."

As if to emphasize her point, the porch step right behind him snapped in half.

Rodney jerked his head around, gazing uneasily at the broken step. He stuffed his hands into his pockets and turned back to Emma. "Look, I never meant to hurt you, okay? I was just confused." His eyes went wide and serious, but she knew that look well. He usually reserved it for telling saccharine-sweet lies.

"Yeah, I can see how being a cheater and a thief might get confusing," Emma said. "Must be hard to keep all the facts straight."

Rodney glanced away. "You were so sad all the time, Emma. With your grandmother dying, and all. You were always crying, and I guess . . . I didn't know what to do. I just felt like I had to get away. I couldn't breathe, you know?"

Of course. It was always about him. "I'm so sorry my grieving over a loved one bothered you so much."

He shrugged. "Hey, it's okay. I just couldn't deal, that's all."

She shook her head in disgust. Typical Rodney. He was so wrapped up in himself that he couldn't even recognize her sarcasm. "What do you want, Rodney?" There was always something he wanted.

He shifted on his feet. "I just wanted to see you. I was thinking of you all alone here, and I wanted to see how you were doing."

"I'm doing great," she lied. There was no way in hell she was going to give him the satisfaction of seeing poor little Emma fall apart. "Everything's going great."

He nodded. "Good, that's good. I'm glad. My parents are giving me a hard time since I got back. My mom's still mad at me for taking her car when I left town, which is stupid since I worked on it so often, it was pretty much mine anyway."

Of course it was. He always found a way to rationalize his actions, because life owed him a living. How silly of her to forget.

"Anyway, they won't let me stay at their house right now, so I kind of need a place to crash until they cool off."

And there it was. Her stomach churned with anger and resentment. How did he even have the guts to ask?

He gave her his best smile. The canned one. A flash of perfect teeth that ended on a smolder. She had seen it too many times to be fooled.

"It would just be for a little while," he continued. "I'm sure I can get them to come around in a week or two. Anyway, I thought of you here, all by yourself."

123

Emma was already shaking her head. "There's no way I'm letting you stay here."

"I don't have to stay in the house," he said in a rush. "To be honest, this place always kind of creeped me out, anyway."

Rodney had never liked visiting. He always had trouble with doors jamming or tripping on the stairs. She used to try to make excuses, but it was pretty clear the house never liked Rodney much. Once, when they were teenagers, he tried sneaking in her bedroom window in the middle of the night. Halfway over the ledge, the window slid shut on him and stuck. By the time they were able to pry the window off him, he was in no mood to stay. Convinced the house was haunted, he never tried to sneak over at night again.

"Just let me hang in the room above the garage for a couple of weeks, all right?" he asked. "You won't even know I'm there."

Emma glanced behind him at the small out-building near the edge of her yard. It was used for storage, but there was a tiny room above it. "Absolutely not. I want you to go. Now."

He dropped his head in disappointment, then peered up at her like a street urchin from a Dickens novel. "I'm sorry to hear that."

Annoyed, Emma bit the inside of her cheek. It was a tragedy that Hollywood had never discovered Rodney Winters, because he'd have made a fortune on the silver screen.

He turned to go, jumping over the broken step. She was about to close the door when he called out, "I've missed you, Angel. I'm going to find a way to make it up to you."

"Don't bother."

She shut the door and leaned against it, staring up at the ceiling. She was so over him, but it was still a shock, seeing him there on her front porch. After all these months, he thought he could just waltz back into her life like nothing ever happened. It was absurd! She thumped the back of her head against the door and groaned. Rodney had a knack for weaseling his way into people's good graces, but she was never going to fall for it again. Not after what he'd done. She was a different person now. A stronger person.

She walked into the kitchen with Buddy at her heels. A few minutes later, she sat at the table with a steaming cup of orange cinnamon tea while he snuffled around near the corner cabinet.

The ancient recipe book thumped open on the counter again.

"I'm just going to ignore that," Emma told the house. She added a dollop of honey to her tea, sighing. "And I can't believe you broke the front porch step just to scare him. As if we didn't have enough things to fix. Was that really necessary?"

The deadbolt on the front door slid firmly shut.

Apparently, it was.

Chapter Ten

"You've got to be kidding me." Hunter gripped his cell phone and sat down hard in the corner chair of his rented room. A frilly nightmare of a pillow jabbed into his lower back and he tossed it onto the floor. "Sam Norton is the owner of the entire waterfront?"

"That's right. All of it," Jim Creese said in his usual clipped tones. The New York native always sounded like he was in a hurry to get things done, which made sense considering he was the best commercial real estate broker Hunter had ever met.

"Are you sure we're talking about the same person? Sam, the old guy who's on the commerce committee? It just doesn't make sense." The few conversations Hunter had with Sam revolved around town gossip, island traditions, and the best places to get a good drink. The man had to be in his eighties. He had never expressed any interest in property investments, let alone mentioned the fact that he owned all the real estate on the wharf.

Jim's laugh was as cold and sharp as the steel beams in Hunter's high-rise penthouse. "Well, we did have to dig pretty deep on this one. Turns out the waterfront is one big lot, and the property hasn't changed hands for several decades. The county clerks had to go into the paper archives for the title, if you can believe it. He's not using a corporate entity or anything, so my guess is that he inherited it."

Hunter mulled this over. It made sense, because Sam didn't strike him as a real estate tycoon. Take the way he dressed, for example. Faded pants and shirts so old, they belonged in a museum. And then there was Sam's car. The Datsun pickup looked about the same age as its owner. But it wasn't just the way Sam looked that made this news so surprising. It was his personality.

Hunter had met many investors in the past few years since he made a fortune with his e-commerce website. He and his college room-mate, the founder of the company, had developed an online retailing business that eventually got bought out after it went public. Those investors had a different vision for the company, and Hunter finally sold off his interest and moved on to other projects.

After several years, Hunter was now the owner of three upscale, successful restaurants in Seattle. One of them was on the waterfront, just steps from the famous Pike Place Market. He'd had a lot of experience dealing with investors, and all of them had a calculating, aggressive quality to their personality that Sam Norton lacked. They were like circling sharks, always searching for the next big bite. Hunter knew this because he swam in their circles. Staying sharp, staying hungry—that's how you made it in the world. Sam just didn't fit the mold. But then again, no one on Pine Cove Island was typical.

"Listen," Jim said. "You already bought the other plat on the wharf there, and that's no secret. If this guy knows you want his properties, too, he's going to try to manipulate you."

Hunter could hear Jim clicking his pen, the way he always did when his gears were turning. It was hard to imagine Sam Norton being manipulative, but appearances could be deceiving. If years of working with cutthroat investors hadn't proved that to Hunter, then his ex-girlfriend, Melinda, had sure brought it home.

Hunter stood and began pacing the small room. He refused to think about his ex's betrayal. After what had happened between them, taking a break from Seattle was the best way to rid himself of the bitter regret so he could just move on. And that's exactly what he planned to do.

"If you really are interested in this place, I think it would be best if we extended Mr. Norton an offer from an 'undisclosed investor,' " Jim said.

Hunter rubbed his face with one hand and glanced at the clock on the nightstand. It was four-thirty in the morning, but Jim had called from the East Coast, three hours ahead. Hunter considered talking to Sam face-to-face. Sam the drinker. Sam the octogenarian. Surely, he'd be reasonable? But then, we were also talking about Sam the real estate mogul who owned half the business property in town. There was a lot more to this guy than Hunter had realized. Jim was probably right.

"Yes," Hunter said. "Extend him the offer and we'll go from there."

"Okay, good," Jim confirmed. "I'll have Trisha get ahold of him later today. One other thing. I'm pretty sure you're aware of your capital situation. . . ." Jim was alluding to the fact that Hunter didn't actually have enough to buy the entire waterfront at anywhere near fair-market value. "You'll need to sell some property."

"The Hornstein brothers still interested?" Hunter asked. They had extended an impressive offer to buy his two larger restaurants a few months ago. At the time, Hunter had been reluctant to cash out and walk away. Now things were different. He not only wanted to expand onto the islands, he also needed the change of scenery. Maybe throwing most of his capital into this new project was his best opportunity.

"I just spoke to them this morning before I called you. Their offer still stands."

Hunter considered the step he was about to take. Pine Cove Island had been on his radar for a couple of years now. He could see the potential in the sleepy island town, especially with all the tourist traffic from both the Seattle area and

British Columbia. Initially, he had only planned to open Haven on the wharf, but after researching the property, he wanted all of it. The waterfront was run-down and needed work, yes. But so much could be done to make it thrive. He had a gut feeling about the place. It would be a huge risk, but one he was willing to take. The timing was perfect, and he wanted nothing more than to throw himself into a new project and watch it succeed. This was what he knew. This was what he was best at.

"Tell them I'll consider their offer," Hunter said. "Let's hear what Sam Norton has to say first."

There was a long pause on the other end of the line. "Hunter, listen. I think you may be onto something huge here. But understand, if this plays out, you'll be all-in on this little backwater town of yours. You know what I'm saying? The only property you'll have left in Seattle might be the bistro and your penthouse."

"I know," Hunter said. "I'll make it work. Thanks, Jim."

After he hung up the phone, Hunter felt a rush of adrenaline over what was to come. Once Sam Norton accepted his offer, the game was on. He could see the waterfront in his mind's eye. A resort and a retreat for the harried crowds from the city. It would be a combination of the comforts of home and an escape from the fast-paced lifestyle on the mainland. The whole idea invigorated him and gave him a sense of exhilarating purpose that he hadn't felt in too many years to count. He would make it more profitable than any of his past investments had ever been, and at the end of the day, it was all about profit, wasn't it? Money talked. It was a language he knew well. Everything else was just noise.

He walked into the bathroom and splashed cold water on his face. It was still dark outside, but he was wide awake now. At this hour of the morning, there wasn't much else he could do yet, but there was one thing.

He could run. Running always helped him clear his head and focus. In Seattle, he had a treadmill in his penthouse so he could run any time of the day or night without being subjected to the rain. Here, he had to make do with what was available. He stretched to ease the tension in his neck and reached for a T-shirt.

Chapter Eleven

It was so early in the morning that the moon was still visible in the dark sky, with just a tinge of light on the horizon to herald the rising sun. Emma trudged after Juliette, her cell phone's flashlight scanning the path in front of her. They made their way down the forest trail that wound along the perimeter of Bethany Andrews's B&B, the rich scents of evergreen and damp earth kicking up around them with each step.

Emma yawned, wishing she hadn't forgotten her coffee in the car. She was barely awake and grossly unprepared for this stealth operation. The soft broomstick skirt she had dragged on over her hiking boots that morning wasn't the best choice, but that's what happened when you had to function before coffee.

"What time is it, anyway?" Emma asked.

"It's almost five o'clock. The sun's on its way," Juliette said, searching the edge of the trail. She always knew when the sun was going to rise. It had something to do with her affinity for plants and their need for daylight.

The trail wound in a circle around a small pond, and instead of staying on the path, Juliette stopped at the edge of a copse of trees. "We need to go this way." She pointed into the thick undergrowth.

"Are you sure?" Emma peered into the thick foliage. "It looks pretty wild and, you know, *woodsy*."

"Exactly. The night-blooming jasmine is growing through there." Juliette charged ahead, ignoring the overhanging branches and thick ferns in her path. It wasn't that she was being careless, she just didn't need to worry about them. Emma watched the ferns and evergreen branches sway as though caught in an underwater current, bending away to let Juliette pass.

Emma, on the other hand, had no such treaty with Mother Nature. She stepped off the jogging trail and tripped over an exposed root. "Jules, hold my hand!" she whispered loudly.

"Are you still afraid of the dark?" Juliette teased.

"No," Emma said testily. Even though she was, a little. She should never have watched that scary movie when she was in fourth grade. Scarred for life by the bogeyman. "It's just that if you're touching me, the plants behave. And I'm not in the mood to be smacked in the face with a tree limb this morning."

Juliette backtracked and grabbed Emma's hand, hauling her across the thick undergrowth. "It's down this way, near the pond."

A few minutes later, Emma could make out a

shimmer of water through the trees. The sky had grown lighter, and she could now see the moonlight reflected off a tiny pond in the middle of a clearing.

The scent of jasmine filled the air, and Juliette let go of Emma's hand, running to the plants. "Here you are," she said to the delicate flowers.

Dropping down on one knee, she pulled cutters from a satchel slung over her shoulder and began clipping sprigs of jasmine. Every once in a while, she murmured to the plants. It would have been unusual for anyone else to see, but Emma was used to it. Juliette always talked to plants, and they seemed to listen.

Emma dug around in the satchel for the bag of blackberries Juliette had brought from her garden. It wasn't even blackberry season, but Juliette's plants either didn't know or didn't care. She bit into the wild berries, savoring the tart, sweet flavor. "These are crazy good."

"I know," Juliette said absently. "I put a spell on the blackberry bushes last year so the birds and rabbits wouldn't be tempted. Now I can pick all the ripest, juiciest berries and they're right up high, out in the open."

"Nice," Emma said around a mouthful of berries. "Can't get much better than that."

"Sure it can." Juliette threw her a mischievous smile. "I also made it so those bushes don't have thorns. Now picking blackberries is easy as pie."

"Mmm, pie," Emma said. "You should make me one for my un-birthday. It's today, in case you're wondering."

"Yeah, I'll get right on that," Juliette said. "Right after I give Icarus a bath."

Emma popped another berry into her mouth. "Who's Icarus?"

"My flying pig."

Emma shook her head. "Meanie." She ate another blackberry. Juliette had absolutely no interest in baking or cooking and they both knew it. Her idea of making dinner involved picking up the phone and ordering pizza.

"Okay, I think this is enough," Juliette said, clipping the last of the jasmine. "Bring me the basket."

Emma crept forward, congratulating herself for only tripping once. She waited as Juliette filled the basket, wondering if their magic "Go Away" cupcake was really going to work.

"Do you know I planted these back in high school?" Juliette said. "I had that crush on Logan O'Connor, remember him?"

Emma took a seat on a spongy patch of moss. "Of course. You used to write his name with hearts all over your notebooks. You wanted him to ask you to the prom."

"At the time, that was my plan. I planted all this jasmine out here, coaxing it to grow and thrive. Then I was going to lure him to this pond for a romantic picnic. I thought if I could surround him with the scent of flowers that bind the heart, he would fall madly in love with me. Jasmine is magical like that. Wherever it shows up, love soon follows. That's why we're putting it in the 'Go Away' cupcake. Mixed with our other ingredients, it's going to make Hunter fall head-over-heels in love with the tropics. It'll bind his heart to the idea so he can't imagine living anywhere else." Juliette gave her a wicked smile. "It's gonna be amazeballs."

Emma frowned. "I don't seem to remember it working out very well with Logan O'Connor."

"That's because I chickened out," Juliette said with a laugh. "I just couldn't get up the nerve to ask him. I waited after school every day for a week, trying to find a way to talk to him. But he had that girlfriend, which sort of put a damper on my plans. And anyway, his parents never would've approved of me."

Emma gathered a sprig of jasmine and inhaled the rich, buttery sweetness. She tucked some behind her ear and stared up at the moon. "Weren't his parents on the town welcoming committee, or something?"

"Yeah, but they weren't very welcoming to our family. They used to cross to the other side of the street if we happened to be on the same sidewalk, remember?"

Emma remembered that part. It always hurt

136

her feelings when people shunned them. She had always wanted to fit in, but that could never really happen. Not when she was a Holloway. There was always someone to remind her that she and her family were the resident weirdos. "It was his loss, Juliette. He probably didn't deserve you, anyway."

"I know." She placed the jasmine into the basket and stood. "He wasn't the guy for me."

Juliette had only had a few boyfriends growing up, but nothing serious. She always said if the right person came along, Mother Nature would let her know. Emma often wondered how Juliette could be so sure. Emma once felt sure about Rodney, and look where that had gotten her. Nowhere good.

Sighing, she slapped leaves off her skirt and stood. Juliette drew a small vial of liquid from her bag and murmured something over it, dropping several jasmine petals into the jar. The wind kicked up and swirled around the women, whistling through the trees like an elusive lullaby.

"What are you making?" Emma whispered, not wanting to disrupt the light magic that ebbed and flowed around the small clearing.

Juliette placed leaves from the plant into the liquid and exhaled softly. "I'm just doing a trial run for the jasmine essence I'm going to make on the solstice. This is supposed to invoke yearning."

"How will you know if it works?" Emma asked.

Juliette screwed the top on the glass vial and dropped it in the basket. "I haven't decided yet. I was thinking I'd mix it in a tincture and sprinkle some on Bonbon, then bring Luna over to visit him."

"If you can get Luna the Hellcat to yearn for Bonbon, then you will be the most powerful Holloway that ever lived." Emma took the basket from Juliette. "We should get moving. Bethany's B&B will be up by now, even if she isn't. It will look really weird if we're seen emerging from the woods in her backyard at this hour."

They walked back to the jogging trail, Emma holding on to Juliette's hand as much as possible. At the edge of the trail, they lowered their voices and rounded the corner to the B&B. The kitchen in the little house was lit from within, and Emma could just make out the cook starting breakfast.

Someone was coming toward them on the jogging trail, moving fast. Emma gripped the basket tighter as Juliette yanked her arm, pulling her toward the trees. The basket wobbled, spilling some of the fresh-cut jasmine onto the path. Emma stooped to gather them up.

"Leave it," Juliette hissed from behind a tree.

But it was too late. Emma stood up fast and the shadowy figure slammed into her, grunting in surprise.

She fell backward, scattering the contents of

138

the basket onto the ground. Strong arms reached out and grabbed her before she hit the ground. She jerked away in reflex, and the man tumbled forward, landing on top of her.

Chapter Twelve

Hunter heard a soft, feminine gasp. He tried to catch his fall, gripping the woman's head in his hands at the last minute before they slammed to the ground.

Emma Holloway's stunned face stared up at him. Her soft curves were pressed against the full length of his body. She smelled like blackberries and wildflowers. *Damn.*

Rising above her, he braced on his forearms to catch his breath. Five miles into his morning run, he had just reached the point where it became less exhilaration and more of a chore. Now he had to work at breathing, but it may have had something to do with lying on top of a beautiful, alluring woman.

Emma didn't move, just stared up at him with her mouth open and a startled look on her face.

"I'm so sorry. I didn't see you." Hunter pulled himself up, noting for the first time that she was surrounded by scattered white flowers. The petals were tangled in her hair, and with her silver eyes and lush mouth, she looked like a magical forest nymph. He scowled and ran a hand through his hair. *What the hell?* The lack of breakfast was getting to him.

She sipped air, as though unable to catch her breath.

He crouched beside her. "Emma, are you okay?"

"You just . . . knocked the wind out of me," she whispered.

An empty glass vial lay on the ground between them. He brushed at his shirt, noting the faint scent of jasmine in the dampness left behind.

Reaching one arm behind her back, he raised her to a sitting position and waited for her to catch her breath while he tried to slow his own breathing.

She sat up farther, fumbling for her skirt and pulling it down over her thighs. Hunter caught a glimpse of graceful bare legs and soft skin. A stab of hot lust shot through him and he fought to get it under control. He noted the exact moment she realized he was holding her.

"I'm okay now." She pulled away and slowly stood, her expression prickly. "What are you doing out here?"

"Running."

She frowned.

"You know, on the running trail." He indicated the path ahead of him.

"Well, you should watch where you're going." She ruffled her hair and slapped dirt off her skirt. Tiny white flowers floated to the ground around them. Clearly, she was disturbed. So was

141

he, but in a much different way. What was it about her? She wasn't anything like the women he usually saw back in Seattle. Those women were the tailored business types with sleek hair and hard edges, just like his ex. The type of woman who calculated every move; who always had an agenda. Emma Holloway, on the other hand, was wild and soft and deliciously carefree. He had no idea how to even begin dealing with her.

"I'm sorry," he said again. "I wasn't paying attention and I didn't see you on the path until it was too late."

"Well, you shouldn't go out running in the dark. What were you thinking?"

If you must know, I was busy thinking of you licking whipped cream off your finger the other night at dinner. He never in a million years expected her to appear right in front of him on the trail at five o'clock in the morning. Come to think of it, "What are *you* doing out here?"

She bent to pick up the scattered sprigs, tossing them into her basket. "We were just going for a stroll. You know, fresh air and all that." She wouldn't look him in the eye, just kept gathering the flowers.

Hunter glanced around. "We?"

"Emma," a breezy voice called. Her cousin, Juliette, stepped out of the forest. "Oh, hey, Hunter. Fancy meeting you out here." Her voice was a little too cheerful and her smile a little too bright. What the heck was going on?

Juliette glanced at the ground and her smile faltered. She looked at Emma. Then him. The strangest expression stole across her face. She pointed at him in accusation. "You have jasmine in your hair."

Hunter reached up and brushed petals off his head. He had the sudden urge to apologize, but he didn't know why.

Juliette put her hands on her hips, the barest hint of a smile ghosting across her face. "And so do you, Emma. You're both surrounded by it. And the vial spilled." She pointed to the wet splash of liquid on Hunter's T-shirt, then at Emma. "On both of you."

Emma grabbed the last of the clippings and turned to go. "Sorry if we startled you. Have a nice run. Gotta go."

She charged down the path in the opposite direction, jerking her head at Juliette to follow. Her cousin stayed for a moment, staring at him.

"What?" He brushed white flowers off his T-shirt. The damn petals stuck like Velcro.

Her mouth curved up at one corner as she turned to leave. "Nothing you need to worry about."

He watched them go, still feeling the warm imprint of Emma's soft curves against his heated skin. His body was on fire, and not because of the run. He was ramrod stiff and one hundred percent on high alert, for a woman covered in dirt with leaves and flowers tangled in her hair.

Emma disappeared around the bend and he waited for his heartbeat to return to normal. He waited a long time.

Chapter Thirteen

Emma stirred her double raspberry mocha, slouching in one of her shop's bistro chairs. It wasn't easy, the slouching. The chair was one of those hard, wrought-iron numbers that people usually reserved for outdoor seating. But she needed to give Juliette a visual. She was completely apathetic about Hunter Kane. He did nothing for her. *Slouch.*

"Juliette, I told you a dozen times, there's nothing going on between me and him."

Juliette uncrossed her arms to grab a quick bite of her cupcake, then crossed them again. She had just arrived as Emma's shift ended and Molly took over. "I don't buy it. Something's definitely brewing between you two. Mother Nature doesn't make mistakes. And two nights ago, you both got hit with my potion. It's a double whammy."

Emma sighed and gave up on slouching. Her back had its limits, after all. Instead she leaned forward and pinned Juliette with a hard stare. "Your potions don't work on me. I'm a Holloway, remember?"

"I remember," Juliette said in a singsong voice. "But you were with me when I made the spell. Both of us together, just like when we used to try stuff back in school. So, it's wild magic. And this time Mother Nature got involved. The vial spilled all over you guys. On a full moon."

Emma clenched her jaw and took a deep breath. She needed to remain calm. "That scene on the running trail last Friday had nothing to do with Mother Nature, and everything to do with you. If you hadn't yanked my arm so hard, I wouldn't have dropped the jasmine in the first place. Then it wouldn't have been all over the ground, and he wouldn't have slammed into me after I bent down to pick them up."

"It doesn't matter how it happened; what matters is that it did. You had jasmine stuck to your hair and clothes, and so did he. It surrounded you guys like a fairy circle, and jasmine binds the heart." She wagged her finger in Emma's direction. "You two are bound."

"We are not—" Emma lowered her voice to make sure Molly didn't overhear. "We are *not* bound. You're being ridiculous." A nervous twinge formed in the pit of her stomach, even as she said it. What if Juliette was right? What if Mother Nature and that full-moon jasmine spell were going to wreak havoc on her emotions and make her fall for him?

No. It was impossible. There was too much at stake, and Emma had already had her moment of idiocy years ago with Rodney. She knew better than to let herself be carried away by a gorgeous face and a mouthful of lies. Plus, she was a

Holloway. She could resist one little messed-up garden spell. No big.

Juliette gave Emma a long-suffering smile, as though she were addressing a toddler. "Deny it all you want, but the wheel's already in motion. Even if you don't believe me now, just wait and see. And from that smoldering look he gave you on the trail, it's totally obvious you've gotten under his skin. Like a thorn." She nodded smugly, grabbed Emma's mocha, and took a sip. "A love thorn."

"A *love* thorn? Okay, do you hear yourself right now? That's not even a thing."

"Sure it is."

Emma sat back and threw her hands in the air.

"It's not a matter of falling for each other," Juliette continued. "Because that's a given. It's a matter of *when*."

She took her mocha back from Juliette. "What do you mean?"

"We have to beat the clock and get him off this island before you lose your heart and common sense. It's imperative. Do you think you can hold off on getting all dopey-in-love-struck until the festival?"

Emma pursed her lips. "Please. When's the last time you've seen me dopey-in-love-struck?"

Juliette opened her mouth.

"Don't answer that." The last thing Emma wanted to do was talk about Rodney Winters, especially after the shock of finding him on her doorstep the other day. Growing up in the Holloway house was never normal. When most teenagers were sneaking beers and dating and going to parties, Emma had been learning kitchen magic with her grandmother or tromping through the woods under a full moon with Juliette, who was always on a quest to find some plant or another.

It wasn't that Emma was antisocial; she loved meeting people, and even had a small circle of friends from school. But nothing thrilling had ever happened to her until Rodney came along. It was almost as if Emma could sum up her entire life into two parts: Before Rodney and After Rodney.

Even now, after everything that had happened, she still remembered that giddy, all-consuming feeling of being hopelessly, deliriously in love. Her grandmother used to worry over her. "You're getting too wrapped up in that boy, honey," she'd say. "If you don't slow down and listen to your intuition, you're going to lose sight of who you are."

But Emma didn't listen. What did her grandmother know about guys, anyway? Her own husband had died young and she had never remarried. Emma believed she had found everything she ever wanted in the gorgeous golden boy, Rodney Winters. She jumped into their relationship with her whole heart, eyes wide shut, believing nothing could stop them from living happily ever after.

She shook her head. If only she had known where that handbasket was headed.

"High school was a long time ago, Juliette. I can assure you, I'm way smarter about men now. Besides, it's not like I'm going to be dazzled beyond reason by Hunter Kane. He's not even all that." The lie tasted like burnt sugar on her tongue, but she forged ahead. "He's just a guy."

Juliette smiled wickedly. "You and I both know that's not true. Just one look, and anyone can see Hunter Kane is most definitely not a guy. He's a *man*."

The wind chimes rang above the door and Mr. Man stepped inside. Today he wore a black T-shirt, black denim jeans, and black boots. All that black made his emerald eyes seem even brighter than usual. He hadn't shaved, which gave him a sexy, dangerous vibe. Maybe he was going for the casual island look, or maybe he just didn't care. Whatever the case, it worked.

Emma's breath hitched and her face flushed. Someone up there in charge of creation got distracted and dumped too much sexy sauce into the Hunter Kane batter. No one should be allowed to look this good.

He gave them a small half smile. "Hi, ladies. Is this a bad time?"

"Not at all," Juliette said. "I was just telling Emma that I need to go check on my garden. I have some flowers to distill." She gave Emma a pointed look and slid out of the chair. "See you guys around."

Hunter nodded, and took a seat. Emma immediately stood up. Too close. He was too close. He smelled like fresh soap and sunshine and something earthy and alluring. She needed a moment to think. "Um, I'm just going to hop in the back and get the files."

The file box was stuffed to the brim with manila folders, which were organized in alphabetical order. Sort of. Emma plopped the box on the tiny table and sat opposite Hunter. "Here we go."

"Listen, I want to apologize again for last Friday on the trail. I didn't see you until it was too late, and by then I couldn't stop myself. Were you hurt? I'm sorry I slammed into you."

Slammed into you. A delicious shiver skittered up her spine. The last thing she needed was a reminder of how he had felt on top of her, the heat of him pressed along the length of her body. Something in his expression told her he was thinking about it, too.

"Nope. No. It was no problem at all." She cleared her throat and dug into the box. "So um, these are the vendors."

Twenty minutes later, she had laid out all the files and walked him through the previous year's festival map.

Hunter listened intently, gathering the lists of vendor names applicable to the current year. "Do you mind if I borrow these files? I'd like to get this information into a spreadsheet. It would be much easier for me to keep track of the data that way. Then in the future, changes could be more easily integrated."

"Knock yourself out," Emma said. If he wanted to go all computery on her, she wasn't going to complain. And anyway, it would be good to have a file on her desktop. Something to keep her Pinterest boards company.

"I'll bring the files back in a few days. Will you be here on Sunday?"

"All morning."

He nodded. "Now, can you tell me how important this Spring Fling is on Saturday? Bethany said it's quite a big deal here."

"Did she?" Not surprised. She was probably hoping he'd Spring Fling *her*. The idea was annoying. Emma frowned, annoyed that she was annoyed. "Bethany runs it every year. It's sort of her pet project. It's a party for just the locals, established decades ago by farming families on the island, as a way to celebrate the end of the rainy season and the coming of summer. Over the years it's sort of become an island superstition. If you're a local merchant, you have to participate in order for the summer's and next year's business to be prosperous."

He sat back and folded his arms. "It sounds pretty important, then."

"It's just one of those things. There'll be food and dancing and drinking. Lots of drinking. Some people bring their homemade beers. Tommy Jenkins has a small brewery in his garage, and he brings all his weird creations for everyone to try. Stay far away, if you want my opinion. There be dragons, I promise you."

"Dragons?"

"Lavender pumpernickel bacon beer," Emma said with a grimace.

Hunter blinked. "Thanks for the warning."

Molly poked her head out of the back kitchen. "I'm going next door to check on Buddy and make sure Bonbon hasn't eaten him. Oh, hi, Hunter." Molly beamed. "Good to see you."

Was Molly batting her eyelashes? Jeez, no one was immune.

He waved as she shut the door, then turned back to Emma. "You named your dog Buddy?"

"He's not my dog. And it's just a placeholder," Emma assured him. "He'll get a better name once he has a real home."

"It's a good name for a dog. I had a dog named Buddy when I was a kid."

Emma tried to imagine Hunter as a child. He

seemed so grown-up and in charge, it was weird to think of him being small and vulnerable. "What kind of dog?"

"He was a mutt, and a complete nuisance. He chewed everything in sight, barked at shadows—even his own—and regularly peed in my dad's shoes."

"Sounds like an honest dog," Emma laughed.

Hunter grinned and she had to look away. Watching him smile was like staring into a roaring fire on a cold winter night. Mesmerizing, but dangerous.

"He was a great dog," he said.

"How old were you?"

"I was around nine." He traced a pattern on the bistro table with one large hand. "That was my favorite year."

"Why? What happened after?"

He shrugged. "Oh, you know. The usual stuff. Parents got divorced, dog had to go."

Emma felt her heart squeeze. "That's terrible."

"It was a blessing in disguise. Not losing my dog, but my parents splitting up. There was always so much tension in our house, and I never realized it until it ended. Not that growing up with my mom was a cakewalk, or anything. She was in advertising, so pretty much never home. Her idea of parenting was Post-it notes stuck to the fridge and a string of nannies."

It couldn't have been easy for him. Even though

she had her grandmother and Juliette growing up, nothing had ever filled the void of not having parents in her life. She wanted to tell him she understood, but how? "Um, I was raised by my grandmother because my mom has wanderlust." Okay, that had to sound weird.

"So, she travels a lot?"

"More like, she never stops traveling. It's just how she's wired. She only comes around"—Emma corrected herself because, who was she kidding?—"*came* around once every few years. I was seventeen the last time I saw her."

After her grandmother died, Emma received a postcard from her mother, who had been in Kenya and hadn't known about the funeral until it was too late. Emma felt an old twinge of melancholy, but it didn't last. She loved her mother, but in the way one loves a distant relation. It was her grandmother who had truly been there for her.

She brushed the memory aside and glanced at Hunter. An awkward silence passed between them, and she wondered if she should've kept her mouth shut.

"What about your dad?" Hunter asked.

"Oh," she said, trying for breezy and throwing his own words back at him, "the usual stuff."

He remained quiet, but gave her an understanding nod.

Emma swallowed. It was crazy, because she never talked about this to anyone. Maybe Juliette was right and Mother Nature had done some tricky bonding thing on them with the jasmine the other night. "I never knew my father," she found herself saying. "Wandering hippie moms aren't great at keeping track of things like that. He was in the Peace Corps. My mom only knew him for a short time."

"I'm . . ." He looked like he was going to say he was sorry, and Emma didn't want to hear it. All her life people told her they were sorry her mom was gone. Sorry she didn't have a dad. Who cared about "sorry"? It didn't mean anything coming from random people who could never understand.

He slapped his hand on the table. "Well, lucky us. Some kids get all the excitement."

A delicious warmth rolled softly over her skin. It was like slipping into a beam of sunshine after standing too long in the shade. Emma smiled. "Lucky us."

Hunter braced his forearms on the little table. He glanced down at her mouth and her breath hitched in her chest. There was an odd, swooping sensation in the pit of her stomach. The air felt supercharged, like they were standing in the eye of a storm and it was moving fast, roaring closer with each passing second.

She licked her dry lips.

His eyes narrowed dangerously and he began to lean closer.

The front door flew open. "We're back," Molly called. "Buddy wanted to come say hi."

The puppy let out a happy bark and scampered toward them.

Emma stood quickly and scooped him up.

"I should get going," Hunter said. "My contractors are down at the restaurant right now, so I'm heading over."

He stood and reached out to scratch Buddy under the chin. Their eyes met over the top of the puppy's head. Emma felt caught in an ocean swell, as if she were rising up, up, gaining momentum to crest the tip of a wave and then hover there, right before the fall.

She tore her gaze away. She was not falling. They were *not* bound.

He picked up the box of files. "See you at the Spring Fling."

Molly followed him out and waved good-bye. When he was gone, she shut the door and sagged against it. "Oh my God, Emma. That man is a hundred million degrees of hot. How can you sit there calmly like it's nothing?"

"It's just business." Nothing calm about it.

Molly glanced out the window at Hunter's retreating back. "Did you see his hair? So glossy and thick. Gertie said she'd offer to cut it, but it was hard to improve upon perfection."

"That's high praise, coming from Gertie."

"As for you." Molly turned and pursed her

lips. "She said to tell you to be at Dazzle at three o'clock, sharp. She has plans for your hair."

Emma tucked a stray curl into the ponytail at the nape of her neck. "I don't really want to change it."

"She says you're getting balayage."

"What the holy heck is balayage?"

"Highlights," Molly said in exasperation. "But way cooler. It's a French thing."

It sounded like an expensive thing, but Gertie never charged her much. And a small change might be nice. Not that there was any reason she needed to look especially good for the party.

See you at the Spring Fling.

No reason at all.

Chapter Fourteen

Hunter dropped the box of files in the trunk of his car and headed down toward the wharf. It was late morning, and he had contractors to meet in just under an hour. They were installing the booths along the back of the restaurant today. The staffing manager was already finished hiring servers, and at two o'clock, Hunter had a conference call with his publicist in Seattle to go over plans for advertising the grand opening. He was swamped.

And yet, his mind kept wandering back to Emma.

Since that moment on the running trail, he couldn't stop thinking about her. Hell, if he was being honest with himself, he'd been thinking about her even before that. There was just something so alluring about her. When she smiled, it was as if her whole being radiated warmth, and it made him want to move closer and bask in it. When she was angry, her eyes flashed fire and even though he knew he was screwed, there was a part of him that didn't care. Being near her was exhilarating, and that was a problem.

He stopped at the top of the grassy clearing overlooking the north side of the shoreline. A path wound down to the little beach and he took it. Maybe the cool breeze would help clear his head.

He really needed to get a grip. Haven was opening in a few weeks and he didn't have the bandwidth to be thinking about a woman. He needed to stay sharp. Focused. Especially now that he was working with Creese on acquiring the entire waterfront. This would be the biggest real estate investment Hunter had ever made. He couldn't afford to get distracted, no matter how alluring that distraction was.

At the edge of the small beach, someone sat on a bench tossing breadcrumbs to a flock of enthusiastic seagulls. Hunter recognized the back of Sam Norton's head. The old man was feeding the birds as he watched a fishing boat troll along the shoreline.

Just that morning, Creese had called Hunter to relay Sam's message about their anonymous offer. His exact response had been, "A man wants to talk about buying my property, that's one thing, but I ain't dealing with no faceless coward hiding behind his agent."

Hunter wanted to laugh. He should have known someone like Sam wouldn't go for the typical approach. This was his home, and the home of his family before him. A man like this would never sell to someone he didn't know.

"Good morning," Hunter said.

Sam glanced up. "Ah, it's you. Have a seat, son."

Hunter moved to the front of the bench and sat down. It was almost as if Sam were expecting him.

A few minutes passed in silence. Hunter studied the waves and tried to find the best way to approach the subject of real estate.

"You ever feed the birds?" Sam asked.

Hell, no, he never fed the birds. Who had time for that? "Not really."

Sam handed Hunter a piece of bread and gestured to the seagulls. The birds crowded around one another, taking flight and landing closer to the bench, then farther away. All of them eyed the bread in Hunter's hand.

"Good for the mind," Sam said. "Helps a person think."

Hunter tossed the bread to the rocky shore and watched the seagulls swarm.

"Not like that," Sam chuckled. "Piece at a time. You have to slow down." He handed Hunter another slice of bread.

Hunter decided to humor him. He tore off pieces, watching as the birds picked them off, one by one. Sometimes they fought over a piece. Sometimes they were fast enough to grab it and fly away. There was a type of cadence to the way they hovered and swooped, vying for the prize. It was oddly satisfying. Maybe Sam had a point.

"So," Sam finally said. "You're that investor who made the anonymous offer?"

Hunter glanced up in surprise. "How did you know?"

Sam tossed a piece of bread at the seagulls and stared out at the water. "You don't get to be eighty-six without learning a thing or two about people." He tapped a finger to his temple. "The way their minds spin."

Hunter waited for him to say more, but he didn't. The silence stretched out between them until it grew uncomfortable. He needed to explain.

"I'm not hiding behind my agent," Hunter said.

"You aren't, now?" Sam was still staring out at the waves.

"It's how the business is done. You extend offers through brokers."

Sam nodded. "And what business do you think this is?"

"Real estate," Hunter said, searching for a way to connect. "Investing."

"Oh, I see."

Sam said nothing more and Hunter tried to find another angle. Any angle. He had no idea how to deal with the old man. He tried again. "I've got investment properties in Seattle, and my current goal is to expand—"

"—Your current goals." Sam turned to face him. "What do you think that wharf is, son?"

He gestured behind them. "You think it's just a bunch of buildings? Just some automatic teller that dispenses dollars so you can live high on the hog? Real estate. Huh." Sam tossed the last of his bread at the seagulls. "So you send your man to try to get me to sell, like pushing a button."

Hunter shook his head. Sam needed to understand his vision for the wharf. It could be so much better. So much more profitable for everyone. "Of course I don't think it's just an ATM. Look, I'm sorry if you were offended because I had my agent extend you an offer. That's my fault; I should have approached you myself. But I know it's more than just a way to make money. Pine Cove Island is only going to get bigger, and more people will come. The wharf isn't ready for it, but I want to make it ready."

"Why?"

"Because it has so much potential and I want to watch it grow and thrive. Not just for me, but for the people."

Sam smoothed the remaining strands of hair on his bald head. "The people. That's what I want you to understand, son. This property doesn't make me tons of money. Oh, enough to get by on, of course." He waved his hand. "But there are families depending on it. This is their livelihood." He shot Hunter a knowing glance. "Let's take Emma Holloway, for instance."

Hunter's heart stumbled at the thought of her.

162

"Her grandmother rented that shop from me, and my father before me. Now Emma's taken over. She's struggling, as you may or may not know."

"I don't imagine it's been easy for her."

"It hasn't. But she's trying, and I'll do whatever I can to help her. The board was divided on allowing you to share the contract. Most wanted to give her the whole thing again, you know. There were a few who proposed that you could cater the whole event yourself, with your fancy new restaurant and all your fancy success. But I made it so you and Emma would have to share. She needs the profits. I couldn't rule her out."

Hunter said nothing, because he didn't know what to say. The truth is, he didn't need the income that the festival would provide. He was only in it for the publicity. If Emma's livelihood hinged on that festival, then he was glad Sam proposed that they share the contract. Sam was a good man.

"Fact is," Sam said, "that girl could be a year late on her rent and I'd still let her stay. Do you get what I'm saying? Now, you might say that's a bad business decision. Kick her out, you'd say. But these merchants have contributed to my own family's success. They've kept bread on my table for generations. I knew Emma's grandmother very well. It would be wrong to turn Emma out now. It's wrong to turn any of the merchants out, no matter how bad the economy gets. I'll do everything I can to make sure they're okay. We all have a history together, do you get what I'm saying?" Sam's blue eyes were watery under his thick white brows.

Hunter recognized Sam's deep-seated love for the people. It wasn't something he came across very often when negotiating for commercial real estate. He needed to find a way to make Sam understand that his offer would benefit the people.

"I understand what you're saying," Hunter said quietly. "But the people would all benefit from the changes I would implement. This place has so much potential. It's not about turning people out, it's about turning this place around."

Sam grunted. "And what makes you different from any other real estate investor who's approached me in the past?"

"That I can't answer," Hunter said. "All I can ask is that you consider my offer and trust that I could make this place prosper. For the benefit of everyone here. My vision is to preserve the nostalgia, but add improvements that will clean everything up and draw more traffic to the area."

Sam was silent for a long time. Finally, he said, "See, this is how business should be. People talking honestly, face-to-face."

"Will you at least consider my offer?" Hunter asked.

"I'm not making any promises, son. But I'm awfully glad you came to feed the birds with me this morning. You should try it more often. It helps with the thinking. Almost as good as bourbon." The old man cracked himself up. He tucked the empty bread bag in his jacket pocket.

"I'll try and do that," Hunter said. He could tell their conversation was over, and it frustrated him. He liked to move fast, get things accomplished. This slow island way of doing business was inefficient, but he knew when to stop pressing.

He smiled and stood. "I have to get to my meetings, Sam. It was good talking to you."

"You have a great day, Mr. Kane."

Hunter paused, then held out his hand. "Call me Hunter."

Sam eyed him for a long moment, then nodded and shook hands. "I'll do that."

Chapter Fifteen

Emma sipped coffee from her travel mug as she turned her car off the highway toward her cousin's cottage. This morning, Buddy sat in her lap, trying to hang his head out the window.

"You're not big enough, yet," Emma told him, stifling a yawn. She had given up trying to keep him on the passenger seat. If he insisted on helping her drive, she wasn't going to argue.

Juliette's mailbox stood at the end of a dusty path near the road. Vines and flowers wound around the post, covering the box in bright yellow blooms. If anyone knew Juliette, they could tell where she lived just by looking at it. When Emma was a little girl, she used to imagine her cousin was the goddess of the spring, and everywhere she stepped, flowers bloomed. While that wasn't quite true, it was close enough. Juliette could make anything grow and thrive.

Rosebushes lined the road that led up to Juliette's house. Even for early June, the bushes overflowed with a profusion of colorful blooms that dazzled the eyes.

Emma parked her car in the drive next to a few other cars. It was only eight o'clock in the morning, but Juliette rose with the sun and she liked to start the planting early. Every year, right before the summer festival, Juliette held a flower-planting party. She was in charge of the two dozen potted flowerpots that would line Front Street during the festival. The pots of flowers would be placed at intervals near shop fronts to help add an air of festivity to the event.

While this might have seemed like a small thing to most passersby, it was a big deal to Juliette and the merchants. Of course, a larger maintenance crew would swoop in and add hanging baskets to all the lampposts, but this tradition of planting flowers with Juliette had gone on for years. The flowers were always gorgeous, never wilted in the hot sun, and were guaranteed to bloom and thrive throughout the summer.

Emma grabbed her coffee in one hand and the basket of muffins in the other. Buddy hopped onto the grass, tail spinning in a happy circle. He immediately began investigating the rhododendron bush that flanked Juliette's front porch. From the sounds of laughter and good-natured banter going on behind the cottage, it was clear the planting party was already in full swing. Last year, Emma missed the party because she had no one to cover the shop. This year, she was grateful Molly had volunteered to open. It had been hard to keep things running all by herself, and Emma thanked her lucky stars every day since Molly had stepped in to help.

Juliette came floating down her front steps holding a pair of gardening gloves. She wore a gypsy skirt and no shoes, which was pretty typical of her, given that it was late spring. Juliette liked to feel the earth beneath her feet when she walked, and she only wore shoes when completely necessary.

She gave Emma a quick hug. "You made it."

"Barely. I'm only on my first cup of coffee, so don't expect coherent speech."

"Babble all you want, honey," a warm voice called. "No one's going to care, because you brought muffins." Romeo Rossi, the owner of the flower shop where Juliette worked, approached from the side yard with Buddy at his heels. He was a handsome man in his sixties, with salt-and-pepper hair, tanned skin and impeccably tailored clothes. It was unusual for an island local to wear collared shirts and pressed slacks, but Romeo was the exception. People often said he looked like an old Hollywood film star. He was also funny, pragmatic, and one of the kindest people Emma knew. If he wasn't gay, she'd have tried to woo him with cupcakes, long ago.

He gave her a Rhett Butler smile and took the basket of muffins. "I'm starving, so I plan on eating at least three of these. They're zero carbs, right?"

"Zero," Emma said, straight-faced. "And they also have negative calories."

"Perfect. I knew I could count on you. What's their superpower?" Romeo was a staunch believer in the Holloway charms, given that he worked with Juliette on a daily basis.

"They inspire productivity."

"Oh, thank God." He put his hand on Emma's shoulder and lowered his voice in a stage whisper. "Have you seen the motley crew Juliette has here this morning? They're going to need all the motivation they can get."

"It's true," Juliette said with a sigh. "You should have made a double batch, Em."

Romeo glanced down at Buddy, who was eyeing the basket of muffins with laser-beam focus. "Come on, little dog. Let's go feed the rabble." He turned and headed toward the side yard with Buddy trailing after him.

Emma followed Juliette inside. Her cottage always smelled like a greenhouse. The damp, pungent scent of fresh earth permeated the air, punctuated by sharp notes of lavender, green herbs, or flowers, depending on where you were standing. Emma inhaled, grinning. Aside from her own house, Juliette's cottage was her favorite place on earth.

"Who's all here?" Emma asked, following her down the hall.

"Um, about that." Juliette spun around to face her. "I may have invited a new person."

Emma stopped fast, her coffee sloshing on

her fingers. She narrowed her eyes. "What new person?"

A burst of laughter erupted from inside the kitchen, and Emma heard loud clapping. She pushed past Juliette to see Hunter standing outside on the back patio in a frilly pink apron.

All at once, he looked out of place, yet perfectly at home. And *scrumptious*. In jeans and a gray T-shirt, with Juliette's gardening apron tied around his waist, he should have looked ridiculous. But the apron just seemed to accentuate his muscular physique. Impossible as it was, he had somehow succeeded in making pink polka dots look masculine and sexy. Emma took a gulp of coffee. Hot guy in frills. Who knew?

"Do it again." Gertie laughed. She was standing beside her husband, Walter, with a half-eaten bagel in one hand and a coffee cup in the other.

Hunter stood on the patio holding three hand shovels. He tossed one into the air, then the next, until he was neatly juggling all three. The small shovels were all sharp edges and angles but he kept up the steady rhythm, expertly tossing and catching, while Gertie and Walter let out enthusiastic praise. With a final flip of one hand, he caught them all together, took a bow, and came up laughing.

Emma couldn't find her voice. Hunter, laughing. It was . . . mesmerizing. Gone was the calculating look in his eyes, the serious expression, the hard-edged businessman. Standing in Juliette's backyard, he just looked carefree and happy. Tiny ripples of pleasure shot through her, warming her insides. She tamped the feelings down and took a huge gulp of coffee. *Calm and steady, Holloway.*

"Where'd you learn to juggle like that?" Walter called.

Emma stepped onto the patio. "Clown school?"

Hunter's mouth quirked up at the corner when he saw her and his green eyes sparkled with laughter. "Nah, I quit clowning a couple years ago. I try not to think about that time in my life."

Emma fought not to smile. It wasn't easy.

Gertie came onto the patio with a tray of lemonade. "Did you say clowns taught you to juggle?"

Hunter took the tray from Gertie, setting it on the breakfast table under the huge maple tree. "No, back in college I had a roommate who was a bartender. He and I used to compete with each other on who could juggle the most bottles without breaking them."

Emma watched them talking and laughing. He looked so at ease in Juliette's garden, but he didn't belong there. The annual planting party was *their* thing. It was weird to see him fitting right in with everyone else. Sam Norton lounged on a gliding patio chair, talking with Romeo and two of the older men from the fire station. Some of the firefighters' wives were setting out platters of bagels and doughnuts on the table, while Buddy wandered the yard. Hunter said something to Gertie, then went to help James Sullivan, the bartender from O'Malley's Pub, carry in the terra-cotta pots from his pickup truck.

It all felt so normal, but it was just wrong. If everything went according to plan, Hunter wasn't even going to be around for much longer. He shouldn't be getting all involved in their traditions.

Emma went back into the kitchen where Juliette was filling a large coffee urn.

"What were you thinking?" Emma demanded.

Juliette gave her a vacuous smile. "That everyone needs coffee?"

"That's not what I'm asking and you know it," Emma hissed. "Why is *he* here?"

Juliette shrugged. "Because when I ran into Sam at the pub yesterday, Hunter was there, too. And Sam started asking what time the party started, and then he did his whole, 'Oh hey, son, you should come along, shouldn't he, Juliette?' blah blah blah thing. You know how Sam gets."

Emma sighed. She knew Sam all right. The old man loved the community. He was always trying to get people to gather and celebrate things. For Sam, it didn't really matter what the celebration was, as long as it brought people together. Baby christening? Splendid! What time should we show up? Your dog had puppies? Marvelous! When's the birthday party? One time, Sam even convinced the veterinarian's office to have a memorial service to honor the town's oldest rooster—an ancient, crotchety thing—who had finally met his end when he decided to cross the road in the path of an oncoming truck.

"I wish you had told me last night when I called," Emma said. "If I knew he was coming, I'd have stayed home."

"Which is exactly why I didn't tell you. I thought you might come up with some excuse, so I decided to omit that bit of information. Besides, think of it as temporary. You're supposed to act nice and get along, remember? This might be a good way for you to butter him up."

Emma didn't like it, but Juliette had a point. It would be a good way to make Hunter feel right at home, without having to exert so much personal energy. It was a party, after all. Everyone was gathered together for a common purpose: potting the flowers for the shop storefronts along Front Street. That was all.

"Here," Juliette said. "Take this coffee to the breakfast table, will you?"

Emma took the urn outside, careful to avoid Hunter. Juliette's garden looked like something out of Shakespeare's *Midsummer Night's Dream*. The grassy yard was surrounded by flowering bushes, with a huge maple tree at one end. There appeared to be no order to any of the plants and flowers, yet everything seemed to exist in harmony. Lilac bushes grew as tall as small trees on one end, right alongside lavender plants and roses. Here and there, fiery pink azaleas bloomed beside tulips and daffodils. There was an arching trellis of jasmine in the corner, and snapdragons along the borders. If anyone cared to point out that some of those flowering plants were out of season, Juliette just laughed and told them she had a green thumb. A select few believed it had something to do with the Holloway gifts, but most people attributed it to lots of hard work and planning.

Hunter and James were setting up the large flowerpots along one side of the garden.

Emma spent a few minutes talking to Sam, trying not to notice the way Hunter's arm muscles flexed under the weight of the planting equipment.

Sam's bushy eyebrows shot up. "And who's this, then?" He grinned down at Buddy, who was attacking Sam's shoelace.

"This is Buddy," Emma said. "I'm taking care of him until I can find him a good home."

Sam reached down to pet him. The puppy put both paws on Sam's knee, wagging his tail furiously. "I like this little guy," Sam said. "He's a smart boy, aren't you?"

Buddy would have agreed, but he caught sight of a squirrel and shot off toward the edge of the garden in a flurry of barking.

Hunter glanced over at Emma and smiled. Again, she felt that zing of warmth all the way to the tips of her toes. Juliette's stupid jasmine potion sure had done a number on her. Maybe it was affecting him the same way. Maybe that's the only reason his gaze seemed to linger on her. Or maybe it was wishful thinking. Except it wasn't. Because she wasn't wishing for it. That would be stupid.

She tore her gaze away and smoothed her sweatshirt down over her hips. Why did she have to wear the crappy jeans with the hole in the knee, today of all days? They were baggy and old, and she had much cuter jeans in her closet. She needed a do-over.

"How are things going with Hunter?" Sam asked.

"Nothing!" Emma felt her ears grow hot. "What?"

Sam's eyes crinkled at the corners. "How are things going with the summer festival preparations?"

"Yes. Good, good," Emma said quickly. "Everything's going great."

"He seems pretty intent on making a splash here," Sam said. "What do you think about his ideas for the festival?"

Emma wanted to tear them down, but she couldn't. Even though she had her own reasons for wishing Hunter would leave, she had to admit his ideas were fantastic. And the money he had donated to clean up the wharf was going to make a huge difference. "I think it's going to be the best festival we've ever had."

Sam beamed, the tips of his ears turning pink in his wrinkled face. "You don't know how happy I am to hear that."

"Okay, everyone!" Juliette marched into the yard. "You all know the rules. Except you, Hunter. You're a newb, but you'll catch on. The idea is to be as creative and colorful as possible. Plant the flowers with the taller greenery toward the back, the lower-blooming flowers toward the front. If you need any help with the design, I'm here. If you need any help lifting heavy objects"—she jerked her chin toward Hunter and James—"ask them. Sam, you're in charge of the breakfast table. Keep an eye on it and don't let anyone loiter."

"Jeez, Juliette. You sound like a drill sergeant," Gertie said.

Juliette put her hands on her hips. "We're on a mission here. I want these finished before noon so we can get the barbecue started. So behave or I'll make you run laps with him." She pointed to Buddy, who was gleefully circling the perimeter of the yard like an Indy 500 speed racer.

"All I want to know is, what's for lunch?" Walter asked.

"New York steak." Sam beamed. "Hunter brought some over from Sawyer's butcher shop."

"And grilled portobello mushrooms," Juliette added. "For the herbivores in the group."

"Yeah, I think that'd just be you, Juliette," James called, hefting a wheelbarrow full of potting soil. "No sane person wants grilled mushrooms when steak's on the menu."

"Good. More for me." Juliette clapped her hands. "Okay, let's get to work."

For the next hour, Emma focused on choosing which plants she wanted from the palettes of flowers, occasionally stopping by the breakfast table for more coffee. The atmosphere was light-hearted and easygoing, and the conversation ebbed and flowed in a lazy rhythm that soothed all her initial worries about having Hunter there.

"Are you ready for this?" His deep voice startled her out of her thoughts. He set the wheelbarrow of potting soil next to the terra-cotta pot on the grass in front of her.

Emma sat back and rubbed her hands on her faded jeans. "Thanks."

Hunter began filling the pot with soil from the wheelbarrow. Emma watched him under her lashes, trying not to notice the way his muscles bunched and flexed from the weight of the shovel. His arms were like Thor's in that movie, which was really saying something. Emma and Juliette had argued for days over who was sexier: Thor or his brother, Loki. Emma was team Thor, all the way. No contest.

Hunter paused and balanced his hammer in one hand. *Shovel.* Shovel in one hand. "Do you want more?"

Lots more. "No, I think that's good."

"Here, let me help you." He kneeled on the grass beside her.

Emma was acutely aware of his body, the nearness of him, the heat of him. She felt loose-limbed and shaky, but in a delicious way that made her want to giggle. Cripes. Juliette's jasmine fiasco had really screwed with her senses.

Hunter looked at the plastic cups of seasonal flowers with reluctance. "So how does this work?"

"You . . . plant . . . them?" Emma said with deliberate slowness. "You know, in the dirt." She gestured to a cup of pink flowers. "And then they grow."

Hunter handed her the plastic cup of flowers, his mouth tilting up at the corners. "You don't say."

She tried not to stare at his mouth. "Haven't you ever planted anything?"

He shrugged. "Not that I can remember."

"Not ever? Not even when you were a kid?"

It seemed weird to Emma, who had grown up around Juliette. As kids, they were always running around, digging in the dirt.

Hunter shook his head and handed her another cup of flowers. "We had gardeners."

Oh. Of course he did. "I should have guessed that."

"It's not like I didn't play in the dirt," he continued. "I mean, I was a regular kid. Climbed trees, skinned my knees, that sort of thing. But the gardens were off limits. My parents wouldn't have wanted me to interfere with the 'aesthetics,' as my mother called it. I could pretty much do whatever I wanted as long as it didn't cause a dent in the glorious landscaping. Same rules applied inside the house."

Emma set the flowers into the soil and glanced up. "Sounds like a lot of rules for a little kid."

"A lot of rules to break." He gave her a wicked smile that made her toes curl in her tennis shoes. He wiped his hand across his forehead, leaving a smudge of dirt. Somehow, it only magnified the rugged, outdoor vibe he was channeling. "I was in trouble a lot."

"Glad to hear it. I'd think less of you other-wise."

He leaned in and lowered his voice. "Once, my GI Joes waged war against my mother's tulip garden right before her summer gala."

Emma could just see him as a little boy,

thrashing through the flower beds. "I'm guessing the tulips lost."

"They never stood a chance."

She tried not to grin, but failed.

"It was total annihilation," he continued. "Flower carcasses all over the grass, dirt and debris everywhere. My mother was crying into her martini, but there wasn't anything she could do because the guests were already on their way. The mayor was the first to arrive. His wife slipped and fell in the mud."

"Your parents must have been furious." Emma laughed.

"They stuck me with the nanny and didn't talk to me for a week." He said it in such a lighthearted way, but Emma could feel the darker, sadder emotion behind his words. How lonely he must have been. "My father called me a tornado on two legs, but what was I to do? Those GI Joes were a bloodthirsty lot. I was just a pawn in their scheme."

"Was it just you?" she asked. "No brothers or sisters?"

"No, but that was a good thing. My parents always said trying to handle me was like herding cats. They never did get the hang of it. Even after they divorced, they each kept a full-time nanny."

"I'm sorry," Emma said softly.

He shrugged. "I was fine. I had friends, and did

a lot of sports in school. It kept me busy and out of trouble."

Emma tried to imagine what it must have been like for him to have two parents who felt he was constantly in the way. Growing up, she always thought it was tough having both her parents gone. But at least she had her grandmother, who had loved her completely. Maybe that was better than having to live every day knowing you were a burden.

"Well, someday when you have kids," Emma said, "you can let them run wild all over the yard to make up for all those pesky rules you weren't allowed to break."

The humor died on Hunter's face.

"Oh, do you already have kids?" Emma felt as if the world slowed on its axis and she held her breath. It made no sense, but somehow his answer mattered to her.

"No, I don't have kids. And I don't plan on it." Clearly, he wasn't comfortable with the direction the conversation was going.

"Well, you never know." She turned her attention back to the planting. "Some people start out saying that, and then change their minds. When Gertie and Walter first got married they never wanted kids, but then they decided—"

"I don't plan on ever getting married."

"Ah." Emma concentrated on laying another row of flowers in the terra-cotta pot. For some reason, his declaration bothered her. If there was one thing she knew about life, it was that anything could happen. Maybe for people like Hunter, with grand bank accounts and worldly views, there was some secret bargain they could make with the universe. Some kind of pact to ensure that all their plans succeeded. If there was such a thing, the universe never offered it to her.

"You seem to have it all worked out, then," Emma said. "Must be nice, knowing exactly what your future holds." Was that sarcasm in her tone? Maybe a little.

He shrugged. "I just know marriage is not a path I want to go down. It didn't work for my parents and it wouldn't work for someone like me."

"Someone like you," Emma said, tilting her head and studying him. "Where have I heard that before?"

It took a few beats for his dark expression to lift, but when it did, wry humor lit his face.

It was like watching a light go on inside him. As much as she wished it didn't matter, she couldn't deny that it gave her pleasure to see the darkness fade and humor take its place.

"When we were kids," she said, "I once talked Juliette into planting M&M's under a wild rosebush because I wanted an M&M tree."

His mouth tilted up at the corners. "And how did that work out?"

Their faces were so close, Emma could see the myriad shades of green in his eyes, noting a thin streak of amber in one. She shivered, trying to pretend his nearness didn't affect her. It had to be the stupid jasmine potion. She'd be so glad when that disaster finally wore off. Usually Juliette's small potions only lasted a few days.

"No M&M tree," Emma said brightly, ignoring her shaky hands as she placed the last cup of pink flowers along the border of her flowerpot. "But the roses smelled exactly like chocolate after that."

"Well, maybe you didn't plant the right kind of M&M's," he said. "You have to get the organic, cage-free kind. Picked fresh from the vine."

She sat back on her heels. "Oh, is that right?"

He nodded, his expression serious. "Uh-huh. It's common knowledge. I'm surprised you didn't know."

"You think I'm making this up, don't you?"

The pirate smile was back in full force. "Not at all."

He didn't believe her. She could tell. On anyone else, she wouldn't have cared. People had such a hard time believing in magic. But for some reason, she wanted him to believe.

"Okay, then." She tossed the hand shovel in the soil and stood up fast, slapping dirt off her hands. "Come with me. I have something to show you."

• • •

Hunter followed her without a second thought. There was no man on earth who could resist Emma Holloway with that mischievous grin on her face. She led him around the front of the house to the edge of the woods. The sun was high in the sky already, but the woods were dark and cool. Beckoning to him, she stepped into the shadows.

He followed her through the deep green foliage. She looked like a forest nymph from a fantasy film, winding through the trees, her hair glowing gold in the dappled sunlight.

They had barely gone a few yards when the tiny footpath opened into a sunny clearing. A wild rosebush grew in the center near an old wooden bench. He watched as Emma strolled over to the bench, then turned.

She was standing in a stray sunbeam, the light kissing her rosy skin and sparking off her head. "Prepare to be amazed."

He already was. There was no denying the attraction he felt for her anymore. He could still ignore it; in fact, he planned to. But he wasn't stupid enough to pretend it didn't exist. She was hands down the most alluring person he had met in a long time. A gorgeous bundle of contradictions. One minute she was cool and standoffish, and the next she slayed him with her intoxicating smile and genuine kindness.

Emma picked a wild rose and brought it over to him. Her eyes were shining with laughter and she held it out.

He took it. What was going on? Was she romancing him? There was no way. She barely liked him.

"Go on," she said, nodding to the flower. "Smell it."

Hunter's eyes never left her face, but he bent to the small red rose. It smelled deliciously sweet. Like a Hershey bar. He frowned down at it. "What is this?"

Emma put her hands on her hips and grinned. "What did I tell you? This is the rosebush where we planted the M&M's."

He sniffed them again. They really smelled like chocolate. Weird. "What species is this?"

"Who knows," Emma said as she began gathering a few of the flowers into a bouquet. "You'll have to ask Juliette. I love them though." She bent her head to the roses and inhaled. "I could just eat them, you know?"

Hunter's heart thumped hard in his chest. She was too luminescent; too lovely, even in her old jeans and blue sweatshirt smudged with potting soil.

He could hear the muted conversations from the group at the back of the house, but it was quiet in the clearing where they stood. He felt like they were in their own little microclimate, and she was the sun around which everything revolved. He stepped a little closer, because she was smiling up at him and it was too hard not to gravitate toward all that warmth.

He glanced down at her mouth. So sweet and soft. What if he stole just one kiss? The thought came out of nowhere.

"We should probably get back," she said quietly.

"Probably." Hunter didn't move. He still held the wild rose in one hand, his other hanging loose at his side, fingers itching to touch her.

She took a shaky breath.

He dragged his gaze up from her mouth.

Their eyes locked.

With infinite slowness, he closed the gap between them and reached his arm around her waist, settling his hand on her lower back. He felt as though he were in a trance, like everything else faded around them and the only thing he could see clearly was her. She was warm and soft, and touching her felt right. A thrill shot through him when she didn't resist. He pulled her body flush against his and she exhaled on a tiny sigh.

Emma tilted her head back, her eyes half closed, her breathing shallow. The scent of chocolate and honeysuckle surrounded him and the urge to taste her was so strong, he almost groaned out loud. If he didn't kiss her now, he'd go mad. The rose fell to the ground, forgotten, as he wrapped both arms around her and lowered his head.

Her eyes fluttered shut.

When he lowered his lips to hers, she grabbed fistfuls of his shirt, pulling him closer. For the briefest, most blissful of moments she brushed her lips against his. The whisper-soft touch of her mouth on his was intoxicating. He was drowning and he never wanted to come up for air. This was *heaven.*

Emma yanked away, breathing hard.

Hunter blinked, frozen in place. Most of his mind was still mush and the only thing that seemed to matter was getting closer to her.

"Fake." She shook her head with a nervous laugh. "This is all fake. It's not real."

Hunter strained against his desire to hold her again, forcing himself to find his voice. "What?"

Emma gestured to him and her. "This whole thing you're feeling," she said in a rush. "It's because of Juliette's jasmine potion."

He frowned and stared down his nose at her, struggling to get his breathing under control. "What?" he repeated in irritation. She wasn't making any sense and he didn't like how nonchalant she was acting, as if the tiniest, almost-kiss didn't affect her the way it had affected him.

"This," Emma insisted, wagging her finger back and forth between them. "This whole wanting-to-kiss-me thing? It's because you slammed into me on that running trail and that jasmine spilled everywhere. Remember?"

"I remember," he said. "But I don't see how—"

"Trust me," Emma said, a nervous smile on her face. She nodded and stepped back, wrapping her arms around her midsection. "Juliette put an attraction spell on that jasmine vial that day, and then it spilled on us. But don't worry. It was an accident. Anything you're feeling right now will fade in a couple of days. This isn't real."

Hunter took a breath, then let it out fast. "Are you trying to tell me that your cousin made some kind of love spell and that's why . . ." he trailed off, shaking his head.

"Yup." She forced a laugh. "Crazy, right?"

"Yeah," he agreed. It was crazy, all right. Because it was a ridiculous notion. Love spells were make-believe and this desire raging through his blood was very, very real.

"Anyway, it wasn't supposed to happen," she said, shrugging. "Sorry for the inconvenience. But it'll be over soon." She waved a hand as though to brush the situation away like a piece of stray lint, and started back toward the house.

Hunter stood rooted to the spot, stunned by his desire to grab her and spin her around and finish what he started.

Sorry for the inconvenience?

Her sweet, intoxicating scent still surrounded

him, permeating all thoughts except his desire to take what she had almost given. He jammed his hands on his hips and glared at the ground, waiting for his breath to steady. It didn't. Her bouquet of roses was scattered at his feet and he bent to gather them up.

It was almost as if an invisible string had somehow woven her and him together, and the farther she walked away, the more agitated he felt. *Jasmine potion, my ass.* She could blame it on whatever the hell she wanted, but he knew desire when he felt it. And he knew what it looked like when he saw it. There had been desire in her eyes. She felt the attraction, too, whether she wanted to admit it was real, or not.

He caught up with her just as they emerged from the woods into Juliette's front yard.

"Here." He held out the flowers. "You forgot these."

"Thanks," she said breezily, not meeting his eyes. He wanted to say something, but what could he say? The moment was over and she clearly didn't want to talk about it. But he'd be damned if he'd apologize for it. It had felt too good to hold her, and he wasn't going to take that back, even if he knew it couldn't go anywhere.

Hunter followed her back to the house, swearing under his breath. So that was it, then. They were going to pretend nothing happened. *Technically, nothing did happen, idiot.* He scowled, frustration and desire tangling inside him like dangerously crossed wires on a ticking bomb. Was he mad at himself for almost kissing her, or mad that he didn't get the chance?

He entered the backyard and his gaze flew directly to Emma, who was already back at her post, planting. A tiny frown creased her brow and she wasn't making eye contact, which was just as well. If she turned those gorgeous gray eyes on him again he'd likely forget to be cautious and end up panting after her like the puppy.

He walked over to her and picked up the shovel.

"You can take some of that soil over to Gertie and Walter now," she said, not looking up. "I'm finished."

Oh, was she? Anger flared, hot and bright. Well, he wasn't damn well finished. He hadn't even gotten started. His heart was still pinballing around in his rib cage, and the memory of her soft curves pressed against his body was burning him like a brand from the inside out. But if she wanted to pretend everything was normal, fine. He could play it that way, even though they both knew it was a lie.

Hunter hefted the wheelbarrow and left her there, trying to ignore the simmering frustration shooting through every vein in his body. He had to pull it together. God knew he had no intentions of getting romantically involved with Emma Holloway, so why was he standing in the woods trying to kiss her like a lovestruck teenager? She could try to blame it on some stupid flower potion, but he knew better. He had been attracted to her from the first moment they met. The truth was, he found her irresistible as hell, with all that golden hair he wanted to tangle in his hands as he watched her expressive eyes go dark with desire. Her lips were so perfect and lush, just the thought of possessing them, possessing her, made another bolt of lust spike inside him. The things he wanted to do to her were hot and carnal and . . . *Fool!* He was a complete fool. There was no room in his plans for her, and he'd do well to remember it.

It was time he focused on the real reason he came to the party.

Hunter clenched his jaw, vowing that for the rest of the day, he would work on getting closer to Sam Norton. Getting the old man to accept him as part of the community was imperative. Sam owned all the properties on the wharf, and if Hunter could somehow find a way to gain his trust, then he could gain everything.

Eyes on the prize. Nothing else mattered. For the rest of the afternoon, he would pretend that Emma Holloway didn't exist. Not that she would care, since it was clear she planned on ignoring him, too. Maybe if they both pretended nothing had happened, the raging sense of lust would fade away. Maybe.

Chapter Sixteen

The next evening, Juliette pulled the car into the community center parking lot and turned off the engine. Loud, thumping music boomed from the double doors of the building. The Spring Fling party was well underway. "We're so late, and this time it's your fault."

"I know," Emma sighed. "Sorry."

She had visited her cousin earlier so they could both get ready for the party together. The decision of what to wear had been long and arduous, with Juliette eyeing Emma's choices like a small child eyeing a plate of boiled vegetables.

"You aren't wearing this," Juliette had announced, picking up one of Emma's dresses between her thumb and forefinger. "This is a peach floral. It looks like something you'd wear to a picnic." She tossed it onto the growing pile on her bed. "If you were twelve."

After a long lecture on why Emma needed to look hot, Juliette finally convinced her to wear a simple red sheath dress. It was fitted, but not too low-cut, which seemed to satisfy Juliette's need to make her look sexy, and Emma's need to not feel like she was interviewing for a job at Hooters. The compromise had been hard won.

Now Emma checked her reflection in the

passenger-side mirror of Juliette's car. The balayage treatment Gertie did had been a genius idea. Her hair still looked the same, but sections seemed more luminescent than before, falling around her face in loose waves. She touched up her lipstick and then got out of the car, repeating the silent mantra she'd been saying for the past twenty-four hours: *Nothing happened with Hunter. It was no big deal.*

Ever since their almost-kiss in the woods yesterday, she had been schooling herself on how to behave when she saw him again. It had all just been a silly fluke. The incident had been a direct result of Juliette's jasmine potion, and it was most likely faded by now anyway. Still, it was impossible not to think about the way he had pulled her against his hard body, and the warmth of his lips brushing against hers. The desire that flared between them felt so real, she had to keep reminding herself it was nothing. The sooner she forgot about it, the better. The only problem was, she'd been "forgetting" about it all day and it wasn't easy.

The party was already in full swing when they entered, and in spite of her mantra, Emma couldn't escape the nervous fluttering in the pit of her stomach. Hunter was going to be there. He was probably there already. *Deep breaths, Holloway. Nothing happened with Hunter. It was no big deal.*

"I bet Hunter is already slipping in a puddle of Bethany's drool right now," Juliette said, snapping Emma's attention, mid-mantra.

A shriek of laughter pierced the air and Juliette groaned. "There she is. Madame Boobs-a-Lot." Another ear-piercing shriek. "Singing the song of her people."

Bethany Andrews was chatting with Hunter near the bar. She wore a lime green wrap dress that showcased her impressive cleavage and perfect tan. Surrounding them were a few of Bethany's minions, every one of them glued to whatever Hunter was saying. Bethany shrieked again, and Emma thought she saw Hunter wince a little. Or maybe it was just wishful thinking.

"Let's get a drink," she said to Juliette. She was going to need it. More than anything, she wanted to block all thoughts of Hunter from her mind, but that was like trying to block the sun from shining. Sometime later, Emma was on her third glass of wine. The girls had gone to dance but Emma had declined, preferring to stay on the sidelines.

Her body was like a Hunter Kane divining rod; she was aware of his location at all times. Try as she might, she couldn't stop sneaking peeks at him from across the crowded dance floor. It would take a superhuman effort for any woman to ignore him. In dark slacks and a cobalt shirt open at the neck, he looked like the love child of *GQ* magazine and Versace.

She deliberately turned her back on him and his gaggle of admirers, concentrating on the buffet table instead. *Oh look, baklava.* She took one and bit into it. *Nice. See?* She could focus on something else besides Hunter Kane. Easy peasy.

"Hey, Angel."

All of Emma's reflexes seized at once. The bite of pastry in her mouth crumbled to sawdust as she turned.

Rodney Winters grinned down at her, his eyes already glassy from whatever he was drinking. His blond hair was artfully tousled, and while he may have still been handsome, Emma no longer felt that giddy pull that used to be there when she was younger. It dawned on her that Rodney had no idea his charm had faded around the edges, like a plastic toy left too long in the sun. He had peaked in high school and was still riding that high.

She gripped her wineglass tighter. "What are you doing here?"

He shrugged. "I ran into Bethany this morning and she insisted I come. Drove me here herself so I wouldn't get away."

Emma resisted the urge to roll her eyes. It was so typical of Bethany. That woman couldn't miss an opportunity to create drama. "I didn't know you'd be here."

He shrugged, eyeing her up and down. "I never did like these parties, but I'm glad I made the exception."

Emma hugged herself, wishing she hadn't worn the fitted red dress. Under Rodney's scrutiny, she felt self-conscious and lacking. It was like the high school prom all over again. Emma remembered when he came to her door to pick her up, their senior year. The front door had stuck, thanks to the house, and it had taken Emma a good five minutes just to pry it open. She had been so nervous, standing in front of him in the blue dress her grandmother had made for her. It had a sweetheart neckline and spaghetti straps, with a softly flowing skirt that ended right at her knees. Juliette had even talked her into wearing heels. Emma had felt like a princess.

Rodney was charming, but once they got to the prom, he sauntered off to talk to his football buddies, leaving Emma to hold her own against the scrutiny of the mean girls who hung around his crowd. Their dresses were store-bought, and they had professional updos from a salon. They whispered and giggled to themselves, ignoring her for so long that by the time they left the prom, Emma felt like a wilted flower.

She was convinced Rodney would never stay with her. Why would he? She was poor and quiet and boring compared to those girls. And on top of all that, she was a Holloway. As much as Rodney told her it didn't matter, Emma knew on some level, it did. Rodney never liked visiting her house, and he never seemed comfortable talking to her grandmother. Back then, Emma had wished with all her heart that she was just a normal girl like all the others. The kind with normal houses and normal parents who went to PTA meetings and threw neighborhood barbecues and went on camping trips. She wanted so badly to fit in; to truly belong. It was the main reason why, later that night, parked in Rodney's car overlooking the ocean, she had given in to him. Deep down, Emma hadn't felt ready to have sex, but she wanted so desperately to hold on to him. He had even said he loved her, and that was all that mattered, wasn't it?

But it hadn't been real love. Rodney had chosen poor Emma Holloway because she believed he hung the moon. And that was very attractive to him, since he rather agreed. Anyone could see just by looking at them that Emma had worshipped him, and Rodney needed to be worshipped. In his mind, he deserved nothing less.

Now Emma set the pastry back on the table. She had to concentrate not to snap her wineglass.

Rodney took a sip of his drink. "I was hoping I'd see you here."

She took a deep breath and let it out slowly, trying very hard not to slap that smug half smile off his face. It was the same smile he used when he wanted to charm his way back into her good graces. But Emma wasn't that gullible girl anymore. Part of her died the day he betrayed her. The words on his "good-bye" note were etched into her memory like cut glass.

"I don't want to talk to you, Rodney," she said. "Stay away from me."

She pushed those painful memories aside and searched the hall, spotting Juliette near the bar. Emma lurched forward and elbowed her way across the room, ducking to steer clear of a couples' flailing arms as they danced to some song about busting a move.

At the bar, an overweight man draped an arm over the back of his chair and leered as Emma tried to squeeze past his giant belly. "Works for me," he said with a hiccup.

"Everything works for you, Lester," James Sullivan said dryly. He nodded to Emma from behind the counter as he filled a beer glass.

"Not true," the man insisted, sloshing some of his drink down the front of his shirt. He smelled like stale sweat and bourbon with a shot of Drakkar Noir. Emma breathed through her mouth and stood on her tiptoes, straining to see over people's heads. Where the heck was Juliette?

The man leaned closer, his belly filling the space between them like an airbag during a collision. "Girl, you must be a parking ticket because you got 'fine' written all over you." He cracked himself up.

Emma blinked through the fumes. "Clever."

"Yeah," he agreed. "My wit pops up at random."

"Like bubbles from a swamp," she murmured underneath her breath, scanning the crowd. There! She pushed past him. Juliette was standing with Molly and Gertie near Tommy Jenkins's beer table.

Emma rushed over to her. "Jules, I have to get out of here."

Juliette spun around, her face red with suppressed laughter as she gripped a small cup of beer. "Emma, you have to taste this. Wait! On second thought, no you don't. I'm not that mean."

"What do you girls think?" Tommy Jenkins shouted above the music. A huge grin split his freckled face, and his red hair had been smooshed down around the edges with some kind of pomade. In his early thirties, Tommy still had a baby face. He looked like an evil Chucky doll, but he was one of the nicest guys they knew.

Molly made a strangled noise that turned into a cough. She set her cup down and excused herself, mumbling something about the bathroom.

"I'm just going to go make sure she's okay," Gertie said, backpedaling.

Tommy glanced hopefully at Juliette. "You like it?"

"Well. It's just . . . it's *remarkable,* Tommy," Juliette said. "What is that odd texture?"

"Chia seeds," he said proudly. "They're great for digestion and they go well with the kale puree I added during the fermentation process."

Juliette coughed. "You are so"—*cough*—"so creative. Emma, you should really try one of Tommy's ales."

"Wow. Thanks so much, Jules." Emma glared, holding up her wine. "Let me just finish this first." She grabbed Juliette's elbow and hissed into her ear. "I have to go. Rodney's here."

Juliette's eyes sprang wide. "What? Where?"

Emma jerked her thumb over her shoulder.

Scowling, Juliette searched the crowd behind her. "How did he get here?" she asked grimly. "Wait! Let me guess. A puff of black smoke?"

"No."

"A crack in the earth opened up and he crawled out?"

Emma took a gulp of wine. "Getting warmer."

"Fine, I give up. Just tell me."

"Bethany brought him."

Juliette let out a huff of disgust. "I knew it had something to do with hell." She stiffened and narrowed her eyes over Emma's shoulder.

Emma glanced behind her to see Rodney weaving toward them.

"Hey, Juliette," he drawled. "Long time no see."

"Yeah, it's been great. Too bad you had to ruin the streak."

"Still a witch, I see."

Juliette wrinkled her nose in disgust. "Still a total assho—"

"—*Okay,* you guys." Emma threw up her hands. "We are done here." She glared at Rodney. "I said I didn't want to talk, Rodney. I meant it."

"Give me a chance to change your mind." He winked and reached for her hand.

She yanked it away.

"Oh my God, hi," Bethany said in a voice high enough to shatter glass. "I see you found Emma, Rodney. I told you she would be here." Bethany swayed up to Rodney and laid her hand on his shoulder, grinning up at him like a shark. She turned to Emma and Juliette. "He was asking about you and I knew you'd have a lot to talk about, so I convinced him to come tonight." The malicious glint in her eyes accented her green eyeshadow to perfection. Leave it to Bethany to accessorize like a pro.

Juliette stepped closer to Emma. "So thoughtful of you, Bethy."

Bethany narrowed her eyes at the familiar nickname, her red fingernails tightening on Rodney's arm.

"But what you may not know is that Emma isn't interested in Rodney. She wants nothing to do with him anymore. So there's one man you can put back on your list of prey. How is that list, anyway? Must be dwindling pretty low by now, considering the way you mow through them."

Bethany shot Juliette an evil glare, which quickly melted into a plastic smile. She tossed her hair and turned her attention to the person at Emma's shoulder. "Hi," she breathed.

"Emma." Hunter's quiet voice near her shoulder was like a lifeline. She grabbed on.

"Hunter! Hi. How are you?" Emma reached mechanically for the small cup of ale Tommy held out for her. Now she had a glass of wine in one hand, and beer in the other. Nothing like double fistfuls of liquid courage.

Hunter glanced at her drinks, then at Rodney and Bethany. "Having fun?"

Hell to the no. "Oh, you know. Just hanging out." She could feel Rodney's indignation, and his cool assessment of Hunter. Emma faked a smile and took a sip of her wine.

Gak! She choked down crunchy bits of disaster. Wrong drink. *So* much wrong.

"Want some?" Tommy held a cup out to Hunter, beaming.

"No!" Juliette cried. "He's, um, didn't you say you were allergic to hops?"

"I . . ." Hunter caught Emma's wide-eyed warning. "I am. Yes, it's a problem for me. Thanks anyway."

Rodney stuck his hand out toward Hunter. "We haven't met. I'm Rodney Winters."

"Hunter Kane." They shook hands, and Emma

would bet money that Rodney was giving Hunter the old death-grip shake. Trying to prove he was the stronger man.

"That's quite a grip you have there," Hunter said.

Nailed it.

Rodney eyed Hunter. "So who are you, now?"

Juliette shot daggers at Rodney. "He's a friend of Emma's."

Rodney gave an unpleasant laugh. "Is that right?" A muscle ticked in his jaw and he squared his shoulders. "And how friendly would that be?"

"Stop it, Rodney," Emma said sharply. This was too annoying to bear.

He put his hands up in mock surrender. "Okay, okay." Then he turned to Hunter as if they shared an inside joke. "She gets feisty sometimes. But I kind of like a woman with some fire in her, you know what I mean? Did she tell you we—"

"—Excuse me," Hunter cut Rodney off. "I just came over to see if Emma wanted to dance." He turned to her. "Do you?"

"She does." Juliette gave Emma a little shove.

Bethany sputtered something unintelligible.

Emma set her drinks on the table. "Fine." She needed to get away, even if it meant she had to dance with the devil himself. Although Hunter didn't feel like the devil at the moment. Compared to Rodney and Bethany, Hunter was a saint at the pearly gates.

She marched out onto the dance floor, passing Molly Owens and some guy who was staring into her cleavage as if it held all the secrets to the universe.

Hunter came up behind her. He slid his arm easily around her waist as they began to sway to the music. "Who was that?"

"An old mistake. A dodged bullet." Her emotions were all over the place. She couldn't believe Rodney. What the hell was he trying to do? It was so over between them. "I have to get out of here," she declared hotly.

"Now?" Hunter asked.

"Yes. No." She let out a frustrated breath. "Right after this song."

"All right."

"I mean it."

"I see that."

"In fact, can you dance us closer to the front door?"

In a few moments, he had maneuvered them to the far end of the building. She half danced, half pulled him even farther toward the doors.

"Are we still dodging bullets?" he asked in amusement.

"Yes."

Hunter placed his hand on the small of her back and spun her in a circle. With the other hand, he somehow opened the door and before Emma realized it, they were standing outside. He held her lightly, but she was suddenly aware of how close they were. How alone.

"Better?" he murmured.

She nodded, speechless. She had been so preoccupied with her resentment over Rodney that she hadn't realized she was standing in Hunter's arms for the second time in the past twenty-four hours. To say it was disconcerting was the understatement of the century. Head spinning from all the wine and commotion, she searched for an anchor. She tried to remember her mantra. Something about *No big deal*. But that was a lie, because this felt like a very big deal.

Hunter drew her closer. They swayed to the muted music until little by little, Emma began to relax. All her frustration funneled into something much different. In Hunter's arms, it was impossible to think about anything except how deliciously warm he was. He was like her own personal furnace.

An old song from the eighties wafted through double doors, surrounding them. Something about being forever young. She had a sudden memory of her mother playing that song when she was a little girl. They swayed together to the music until all her earlier tension eased. Emma felt warm and safe and protected.

When the song ended, he stepped away, taking all the warmth with him. "Come on, I'll walk you out."

Crap. She didn't have her car. "You can't. I didn't drive here. I have to get Juliette to take me home."

"I'll take you. I'm leaving anyway."

Five minutes later, they were on the highway heading toward her house. Emma called Juliette to let her know she was heading home, then stole a glance at Hunter from beneath her lashes. He seemed completely at ease in the black sports car. It smelled like leather and something spicy and elusive, and very male. It was probably just him.

"Sorry about all that back there. Rodney's my ex. I haven't seen him in a long time, and he just showed up in town again. It's been over for a while, but he's not making it easy."

"You don't have to apologize."

She shifted in her seat, feeling like she needed to give him an explanation. "We were together in high school. And then on and off for a few years after that."

"Uh-huh."

"And then my grandmother got sick and he asked me to marry him, and it seemed like a good idea at the time. I needed help and I thought he'd be supportive." She needed to shut up. Why wasn't she shutting up? "How was I supposed to know he'd steal all my savings and leave town with another woman? I mean, who *does* that? Just people on TV, I thought. Or I don't know, maybe it happens all the time. You just never think it will happen to *you,* you know what I mean?" Okay, now she was babbling. Damn those glasses of wine.

Hunter was quiet. She wished he would say something.

"Anyway, it's totally over." She ran her hands through her hair and smoothed her red dress over her thighs. "I have no idea what he wants."

Hunter turned, piercing her with his emerald gaze. "Don't you?"

Emma felt light-headed, and it had nothing to do with the wine. The air seemed to spark between them and the temperature in the car went up a few degrees. She licked her suddenly dry lips. It had to be her imagination.

She tore her gaze away and stared out at the highway, grateful when her driveway appeared around the bend.

"That's me, right there." She pointed to the gravel road and he pulled the car to a stop in front of her house.

The porch light was on, illuminating the peeling yellow paint and sagging front step. Even in the dark, it was obvious the house needed work, but Emma didn't care. To her it was the most beautiful place in the world, with its Queen Anne turret and "good bones," as her grandmother used to say.

"Thanks for driving me home," she said with a

hiccup. "And for, you know. Helping me dodge bullets."

He nodded once, studying her.

Emma bit her bottom lip. Was he going to kiss her, finally? Ridiculous! Of course not. It was the wine. It made her think stupid things. Did she want him to kiss her? Of course . . . not.

The silence stretched out between them. He leaned just a fraction of an inch closer. She hiccupped.

He blinked as if coming out of a fog, then turned and stared straight ahead, gripping the steering wheel with both hands. "Good night, Emma." His voice sounded strained.

Back to reality. "Yeah. G'night." She jumped out and ran up the steps, careful to skip the broken one. She could feel him watching her.

When he drove away, she let out the breath she had been holding. Jeez. Maybe Juliette was right. Maybe that stupid jasmine fiasco had something to do with her annoying, but persistently growing infatuation with the man. *No big deal.* Yeah, right.

Emma set her purse on the entry table and walked into the kitchen. Buddy ran circles around her ankles, trembling in pure joy at her existence. She took him to the backyard to do his business, then opened a new bottle of wine and poured herself a glass. Why not? She was heading to bed, anyway. And if she dreamed about Hunter's full lips on her skin, his warm hands roaming over her, the delicious scent of him, who cared? No one ever had to know.

"They're just dreams," she said out loud, staring into her wineglass.

Bottoms up.

Chapter Seventeen

The next morning, Emma sat in her favorite overstuffed chair in the living room with a mug of Earl Grey tea and the tail end of a hangover. Thankfully, Molly had agreed to take her Sunday morning shift. The Tylenol had finally kicked in and Emma was feeling pretty good, all things considered. Buddy was hard at work, sleeping on the couch beside her.

She smoothed the fleecy fur on his back, loving the silky texture of it, and the softness of his ears between her fingers. When Juliette had first brought him, all Emma could think about was how she had to give him away to a real family. And even though she still felt like he deserved better, she had grown accustomed to having him around. Last week, he had somehow wiggled his way into her bed and now he was a permanent fixture on top of her comforter at night.

On the evenings she sat alone at her kitchen table, she was grateful for the snuffling noises he made as he searched the floor for stray crumbs around her chair. Reading her latest overdue bills was less painful with his warm little body curled up in her lap. For some reason, even though she knew it wasn't going to last, Emma took comfort in feeling like she and Buddy were a team. Things felt less bleak with him around.

Even the house liked him, which made things so much easier. The biggest perk of all was that the house seemed to know exactly when the puppy needed to go outside. Every once in a while, the front and back doors would swing wide open and the puppy would go running into the yard. It was amazing how easily he slipped into her life. She almost couldn't imagine her home without him now.

Emma snuggled deeper into her chair with a contented sigh. It was close to eleven o'clock, but she still wore her pajamas—flannel pants with pink doughnuts on them—and a cat tank top that read CHECK MEOWT. She had just arranged a knit throw blanket around her and picked up a new romance novel, when the doorbell rang.

A burst of dread washed over her, and she forced a couple of deep breaths. If it was Rodney again, she would stay exactly where she was. He could ring the bell all day long if he wanted to. She wasn't answering.

Buddy, on the other hand, was happy to investigate. He barked in glee and scampered into the foyer, pawing at the front door.

After several moments, there was a polite knock on the door.

Emma frowned.

The house seemed calm and no lights flickered. She tiptoed to the door, but before she had a chance to peer through the peephole, the door swung wide open. *What the heck, house?*

Hunter stood on the front porch with her file box. He wore a flannel shirt and faded jeans, with windblown hair and a slight stubble that gave him a rather disheveled appearance. Sort of a "Hot Lumberjacks 'R' Us" vibe. It must be his weekend look, and it was a good one. Not that Emma was keeping track, or anything.

Buddy leapt over the threshold, his whole body wagging in joy at the miracle that appeared before him.

"What are you doing here?" She tried to close the door a little, mostly to hide her pajamas and the puppy-chewed slippers on her feet, but the door wouldn't budge. The house wanted to let him in.

Hunter's gaze swept over her and his mouth kicked into a grin. "Juliette was at the shop. She told me to come over."

No more cupcakes for Juliette. "Why?"

"I went by to return the files and she said to bring them here, since you weren't going in this morning. She also wanted me to give you this." He held out a small vial of amber liquid. "For your headache?"

Emma took Juliette's headache remedy. It wasn't charmed, but it worked like one. Her cousin always seemed to know when she'd need it. "Sorry, I wasn't expecting visitors." She crossed her arms over her tank top and shivered. Storm clouds were rolling in fast, and the morning air had grown chilly.

Upstairs, the floorboards creaked and a door shut.

Hunter glanced behind her. "Do you have company?"

"No. It's just the wind," she lied. How do you even begin to tell someone that your house is sentient? Just add that to the crazy Holloway rumors.

Somewhere in the distance, thunder rumbled.

Please, not now. Emma stared at the darkening sky, calculating how much time she had before the rain came. It had been days since she checked the leaks in the attic, and one of the windows had a hole in it. She hadn't expected a storm to brew so quickly. She needed more time.

Before she could thank Hunter and send him on his way, a flash of lightning cracked and the sky opened up. Emma knew she was in for it. The spell she had done to keep the storm at bay had finally run its course, and now it was back with a vengeance.

Buddy yelped and ran back into the living room. In a matter of seconds, a torrential downpour surrounded the house.

"The attic!" Emma cried. "I have to go." She tried to shut the door, but it wouldn't budge.

Another crack of lightning split the sky and she gave up with a frustrated groan.

Hunter stepped inside and put the file box on the entry table. "Do you need help?"

She was about to say no, but the word died on her tongue. He was there and he offered help. She'd be stupid to turn him away. "I just have to nail a board to one of my windows. The glass fell out last week—" Rain began pelting the front porch, and the door swung shut behind him.

He glanced back with a tiny frown.

"The wind," she lied. There was no time for this. If the patches in the ceiling didn't hold, the attic would be flooded. Emma darted up the stairs, praying she wouldn't be too late.

Thunder rumbled, loud and ominous, as she flung open the attic door. She was vaguely aware of Hunter following her. Heavy sheets of rain poured in through the broken window, drenching the floorboards.

She whirled and ran down the hall to fetch a stack of towels, returning to throw them onto the growing puddle. It was no use; the rain was coming in too fast. Another bolt of lightning cracked across the sky outside and the sound of the storm echoed off the attic walls.

"We have to block the opening," Hunter shouted. Somewhere in the house, doors slammed, adding to the noise.

Emma flew across the room, pushing old

trunks and dusty boxes out of the way to grab her toolbox.

Hunter lifted a piece of plywood from a scrap pile in the corner.

She nodded, and together they positioned it over the broken window as the driving rain hit them full-on. Emma gasped. The plywood slipped from her hands. Icy water drenched her face and hair, soaking through her clothes. She grabbed it and tried again, holding the plank firmly as Hunter slammed the hammer over and over.

Her arms began to ache, but she held on until the steady flow of water became a stream, and then a trickle. When he nailed the last section of plywood to the window frame, they stood shivering in the half dark, cocooned by the muted sound of the rain.

Breathing heavily, Hunter set the hammer on the floorboards. His shirt was plastered to his very broad, very muscular chest. They were soaked to the skin, their faces only inches apart. A dark lock of hair fell across his forehead. "This isn't going to last," he said quietly.

Emma swallowed hard. "I know."

Slowly, he lifted a hand and brushed a strand of wet hair from her eyes. The roar of the storm outside was nothing compared to the staccato thump of her heart.

"You need something permanent."

"I know," she whispered. "But this works for now." She wasn't even sure they were still talking about the window. All she knew was that he was so close she could feel the heat of his body against her chilled skin.

Hunter lowered his gaze to her lips, his expression fierce in the half light.

She trembled with delicious anticipation.

He cupped her cheek with one large hand, his thumb stroking once, featherlight, across her lower lip. "Is this okay, then?" he murmured.

It was the smallest, simplest word. *Yes.* But Emma knew if she said it, a floodgate would open between them that she might never be able to close.

She took a shaky breath.

He watched her. The cords of muscle on his neck tensed, but he held very still. Waiting for her answer.

Alarm bells went off inside her head, but Emma shoved them aside. She wanted him. And suddenly, even if it was wrong, she didn't care. For once in her life, she was going to live a little. "Yes."

The moment his lips touched hers, she felt as if she were dipped in warm honey. The warmth of his mouth, at first a soft pressure, then more demanding, made heat pool low in her belly and her limbs shake from something far more powerful than the cold air surrounding them. He smelled like rain and wet wool and something darker and more alluring, something completely masculine and just, *him*. Emma gripped his shoulders and instinctively pressed closer. He tasted wild and dangerous and more delicious than anything she'd ever tried before. She wanted to inhale him. Suck him in. Lick him up.

A sound like a low growl escaped him, and he deepened the kiss, wrapping his arms around her waist, smoothing his hands up under her wet shirt to slide across her bare skin. When he pulled her against him, a lightning-hot desire shot through her body and she couldn't seem to get close enough. He was like a storm crashing over her, but this time she didn't care. This time, she welcomed it.

Chapter Eighteen

Emma didn't know how long they kissed, but by the time he pulled away, she was liquid from head to toe. Where did he learn to kiss like that? On second thought, better if she didn't dwell on it. She could just imagine the string of supermodels in his life. The tall, leggy types with sleek hair that never frizzed. Probably had names like Suzette or Giselle.

She crossed her arms and shivered, all too aware of her bedraggled appearance. "Um, I'll go and get some towels." She ran out of the attic before he had even had a chance to stand.

Down the hall, Emma leaned against her bedroom wall and waited for her pounding heart to slow. What the hell was wrong with her? He was supposed to be the enemy, and she needed to remember that. If she got all lovestruck over this man, nothing good would come of it. Sure, he had just helped her patch the window, and then kissed her into kingdom come, but she had to pull herself together.

After drying off, she slipped on a pair of blue jeans and a T-shirt, then grabbed a few towels from the linen closet. When she didn't find him in the attic, a brief pang of disappointment shot through her. She tried to ignore it. Maybe he had already gone home. Downstairs in the kitchen, she heard movement, and she found him tinkering with the ancient coffeepot in the corner.

Years ago Emma had painted the little room a sunny yellow with glossy white trim. Crisp Battenburg lace curtains framed the window, and a collection of blue and white china plates hung on the wall above the small kitchen table. Aside from the industrial-grade sink and double ovens she used for baking, it had a quaint, homey feel to it. It was the same kitchen her grandmother had used for decades, and many other Holloway women who had come before her.

Hunter Kane, shirtless and leaning over the coffeepot in the middle of the kitchen, looked completely out of place. And hot as sin.

Beside him, her spell book lay open to that same old "Day of Bliss" recipe. As usual. The house still hadn't given up on it and Emma had stopped bothering to put the book away. It seemed like every time she walked into the kitchen, there it was. She ignored it now, like she always did. "It's not going to happen," she told the house under her breath. "Quit trying."

"What's that?" Hunter asked, shaking water droplets from his hair with one hand.

"Oh! Um, you won't get dry without these." Emma held up the towels. "So, you know, quit trying."

He took the towels and began rubbing down his

hair. The intimacy of the moment wasn't lost on Emma. She could almost imagine him stepping out of the shower, except she wasn't going to. That would be ridiculous. Nothing good could come of her imagining Hunter gloriously naked, surrounded by steam with water dripping down his muscular torso—

"I thought coffee might be a good idea." His deep voice startled her out of her thoughts.

"Coffee!" she said a little too brightly. "Yes, I'll just make some." She flew to the cupboard and pulled down a tin of gourmet coffee, aware that he was watching her every move. Emma felt flushed and jittery. She forced her hands to remain steady as she measured coffee into the machine. Being in the tiny kitchen with him felt like being in a room with a wild lion. It was unsettling. Because she sort of wanted the lion to pounce.

Outside, the rain continued to pour in gray, icy sheets. Emma sighed. "If all goes well, I'll have a contractor fix that roof before the end of the summer. Good thing Sam's been so easy on me with the shop rent."

Hunter straightened. "Sam seems to really love this town, and the people in it."

"Well, yeah. He owns the whole waterfront, aside from your restaurant. His family was in real estate, and he inherited it. Sam's a lot different than his parents. At least, that's what my grandma always told me. He's kind of a simple guy, and genuinely cares about the community. I'm just so grateful he's my landlord and hasn't kicked me out yet."

She frowned at the storm outside. "I better bake something fast, or that patchwork job we did in the attic is never going to hold. The only problem is, if I force the storm away it will just come back worse, later."

Hunter was silent for so long that when she finally glanced up at him, she almost spilled the coffee grounds. He looked completely baffled.

"You say the weirdest things," he said.

"Get used to it. The Holloways are the resident weirdos, haven't you heard? Wait, you've spoken with Bethany Andrews. Of course you've heard."

He leaned against the counter and folded his arms, a playful smile curving his lips. "I've heard a few things, yes. I've heard you are a magical creature who lives all alone in this big house and bakes spells into cupcakes."

She eyed him carefully. Of course the townspeople talked. But he obviously didn't believe it. Nobody with any sense ever really gave it much credit, except a few of the locals. Most visitors just found the story charming and bought cupcakes for the fun of it.

"And you don't believe it," she said.

His smile broadened and he took a step

forward. "Who doesn't like a good story? And it's no wonder they chose you, Goldilocks, to be the resident fairy-tale character. You're perfect for the part." He smoothed his fingertips down a lock of her hair.

"Fairy tales are make-believe," Emma said solemnly, stepping back. It was important that he understood. "What I do is real."

His laughter was low, a deep, rich sound that resonated through her bones. He was special, too, this man. Something about him made her want to melt into him, and no one had ever made her feel that way before. But he didn't know her. Not really. He didn't accept who she was.

"You don't believe me, do you?" She felt as though she were hanging from the edge of a cliff, holding on by just one hand. His answer would have the power to lift her up, or send her plummeting.

Hunter gave her a half smile. "Sure, I do."

Her hand slipped on the cliff's edge. "No, I'm being serious. I'm sure you've heard all the stories by now. Do you believe them?"

Hunter took a deep breath and gazed out the window, avoiding her face. "You know what I believe in? Facts and numbers. The logic of A plus B never changes. It's steadfast. You can hold on to it. You can build from it."

"Numbers?" Emma echoed. She was asking if he believed in her and he was talking about accounting? Her fingers slipped off the edge of the cliff and she began to fall.

"Exactly," he said. "In my experience, people are mercurial by nature, but you can always count on numbers to tell the true story. Profits, overhead, bottom lines. I pay attention to those things and I stay on top. Everything else is just window dressing."

Emma felt as though she were plummeting to the bottom of a ravine. All her hope dropped to the pit of her stomach. They were so completely different. A man like him could never live in her world, nor she in his. She hadn't even realized she'd hoped it. *Stupid!*

"Look, Emma. I can see you're struggling to make ends meet. What I'm trying to say here is, I know how to make money. It's what I'm good at. And it's clear you need help. I can help you."

She shook her head. "What are you talking about?"

"You're obviously having financial troubles. Your house needs repairs and your business is failing. You need to start thinking about making serious changes. I know you haven't had an easy time of things since your grandmother died."

A sudden ache unfurled inside her and she fought to breathe around it. "I'm managing just fine."

"Maybe for now, but it won't last. Your grandmother's way isn't working anymore. The world's moved on, and you're going to need to update your business model. I can help you do that. I've already organized those vendor files and e-mailed you the new spreadsheets. Haven isn't going to be the only establishment you'll have to contend with. Bigger businesses will come. You need to consider what you're going to do in the long run. This magic act you've got isn't going to work forever. You need to be more realistic."

Magic act? Her cheeks burned with humiliation and something sharper. Anger flooded through her. "You've barely been on this island for longer than two minutes, and yet you want to tell me how to fix my life? My shop, my house? They're mine. This is *my* life."

To her complete horror, she felt tears prick the corners of her eyes. She suddenly felt as small as she'd been when her mother left; as hopeless as when her grandmother died. Why did she ever imagine he could believe in her? "You think you have it all figured out. But there are some things in this world that are just as important as your precious numbers and profits—no—*more* important. Like friendships. And community. And trust. Without any of that, nothing else matters. I'm sorry if my way of doing things doesn't measure up on your spreadsheets." She swiped at her eyes.

"Emma." Hunter took a step forward, a stricken

look on his face. "I don't want to upset you. It's just hard for me to watch you struggle." He ran his hands through his hair and let out a frustrated breath.

She shook her head. They were so different. He had the whole world organized into neat categories that could be calculated and measured, and he was convinced that was how the universe worked because it worked so well for him. But she wasn't him. Her life was nothing like his. In fact, Emma was pretty sure the universe had been laughing at her for years. The only thing she knew for sure was that she was born a Holloway, and she'd been given a gift. It wasn't just a "magic act."

"You can't do it, can you?" she blurted. "You can't step outside of yourself for just one moment and believe that what I do is real."

He threw his hands up in the air. "Believe what, exactly? What do you want me to say? That I believe in *magic?*" His expression was one of incredulity.

She lifted her chin, grateful that her voice was steady. "Some things can't be explained, but that doesn't make them any less real. Maybe you're just afraid it might be true."

"I'm not afraid," he said in exasperation. "It just makes no logical sense."

"So what? Believe anyway." She knew he was going to walk away and that it was probably for the best, but a tiny voice inside of her urged her to try one last time. She gathered her courage. "I *dare* you."

He was quiet for a long time, and Emma wondered if she had pushed him too far. Maybe this was the part where he told her she was a freak and walked out the door. She waited for what felt like an eternity. Each tick of the clock above the kitchen door made her feel one step further away.

"Okay," he said softly, nodding.

She sucked in a breath. The smallest tendril of hope spiraled through her and she exhaled, afraid to embrace it in case it was her imagination.

Hunter nodded and looked her straight in the eyes. "Show me. I'll try to keep an open mind. I promise."

Emma grabbed a mixing bowl from the bottom cupboard and slapped it onto the counter. When the full moon came, she and Juliette would see him gone. But here in this kitchen, surrounded by the storm outside, time stood still. For just a moment, she wanted to show Hunter Kane the truth. She wanted him to believe in her.

An hour later, Hunter sat shirtless and barefoot at the kitchen table with a steaming cup of cinnamon-infused coffee. A deep sense of warmth enveloped him as he watched Emma in the kitchen. She was all fluid grace and movement, whipping up a bowl of frosting until the zesty scent of lemons and vanilla filled the air. Occasionally, she would brush past him, and it was all he could do not to grab her and draw her closer. The kiss they shared in the attic was seared into his mind and his body was still thrumming from the memory of it.

A single ringlet fell over one of her eyes, and she sucked her lower lip in concentration. He shifted uncomfortably and took a quick gulp of coffee, scalding his tongue. She was the most intriguing, alluring woman he had ever seen, and that was the problem. He had no business even thinking about her, not when he didn't even plan on staying. He suddenly wondered how she'd react if she knew his real plans. If all went well, in just several weeks his restaurant would be booming, along with the rest of the wharf properties once he acquired and upgraded everything. When things were running smoothly, he'd move on to his next project. Maybe he'd scope out other islands in the Puget Sound to expand his businesses, or maybe he'd move south to Portland. A pang of guilt flooded him and he pushed it away. This was what he did; what he was good at.

"Okay," she said brightly. "Bring me two of those cupcakes on the table. You, Mr. Skeptic, are about to be dazzled by the Holloway magic." She brushed the curl off her forehead with the back of her hand and beamed up at him.

Hunter sucked in a breath. God, he wanted to kiss her again, but she was like a scared rabbit now. The moment in the attic had passed, and he could sense her nervousness. It made him want to hold her until her tension fled. He wanted to unlock all that wildness that lay just beneath her surface.

He brought two warm vanilla cupcakes to the counter and she began frosting them with simple swipes of a butter knife.

"They're not going to be pretty because I didn't have a lot of time, but it really doesn't matter," she said. "They should work just fine."

The storm still raged outside, charcoal clouds roiling on the horizon. Every few minutes, thunder rumbled and lightning shook the house.

"What exactly are these supposed to do?" he asked, distracted by the way she bit the tip of her tongue while icing the last cupcake. He wanted her mouth, and that tongue. Again.

Emma held out a frosted cupcake and winked. "You'll see."

He took the cupcake and bit into it, his eyes never leaving her face. It was delicious, and the blend of lemon zest and creamy vanilla warmed him to his toes. "Delicious."

"I know." She bit into her own, and for several moments they chewed in companionable silence, with only the sound of the storm outside. Hunter glanced out the window and stopped chewing.

He stared in surprise as the black storm clouds seemed to roll backward toward the horizon, as if being pulled back from where they had come. It was the oddest thing he'd ever seen. The sky looked like a movie reel on rewind.

"See." She pointed out the window. "The storm is leaving. That's why I call these 'Summer Sunshine.' "

He swallowed, frowning as the fog dissipated on a spring breeze. Clouds parted overhead and the sky dawned a clear, crystal blue. The rain droplets on the grass and trees outside sparkled like crystalized sugar. He licked the last of the frosting off his fingertips just as a brilliant rainbow arced across the sky.

Very slowly, Hunter turned to Emma. She stood in front of the sunlit window, glowing softly around the edges as though lit from within. In that moment she looked so much like an angel, Hunter could almost believe in anything. "You did that?"

She gave a half shrug. "I told you. This is what I do."

Hunter felt his mouth go dry and he swallowed once. Twice. "How?"

She shrugged. "I don't really know. I've just always loved baking, and my grandmother explained that my good wishes and hopes sort of flowed over and around me whenever I made something in the kitchen. That's how it starts.

The Holloway abilities. It's something we are naturally born to do."

A bird began singing in the maple tree outside. Hunter ran a hand through his hair, roughing it up as if to clear his mind from the fairy-tale fog he was in. "How long will it last?"

"Only a few days, if we're lucky. Mother Nature always has a way of taking back control."

He stared into her liquid silver eyes and wanted, more than anything else in the world, to understand. "So you bake these, and then things happen when people eat them?"

She nodded and began clearing up the kitchen, as if it were any other normal day. Maybe for her, this was business as usual. Hunter felt a strange yearning somewhere in the region of his chest. It was not unlike the feeling he remembered when he was a kid on Christmas morning. All the bright, shiny packages he couldn't wait to open. The mystery and the surprise, mingled with the bittersweet knowledge that the day would end and the joy couldn't last. He remembered that hollow feeling when his parents would start the drinking that would eventually lead to the arguing. For a few shining hours he could pretend things were good and that they were a real family, but it didn't last. He wished it could.

For the next half hour, Emma explained her different recipes and how they helped people. He watched in fascination as she flipped through her grandmother's ancient recipe book. He could barely grasp what she was saying. If it really was all true, then why wasn't the world banging down her door for her creations?

"You could sell your cupcakes on a grander scale, you know." The idea was almost too overwhelming to contemplate. "The entire world would fight for these."

"No," Emma said. "It doesn't work that way. If I tried to exploit it, it would fade away. That's just the nature of it. And it doesn't work on me, either, which is ironic. I can make other people feel good or have good luck, but I'm immune."

"But you just changed the weather. That was for your benefit."

"For the *house's* benefit."

He frowned in puzzlement. "The house?"

"It's hard to explain." She began filling the sink and placed the mixing bowls in the soapy water. "It's going to sound weird."

"I can assure you it won't be the first weird thing I've heard today." A mischievous humor filled his voice.

Emma turned, wringing a dishrag in her hands. "My house is sort of . . . sentient. By fixing the weather, I was easing its distress."

A door shut quietly upstairs and Hunter glanced up toward the ceiling. "It's haunted?"

"No, no. That's what Bethany Andrews would say. Or small-minded people who are afraid of things they can't explain. But it's not haunted. There aren't any ghosts or anything like that. It's just . . . opinionated. It always has been. It's been in my family for generations. Just another weird Holloway quirk." She tried to laugh it off, but Hunter could see she was afraid of what he would say. He suddenly saw the little girl she must have once been. Big eyes, hopeful, wanting so badly to be accepted. It made that place inside his chest ache again.

He laid a hand on her arm. "Why are you telling me all this?"

"I don't know." She focused on the dish towel in her hands, twisting it nervously. Her voice dropped to a whisper. "I guess I just wanted you to believe in me."

He couldn't wait any longer. Hunter pulled her into his arms and a lightning-hot energy seemed to radiate outward, fusing them together. None of what he had just witnessed made logical sense, and he couldn't care less. In this moment, with her in his arms, all he could do was believe.

He pushed her up against the counter and kissed her slowly, savoring the sweet taste of her, the softness of her skin, and the unbelievable feeling that everything with her felt so *right*.

The overhead lights in the kitchen dimmed and winked out as the back door swung open to let the puppy into the garden. Soft music began to play on the living room speakers and all the curtains in the downstairs windows drew quietly closed. It was odd, to be sure. But with Emma in his arms, Hunter just didn't care.

Emma woke the next morning, feeling deliciously warm and floaty. Her skin felt flushed, her leg muscles shaky, and for several moments she kept her eyes closed and savored the complete sense of contentment that settled over her. It felt good to be alive. She yawned and snuggled deeper into her comforter, hovering on the edge of sleep. But sleep didn't come. Something niggled at the back of her mind. . . .

Crap! She sat bolt upright in bed, hand covering her mouth. *Crappity crap crap.*

She had sex with Hunter Kane.

Sex. She pulled the comforter up under her chin, eyes wide, toes curled.

With *Hunter.* She yanked the comforter over her head, but it didn't help.

Visions of the night before began flipping through her mind like an erotic movie reel. Hunter's torso flexing as she ran her hands over the smooth ridges of muscle. The slick glide of his tongue against her skin. The dark, sensual taste of him. His hands guiding her back against the counter. The weight and heat of him as he covered her body. His mouth. His mouth on *her.*

Emma had the sudden urge to fan herself because, holy heart attack. In all her adult life, she had only ever slept with one man, and it had never been anything like that. Last night she had acted like a lusty nympho, and he had been demandingly, deliciously game. This. This was what everyone talked about. The all-consuming sexy thing that made really bad decisions seem like good ones, in the moment.

She stood and walked over to the mirror above her dresser. Yep. There was no denying that some bad decisions were made last night. Her hair was the epitome of bird's-nest chic, her lips looked swollen from all the kissing, and there was a faint mark at the base of her neck and another, lower on her stomach. A residual flutter of lust at the memory of Hunter licking his way down her body washed over her. For a few seconds, a goofy grin spread across her face, but she shut it down, fast.

Okay, okay, okay. She launched out of her bedroom, grabbed a towel from the hall closet, and strode to the shower. What the heck had she been thinking? She turned on the shower and immediately stepped in, gasping as cold water hit her in the face. Swearing, she adjusted the water nozzle. She hadn't been thinking. That was the problem. But it didn't have to be a problem. Because she could totally handle this. A faint thrill shot through her. Whatever *this* was.

Shrugging, she poured vanilla shower gel into her hands, trying to mentally lessen the impact of what had happened between them. So they had sex. It wasn't that big a deal. Normal people did this kind of thing all the time. Maybe not her, because she wasn't super normal, but whatever. No big. She closed her eyes and massaged shampoo into her hair, practicing what she would say. What did a person say after something like this? How did you move on from it?

Hey, Hunter. Thanks for the ride, but this is where I get off. Sure, that would be awesome. If she were Rizzo from *Grease*.

Hi, Hunter. I'm a professional, so let's get down to business. Straightforward. Nice. It worked in *Pretty Woman*. Then again, prostitute.

Hi, Hunter. What? Oh, I barely remember . . . Bingo. Sex amnesia. It could happen.

A soft smile played around Emma's lips when she finally stepped out of the shower. The weirdest thing of all was that she didn't truly regret it. Once she got over the initial shock, she rather liked the memories of what they'd done last night. Every reckless one. No matter what happened afterward, those memories were hers to keep. Even if he wasn't.

Chapter Nineteen

"Wait, you *kissed* him?" Juliette dropped the rose she was pruning in her garden and gaped at Emma.

"It just kind of happened." Emma stooped to pick up the flower, placing it back in Juliette's basket. It had been less than twenty-four hours since Hunter had shown up at her house. Since she had first kissed him right there in her attic. Just the memory of it gave her butterflies in her stomach. And then there was the kitchen thing. That had been mind-blowing. The butterflies started doing synchronized backflips. She took a deep breath and tried not to think about what it all meant. With barely two weeks left before the summer festival, Emma was all too aware her time with him was running short.

"What about the good-bye–forever plan?"

"I'm not changing the plan, Jules. I know what has to happen." Emma fiddled with a rose stem, careful not to touch the thorns. "Go ahead and tell me. I'm being a fool."

Juliette continued pruning. "Oh, I'd never say that. Everyone's a fool for love."

"I'm not in love. I'm just—"

"—lusting?" Juliette gave her a sly grin.

"I was going to say *living*. Look, you're the one

who's always telling me I need to shake things up a little. I think this counts."

Juliette sighed. "Oh, it counts all right. Lord knows it's high time you did something. I bet even Mrs. Mooney's had more action than you."

"Thanks a lot."

"We both know how this has to end, right? I just don't want you getting in over your head and getting hurt."

Emma flopped on the garden grass and stared up at the sky. "I'm not in over my head. Just, maybe knee-deep. Or . . ." She stole a sideways glance at Juliette. "Neck-deep?"

Juliette stopped cutting the roses and narrowed her eyes. "What exactly does that mean, 'neck-deep'?"

"Well . . ." Emma stared back up at fluffy clouds, afraid to see her cousin's face. "We kind of had sex, too."

"What?" Juliette's shriek sent a bird fleeing from a nearby tree. "Kind of? Okay, spill, you tramp. I want every detail. Was it what you expected? Is he as good as he looks?"

Emma couldn't help the huge grin that spread across her face. "Better."

Juliette gave a theatrical moan and landed in a heap beside Emma on the grass. "Why didn't you tell me yesterday?"

"I'm telling you right now."

"Yeah, but you waited until today! That's like, a bazillion hours of withholding important information from me, your dearest friend and relative."

Why hadn't she told Juliette after Hunter left yesterday evening? Maybe because she wanted to hold the memory close and keep it special, all to herself. It had been so unexpected, and he was like some exciting, unbelievable surprise. That morning he had called to tell her he was moving into a furnished waterfront condo down by the wharf. It rented by the month, which Emma thought was a good sign. He wanted to see her again tomorrow, and he seemed genuinely interested in the town, and her. Perhaps she didn't tell Juliette right away because for just a little while, she wanted to pretend it wasn't going to end.

"It wasn't planned," Emma said. "Just kind of an accident."

"Yeah," Juliette snorted. "Gotta watch out for those accidental sexcapades. How exactly did it start?"

Emma shrugged. "He helped me patch a window in the attic when the storm rolled in. Then we were in the kitchen and I had just told him about the house, and my baking magic. Then I made those 'Summer Sunshine' cupcakes again to chase away the storm, you know? And then he kissed me. And before I knew it, I was on the kitchen island kissing him back and it just sort of escalated from there."

Juliette let out a *whoop* of laughter. "On the kitchen island. Very kinky of you guys. Did he say, 'Gimme some sugar, baby'? Just tell me he did, even if he didn't."

Juliette was on a roll, talking so fast Emma could barely get a word in edgewise. She proceeded to grill Emma on every sexy detail she could think of, until both of them ended in a fit of giggles.

Finally, Emma sighed. "I can't believe I did it, Jules. I'm going to see him in person tomorrow. We have a meeting after I close up. I'm going to have to tell him it was a mistake."

"I'm sure that'll go over like a lead balloon," Juliette said wryly.

"No, he'll understand. I'll just tell him I'm not normally like that, and I don't want to mix business with my personal life. He seems pretty reasonable, all things considered."

"I'm not sure reason has a front row seat at the show when hot sex is on the menu."

"There's nothing on the menu, Jules. Not anymore. It was just one of those crazy things and I don't plan on doing it again."

Juliette gave her a look. "Uh-huh."

"Shut up, I'm serious."

"I believe you're serious now. But what's going to happen when Mr. McSexy is standing in front of you, all godlike, and all you can think about is your 'accidental' excursion in the kitchen? And speaking of that, one more thing. Did you actually *do it* on the kitchen island? Cuz that's really the largest surface space and granite's pretty cold, right? I mean, how was that? I guess with a hottie like him, the cold probably didn't register. But seriously, Emma, you're not going to be able to just cut it off that easily."

"Look, yesterday was a fluke. It probably only happened because we were suffering from the residual effects of that jasmine potion you spilled on us in the forest. Every day that passes will only get easier." Emma lifted her chin, trying very hard to believe it.

"I hate to break it to you, but that little jasmine spell wore off days ago. And even if it did set you two in motion, everything that happened yesterday and everything that happens next is all going to be your own doing."

"Say whatever you want," Emma said. "I'm going to lay down the law tomorrow evening and it'll work out. It'll be totally fine."

Except it wasn't.

Chapter Twenty

"You have to understand he lacks good breeding," Mrs. Mooney announced, clutching Bonbon in one hand. "But Buddy is a sweet dog, in spite of that. Has anyone answered your ad in the paper for him?"

"Nothing yet. One person showed interest but they were single and had four cats. I'd like to find him a family." Emma wiped down the pastry case and glanced at the clock. It was almost six and she felt like an exposed nerve. Hunter was going to walk through the door any moment, and she had been preparing for it all day. Two days had passed since their kitchen "sexcapade," and she had been practicing telling him it was a mistake.

Bonbon sneered down at the cupcake case. Mrs. Mooney patted him on the head and droned on about the importance of good breeding. Emma wished the woman would just hurry up and go. With Hunter on the way, she didn't have the extra brainpower to devote to conversations about Bonbon's impeccable lineage. She needed to gear up for "the talk." Maybe if she slapped herself on the face, kind of like a boxer did before a big fight, it would help her focus. She was willing to give it a try.

Mrs. Mooney *tsked*. "Don't touch your face

with your hands, dear. It puts your delicate skin at risk for breakouts. Fingertips have more germs than a dog's mouth, did you know?"

Emma glanced dubiously at Bonbon. Drool oozed from between his snaggled front teeth. She'd risk the fingertips.

"Would you like anything before I put the cupcakes away, Mrs. Mooney?" Emma took a quick sip of espresso. She had probably had one too many that afternoon, but she needed strength to face Hunter.

"Got anything for hemorrhoids?"

Emma choked a little. "Um, for Bonbon?" Did dogs suffer from hemorrhoids? She didn't care enough to check and find out.

"No, of course not. For *me*. I've had the worst time of it lately. Tried everything. There's these witch hazel pads you can buy to help with the swelling, but I'm still not comfortable."

Dear Lord, Emma prayed. *If you can stop Mrs. Mooney from launching into a detailed description of this ailment, I will be the most devoted—*

The wind chimes announced his arrival, but it wasn't necessary. Emma's body was a tuning fork, humming the moment he stepped inside her shop. Hunter's chiseled face was handsomer than she remembered, if that was even possible. All of him was better than she remembered.

He nodded at Mrs. Mooney, then his gaze

settled on Emma. A half smile hovered at the corner of his perfect lips, and Emma felt the magnetic pull of him all the way from her stomach to the tips of her fingers and toes.

"Mr. Kane, how nice to see you," Mrs. Mooney said, beaming. Bonbon snarled like a perfect angel. "I was just telling Emma about my—"

"—I'll be right with you," Emma sang out. Never could tell where Mrs. Mooney drew the line at polite conversation. "Um, let me just finish up here." She grabbed the tongs and yanked out a "Nighty Night" cupcake. It wasn't for Mrs. Mooney's particular ailment, but it did help a person have a peaceful night's rest. At least for that night, Mrs. Mooney would sleep well and not be uncomfortable.

"Here you go." She pasted a smile on her face and boxed the cupcake. "On the house."

"Well, isn't that sweet. Thank you, dear. Lovely to see you again, Mr. Kane." Mrs. Mooney bustled toward the door, then turned at the last minute. "Oh, and Emma, I do think you ought to consider Tommy Jenkins. He's a sweet young man and he makes his own beer, did you know?"

"How fascinating." Hunter's green eyes sparkled with humor but his face remained deadpan.

"Yes. A very creative young man," Mrs. Mooney added. "I told him he should call Emma. She deserves someone who's not a hooligan. And there are so many hooligans out there, don't you know?"

"Truer words have not been spoken," Hunter said.

"Thanks so much, Mrs. Mooney," Emma said. "Have a great night."

When Mrs. Mooney was out the door, Emma threw Hunter a look.

He walked toward her, all lazy-lion smile and tractor-beam magnetism. "Hi."

Emma swallowed. "Hi." *What sex? I barely remember.* "Um, how are you?"

"I'm good."

He was. He really, really was.

"You?" He leaned his forearms on the counter, his shoulder and arm muscles stretching his blue T-shirt in very delicious, memorable ways. Emma had a flashback of those same arms wrapped around her naked back, pulling her closer. She shook the memory off.

"Oh, I'm fine. I've just been working a lot. Nothing big going on." *Except crazy lust-filled dreams about you.* "Uh, what have you been up to?"

"I was in Seattle yesterday, taking care of some investment details. Everything's right on schedule for opening day."

"That's great," Emma said. Nice to know his business that would ruin her own business was coming along swimmingly. The thought was sobering. It snapped her out of her erotic haze.

"We should probably, you know." She swallowed hard. *Discuss what happened between us.* "Discuss the festival." *D'oh!*

His lids lowered just a fraction of an inch. "Okay."

For the next twenty minutes, he filled her in on the schedule for the following week. They talked about the painters hired to whitewash the fence down by the wharf. He gave her a USB stick with a vendor booth layout for the summer festival. They discussed store signage updates and crowd control and hiring musicians. And all the while, Emma tried to ignore the tiny licks of pleasure she felt in his presence.

There was an undeniable attraction she couldn't shake off. That was the problem. Any other man would have been easy to ignore, but being in such close proximity to Hunter made her edgy. She felt like a baby zebra in an open field with a hungry lion tracking her. And she now knew what that hungry lion could do.

When they finally finished discussing the plans, she gave herself a mental heave-ho. Time to lay down the law. It was now or never. She stood up and gathered her paperwork, then leaned against the counter and took a deep breath. "So, about that day you came over. We should probably talk."

That half smile ghosted across his face again

and he crossed his arms. It was a simple gesture of relaxed ease, but Emma didn't buy it. There was a hunger in his dark green gaze that she remembered all too well. The lion was on high alert.

"What did you want to talk about?" he asked.

"It was wrong," she blurted.

Hunter's posture shifted slightly. "You think it was a mistake."

"Totally. I mean, I never do that kind of thing. Ever. I don't know what I was thinking, you know?" Here came the babble. She always babbled when she was nervous. "But I know it's not a good idea to mix my personal life with business. And you and I are just business, so I hope you understand it's not going to continue because, you know, I can't really believe it even happened in the first place."

His gaze was intense, like he was imagining the things they could do. The things they *had* done. A delicious shiver skittered up her spine. She forged ahead. "I mean, I just don't think it should have happened at all. It was kind of crazy and well, contrary to what you may have heard, I'm not actually crazy. Weird, sure. But not reckless like that. At least I never have been in the past. So anyway, I would like to forget about it and, you know, just go on like before," said the queen of Babble-on. "Normal and stuff."

Hunter nodded once and glanced down at the

floor. He seemed deep in thought, as if he was trying to make a decision.

Emma tried not to notice his muscular arms, crossed against his chest. *Nothing sexy about those. Nope. La la la.* She could hear the second hands ticking on the wall clock. *Tick. Tick.*

He pressed his lips together and she suddenly remembered the feel of them, warm and hot against the sensitive spot on her neck. *Focus!*

When he finally lifted his head, her knees almost buckled. The lion stared back, all wild and hungry and seductive, like he was about to lick zebra chops. He leaned closer.

She should probably back away.

He watched her beneath thick, dark lashes and lowered his gaze to her mouth.

Yup. Definitely backing away soon. She could almost feel the heat of his body on hers and her traitorous limbs ached with the desire to step closer.

His face hovered inches from hers, as if he was waiting for some sign.

Any second now, she would back away. Any second. Emma's mouth opened on a tiny indrawn breath.

It seemed to be exactly what he was waiting for. The moment his lips touched hers, her limbs flooded with heat. Her body remembered him and was instantly ready.

He gripped her hips and lifted, pulling her

flush against him. She wrapped her legs around his waist, completely lost in the kiss that spread like wildfire through her blood. He carried her to the back room, knocking over a bag of sugar on the way as he braced her up against the pantry wall. She gripped the edge of the shelf, sending stainless steel mixing bowls toppling to the floor. The two of them were like a hurricane, demolishing anything that got in the way, and she was helpless to do anything but hang on.

Emma suddenly wanted to feel his skin against hers. She grabbed the hem of his shirt and yanked it up, breaking away from their kiss just long enough to tear it over his head.

A low growl escaped him as he ran his hands up under her apron, sending a jolt of pure desire rocketing through her.

Screwed. She was so screwed. But in this moment, who cared?

She smiled against his mouth and licked his lips. If he was the hungry lion, then she was happy, slow-roasting zebra chops.

The zebra drove home sometime later, her hair a tangled mass down her back. They hadn't even spoken until they said good-bye. He had cupped her face and kissed her, then whispered, "Come out with me tomorrow."

She said yes, because it was her day off. And because in spite of her determination to break things off, she wanted to see him again. What was it with her and sex in kitchens? Her face flamed with the memory of what had just happened on the kitchen floor as she brushed spilled sugar from her hair. He was like a drug and she couldn't seem to get enough of him.

Buddy was curled in the passenger seat next to her when she pulled up to her house. She gathered him up in her arms. "Buddy, am I crazy?"

Always supportive, he licked her chin, clearly appreciating the sugar coating that still clung to her clothes and hair. Buddy wasn't going to judge her. He never did. Emma smiled and stroked his soft fur. The best thing about him was that he seemed to love her, no matter what.

Maybe being with Hunter wasn't such a bad thing, Emma thought as she climbed out of the car. People had flings all the time. Maybe she should just go with it and enjoy it while it lasted. Hunter Kane could be her secret fling. A thrill shot through her, ricocheting from her head to her feet. She liked the idea of having a secret fling. It made her feel wild and strong and somehow . . . normal.

Emma walked up to her house, stopping on the porch. A large bouquet of red roses sat on the doormat. Something unpleasant twisted in her stomach. Rodney always gave her red roses when he felt guilty or needed to apologize. She'd had a lot of them over the years. With great reluctance, she pulled the note card out of the envelope and read:

Angel, please don't shut me out forever.
I'm not going to give up on you.—Rodney

The note was like a bucket of slimy mop water dumped over her head. Just. Yuck. She crumpled the card in her hand and entered her house. The roses went straight into the trash. Juliette would kill her for tossing fresh flowers, but she didn't have to know. Emma stifled a pang of guilt. There was a lot Juliette didn't have to know. Mood already ruined, she sat down at the kitchen table and began opening her mail. The overdue mortgage notices were just par for the course. Once, the Holloways had owned the house free and clear, but Emma and her grandmother had been forced to take out a loan against it when all the medical bills came rolling in. Between the two of them, they had struggled just to make ends meet. Now, as she glanced down at the bills, she felt more alone than ever.

Chapter Twenty-One

When Hunter approached Emma's house on Wednesday morning, the door swung open before he reached the porch. He half expected to see her on the other side, but nobody was there.

The house was letting him in, it seemed. He paused in the doorway. "Thanks?"

If someone told him he'd be talking to inanimate objects a month ago, he'd have said they were crazy. Now the rational side of his brain was telling him he was the crazy one. After all that stuff about magic Emma had shown him, he was still trying to find logical answers.

Old houses settled. He crossed the threshold. Old houses were drafty. He stepped into the foyer. Old houses—

The door shut quietly behind him.

All right, fine. This was not an ordinary old house. He shook his head and ran his fingers through his hair. It was unbelievable. None of this made sense. And yet, when Emma entered the room barefoot in a soft white sundress, he simply believed.

Her face was like sunlight. "I see the house let you in again. It keeps doing that."

"Maybe it likes me."

"Or maybe it just wants you to do more repairs.

It's resourceful like that." A door shut firmly upstairs and Emma laughed.

Hunter wanted to pick her up and spin her around like a fool, but he held back. Something about her really messed with his common sense. He wasn't used to feeling so out of control.

"What is that?" She pointed to the bundle in his hand.

He held out the five rawhide bones tied with a red ribbon. The woman at the pet store had done it when he told her it was a gift. "For Buddy. I thought he'd like it." He suddenly felt like an idiot. When was the last time he'd given a woman something so stupid? Women wanted flowers or jewelry, not chew toys for their dogs.

Emma took the bouquet of bones and held them down for Buddy to sniff. The puppy gnawed at the ribbon, tail spinning with joy.

"They're so perfect," Emma said. "Thank you." A tremulous smile stretched across her face and Hunter reached down to pat the puppy's head, avoiding her gaze. She was so beautiful, when she looked at him like that, it did things to his sanity. If they didn't leave soon, he was going to toss her over his shoulder and carry her up to her room.

"You ready to go?" *Say no. Say you want to go upstairs instead.*

"Okay."

Fine, he'd wait. He wasn't a panting teenage

boy, dammit, even though she made him feel like one. It seemed like every time he saw her, all he could think about was getting her naked. But she deserved more. Besides, the idea of spending the afternoon with her on a picnic was almost better than the alternative. Lately, he just wanted to be near her. It didn't even matter what they did. That was the damned mystery of it. He couldn't remember the last time he'd felt that way about anyone, if ever.

They drove out to Siren Point, a park with a lighthouse that overlooked the north side of the island. It was a gorgeous day with not a cloud in the sky. A soothing breeze blew in off the shore and a pair of dragonflies flitted over the grass. Emma set Buddy loose to run around while she arranged a picnic basket on a blanket.

"Is that lighthouse still in use?" Hunter asked.

"No, it's just a landmark now. They keep it locked, but Juliette and I snuck in once when we were kids. It was kind of disappointing. No hidden pirate treasure or ghosts rattling chains. Just a bunch of cobwebs and dust, and it's empty now. But a man and his wife used to live here, or so the story goes."

Hunter stretched out on the blanket and plucked a grape from the basket. "What's the story?"

Emma poured them each a glass of wine, then sat cross-legged beside him. He wanted to reach out and draw her closer, but he stopped himself.

If he wasn't careful, he'd be fawning over her like a lovestruck teenager. He sipped his wine instead.

"Over a hundred years ago," Emma began, "a young man lived in the lighthouse. He kept the ships from crashing against the rocks in the winter, when the fog rolls in so thick sometimes you can't even see your hand in front of your face. He was a young man, having taken over the lighthouse after his father died. One day, he saw a woman on the rocks, washed in from the sea. According to the story, he rescued her and they fell in love.

"For several years, they lived happily together beside the ocean. On the seventh year, a big storm hit the island. The man woke in the middle of the night to find his wife gone, and he ran into the storm to find her. She was standing at the edge of the rocks, staring longingly out at the thrashing sea. Before he could stop her, she blew him a kiss good-bye, and dove into the waves. By the light of the full moon, he saw her come up for air several yards from shore. She dove up out of the waves and that's when he saw her pearly, shimmering tail. She was a mermaid, and the ocean was calling her home.

"For the rest of his life, the man lived in the lighthouse, always watching the horizon, always hoping she would return. As time passed, the villagers felt sorry for him. They tried to set him up with nice women from the village, but the man could never love anyone again. He really had no choice, because he had been touched by magic. He would spend the rest of his days pining away for his impossible girl."

"That might be the most depressing story I've ever heard," Hunter said.

Emma laughed. "I guess it is, but it's tragically romantic. A typical old island fable. They were star-crossed lovers, doomed from the start."

"Like I said, depressing." He grinned and popped another grape into his mouth.

She stretched beside him on the blanket. "Yes, but at least the man got a nice, joyful seven years with her. What if he had never loved at all? It could've been worse."

"Not really. I think it's worse to find someone you can't live without and then lose them. Better not to have met them at all. Then you don't know what you're missing."

Emma sighed. "That's the thing about fairy tales, especially the original ones. Someone is always getting hosed."

He laughed suddenly. It was yet another unfamiliar feeling, and he marveled at it. "You're really different, you know that?"

"Tell me something I haven't already heard my entire life. Imagine what it was like for me, finding out my grandmother bakes spells in the kitchen. And I have the same gift. Not exactly a typical childhood. 'Different' is probably one of the nicer adjectives to describe the Holloway women."

Buddy came bouncing up and snuffled inside the picnic basket. Emma patted her lap and the little dog curled up in her skirt, then let out a sigh of contentment.

Hunter felt the same. Just being around her was like a weight lifted from his shoulders. "Was it really hard? Finding out about the whole"— he waved his hand as if searching for a word— "gifted thing?"

Emma shrugged, stroking the puppy's soft fur. "I guess I never really knew anything different. My mother had a gypsy soul, so my youngest memories are traveling with her. So many different, exotic places. We lived in Sri Lanka and Guam. A couple of places in India and Egypt. Even Paris, for a little while."

"That's incredible," Hunter said. "To have those experiences at such a young age."

"I suppose it was, but it wasn't always easy. Sometimes we got sick, or had to leave the places we were staying without notice. Sometimes we had money problems. My mom always found a way to keep going, though. I guess that's just part of her gift. And she always found ways to help people wherever we went. It's like she just knew when it was time to go, and where she'd be needed next. She used to tell me how wonderful it was, and how lucky I was to see the world. Like she was hoping really hard that I would have her same gift of wanderlust."

"But you didn't."

She dropped her head, her voice getting softer. "I wanted to. I could tell she hoped I would. But by the time I was six, I couldn't help it. I hated always moving, always saying good-bye. And my mother knew it. She didn't want to give me up, but that year she started telling me a bedtime story. It was an old story she had learned from one of the African villages she visited, about how the sun loved the moon so much, he died every day to let her live. And when I turned seven, she brought me here to my grandmother, and let me go. I didn't want her to leave, and she didn't want to move on without me. But she wasn't going to keep me from my own life's path."

"But she barely visited you over the years." Hunter couldn't help but feel angry at a woman who could abandon her child like that.

"True," Emma said. "And when I was younger I resented her, until I really grew to understand what the Holloway gifts meant. It's not just a preference; it's a calling. There's no happiness unless you learn to embrace it."

Hunter wasn't sure he agreed. She was an angel of forgiveness, this one. "So your grandmother raised you."

"Yes. It was always me and her, together."

Emma stared out at the ocean. "Then a couple of years ago she was diagnosed with cancer. 'Stage IV melanoma,' the doctors said. She died within the year. It's mainly why everything's falling apart with the house and . . ." She shook her head. "I just didn't have a lot of time to devote to shoring other things up. And then there was Rodney."

Hunter felt a pang of jealousy. He didn't like the man, and hated that he had caused Emma grief. "What happened with him?"

She stroked the puppy in her lap, head down. "Oh, I was naïve and believed he was right for me. Plus, I didn't want to be alone. And he had always been around, on and off. So when he proposed, it just seemed like the right thing to do. But it was the worst mistake. He made it harder, always complaining that I spent too much time with my grandmother and didn't have enough time with him."

Hunter felt a stab of anger at the idiot. The man didn't deserve her.

Emma glanced up and shrugged. "And then one day he got tired of the scene, and ran off with someone else."

"He was a fool," Hunter said.

"*I* was more the fool. I kept a large amount of cash in a special tin above my kitchen cupboards. I told him I was saving it for our future. I guess he thought that meant he had a right to it when he left."

Hunter ground his teeth together. Rodney was not only an idiot, he was an idiot that needed a serious punch to the face.

Emma shook her head. "Well, that was a pretty maudlin story. What about you? What's yours?"

He laid back on the blanket and stared up at the cerulean sky, his hands behind his head. "It's not as interesting as yours. My parents divorced when I was young, and my mother raised me. I didn't know my father well, as he wasn't too keen on having a child in the first place. Now that I think about it, I think my mother did it just to spite him. They were always fighting. In a way, I got lucky that they divorced."

"And you've never been married," she said.

"*God,* no."

She stopped petting the puppy in her lap and glanced up. "Oh, that's right. You don't believe in it."

"I don't, really. I don't have any experience with a good one, and the people I do come across who are happily married, well . . . I think they're just wired differently. Like maybe they got lucky or something. But for me, no. I don't ever want to be like my parents."

"So you never even came close?"

"Once, but for all the wrong reasons."

"What happened?"

Hunter paused, uncomfortable. "It just didn't work out."

Emma waited patiently, and he found that he wanted to tell her. She was so easy to talk to and he didn't feel like he had to guard himself the way he did with other people. "When Melinda and I first met, I thought we understood each other. She knew my business was important to me, and she was deeply involved in her own career as a lawyer. We were together for over two years. But she was . . ." Hunter clenched his jaw, hating the memory of what had happened between them. "She was driven. She always had a plan and never deviated from that. It's one of the things that made it work so well in the beginning. We both wanted the same things." He stopped, not wanting to ruin the picnic.

"So why aren't you still together?" Emma asked quietly.

Hunter took another sip of wine, only it was more of a gulp. He might as well tell her. "She got pregnant."

He didn't miss the tiny gasp that escaped her. "You had a child?"

"No." Regret flooded through him. "No, I didn't. Melinda got pregnant, but she didn't want the baby. She never wanted to be a mother. She just wasn't the type." He finished his wine in one gulp. "I didn't even find out until it was too late. She decided to abort. She got rid of it, and I never even knew until afterward." The old feelings of anger and betrayal came bubbling to the surface and he forced them down. "She told me a week later, like it was no big deal. Barely even worth mentioning. I was so angry. Our relationship just changed after that."

"Did you want the baby?" Emma asked. Her huge gray eyes were filled with sadness.

"I . . ." He shifted uncomfortably. He had never told anyone about what had happened. It was unnerving to be sitting across from someone who he could be so open with. "Yes, I guess I did. Which didn't make any sense because I never planned to be a father and certainly never wanted to be married. But the idea of a child . . . my child . . ." Even after all this time it was difficult to think about the loss. Or what could have been. "Anyway, I couldn't help how angry I was that she kept it from me, and Melinda resented me for it. I couldn't get over the fact that she never even discussed it with me. She asked what I would have done, had I known. I told her I would have offered to marry her, and she laughed in my face. She said we both knew what we had wasn't really love. I was so angry. Mostly because I knew she was right. But I couldn't be with her anymore. Not if we couldn't be honest about the important things. The things that really mattered."

He shook his head and took a deep breath. "So that's it. We went our separate ways. Now she's a senior partner at a law firm somewhere in Seattle. Engaged to the CEO, last I heard. And the weird part is, I don't miss her at all. I'm relieved that whole part of my life is behind me. But I feel guilty about what happened. I don't know. It's just really messed up."

Emma bit her lip and stared out at the waves. "I think I understand."

For a very long time, neither of them spoke. Hunter let the sound of the ocean and the cool breeze float over him until the harsh memories faded, and all he saw was Emma sitting before him. In that moment, she was so pure and real that it made his heart constrict with yearning. The feeling was completely foreign to him. He didn't know what it was.

"It's all so uncertain, isn't it?" she murmured. "Sometimes I wish life was like a book, so even though terrible things might happen, you could flip to the end to make sure everything was going to be okay."

The sunlight glowed off her golden head and he wanted to hold her and promise her that everything was going to be okay. It was another feeling that came unexpectedly, surprising him. He couldn't remember the last time he felt protective over anyone. "Everything is going to work out," he found himself saying.

She grinned wistfully. "I wish that were true."

He thought of her struggles, and all she had overcome. He thought of his investment plans, and how much he wanted to help her. In just a few days, he would be able to tell her his news. It would solve all her problems. "It is going to be okay. I know it."

"How do you know for sure?" she asked impishly. "Did you flip to the end and peek?"

"Maybe." He wanted to kiss the dimple near her mouth. "Come here."

She lifted her chin, mischief dancing in her eyes. "No."

Hunter sat up. "Yes."

"Nope," she laughed.

"Are you going to come here, or are you going to make me chase you?"

"There's something else you need to know about me." She leaned in close, her lips hovering just inches from his, and whispered, "I'm very fast."

"I like fast women." Hunter reached for her.

She bolted up and ran, laughing across the grass.

He sprang after her, because what else could he do? When a man was lucky enough to be touched by someone as enchanting as Emma Holloway . . . he really had no choice.

Chapter Twenty-Two

Emma and Juliette sat at the makeup counter at Dazzle on Wednesday afternoon. They were waiting for Gertie and Molly to finish closing up the salon so they could all grab dinner together.

Molly brushed a second coat of mascara on her already sooty eyelashes. She blinked several times, deciding more was more, and went for a third coat. "Did you lay down the law with Mr. McSexy?"

"*Something* got laid down," Juliette said.

Emma shot her cousin a look. "Not yet. I got distracted."

"She got distracted by his hot bod and forgot the plan." Juliette rummaged through the lipstick drawer. She chose a hot pink shade and leaned closer to the mirror, talking through carefully stretched lips. "So now they're kind of dating."

"Girl! Look at you go." Molly beamed. "I didn't know you had it in you. See, Gertie?" she called to the back of the salon. "I told you Mercury was retrograde. That's why all this weird stuff is going on."

"What weird stuff?" Gertie stepped from the next room holding a broom and dustpan. The tips of her hair were a shocking shade of lime green.

She caught sight of Juliette and Emma and gave each a hug. "Hey, gals, what's up?"

"Your . . . hair is new," Emma said.

Gertie patted it proudly, turning her head this way and that. "I did it on a whim last night. Got so sick of my pink highlights. I mean, who wears pink streaks anymore besides angsty tweens, you know what I'm saying? What do you think?"

"It's very edgy," Emma offered politely. "And with your pixie cut, it really suits you." Gertie had that tiny, willowy figure and elflike features that made any combination of wild just look adorable. She could pull off anything, even Lime Juice Tinker Bell.

"So what's going on with Hunter Kane?" Gertie asked.

To stave off any further comment, Emma decided to spill. "We are sort of seeing each other. I don't know exactly how it started."

"Yes, you do," Juliette piped up. "It started when he showed up at your house and helped you in the kitchen."

"Okay, yeah," Emma said quickly. "So it started then, but I was planning on calling things off, and then he kissed me and I sort of forgot." Emma waved her hand impatiently. "It's hard to explain how it all happened. I'm just sort of going with it."

"And well you should," Gertie said. "Who in their right mind would turn down a fling with someone like him?"

Molly nodded eagerly. "I know, right? Please allow us to all live vicariously through you. I don't suppose there's any chance he has a brother? I'm still SOL with Match.com. Last weekend I went to O'Malley's on a blind date and it was a nightmare."

"What happened?" Emma asked.

Molly rolled her eyes. "Online this guy seemed super nice and normal, right? I mean, his dating profile wasn't sleazy. He didn't live in his parents' basement. He said he liked ball games and sports and pets. You know, all the typical stuff. So we started chatting and he seemed kind of romantic. He said he just wanted to find the right person to share all the magic life has to offer."

Juliette gave her a dubious look. "And I'm guessing there was no magic?"

"Oh, there was magic, all right." Molly grimaced. "I went to O'Malley's to meet him, but I got there early. James Sullivan was bartending so he made me a drink and we talked for a while, then his face got all weird. Like he was trying not to laugh, you know? So I turned around to see what he was staring at, and it was my date. Standing there. Dressed like a magician."

Emma gaped. "You're kidding."

"I wish! He had on the satin cape, gloves, everything. Said he just got done with one of his gigs. And for the next fifty-two minutes, I had to sit there while he shared all the magic he had to

266

offer. And there was a lot, let me tell you. We're talking, 'pick a card, any card' type stuff."

"That's crazeballs," Juliette said. "I thought he was normal and he liked ball games and sports."

"Yes, he was quite the champion juggler."

Emma started to giggle. She slapped both hands over her mouth and spoke through her fingers. "What about pets?"

Molly narrowed her eyes. "You mean the rabbit he pulled from his hat? David Hopperfield?"

"Wow." Juliette grinned. "That's impressive."

"What was James doing the whole time?" Gertie asked.

Molly scowled. "Being a total dillhole, is what he was doing. Like, he'd come over and ask me if I wanted another drink, then whip a towel out of his sleeve with a flourish—all magicianlike—to wipe down the counters. And once, I caught him at the end of the bar with three upside-down beer glasses, sliding them around one another. He was pretty much teasing me the entire time."

"Hold on," Gertie said. "I get that having a date with a magician is a little weird, but maybe underneath it all—"

"No," Molly said. "The guy had no redeeming qualities. And he never even asked me about myself, except to find out if I was limber."

"Limber?" Juliette scrunched up her face. "Like, for sexy reasons?"

"Worse. He wanted to know if I could fold

myself into a box for his Saw-a-Person-in-Half trick."

"Okay, that's kind of creepy," Emma said.

"Yeah." Gertie nodded. "It's a flaming red flag when a guy you just met says he wants to saw you in half, even if it's pretend."

"And if that wasn't enough," Molly continued, "when James brought over the bar tab? The guy drew a credit card from behind my ear going, 'Is this your card?' And surprise! It *was* my card. He'd somehow taken it from my purse when I wasn't looking."

"Oh, screw that guy." Juliette sliced a hand through the air. "Hard pass."

"It was a total disaster," Molly said. "James finally kicked him out, saying rabbits weren't allowed in the bar. Then he wouldn't stop laughing at me. I was so annoyed, I wanted to toss my drink at him, but I had already finished it so there was nothing left to throw. That Zombie Mojito he makes is so good. But anyway, I'm still pissed at him. Maybe I'll go in next weekend and order something huge, like a Long Island Iced Tea, just so I can throw it in his face."

"Well, it's always good to have goals," Juliette said. "I'm sorry it didn't work out with the magic man."

Gertie patted Molly on the back. "You'll find someone, hun. Just give it time. Someone perfect for you."

Molly rolled her eyes. "I felt like such an idiot. And now James has something to hold over my head. I'm so going to kill him next time I see him."

"What about you, Emma?" Gertie asked. "You and Hunter are a thing?"

Emma shrugged it off, trying to appear nonchalant. "I wouldn't call it that. We're sort of dating, but nothing serious."

Juliette gave Emma a sideways glance. "I told her just to go for it. I mean, who knows? Maybe things will work out between them."

"Why shouldn't they?" Molly said. "It's high time Emma had someone in her life. A *nice* someone. And even though he's a little citified for Pine Cove Island, he'll settle in."

Emma felt a strange sense of trepidation come over her. "Don't get all excited, you guys. We're just dating for now. I have no intentions of it going anywhere." But the idea of him settling in and them staying together made her heart spin like a weather vane in a windstorm, no matter how hard she tried to steel herself against it.

Gertie stared in the mirror, arranging her green spiky hair. "Well, it sounds to me like you don't have a lot of control in this situation. You may not intend it to go anywhere, but be open to the possibility."

Emma shrugged and pretended to dig through the eyeshadow palettes. The last thing she wanted to do was discuss her possible future with Hunter. She felt bad enough hiding her secret agenda from her well-meaning friends. What would Gertie and Molly think of her if they knew she planned to send him away forever? Juliette was the only one who knew, and the more Emma thought about it, the rottener she felt.

Later that evening, Emma sat in Juliette's garden with a steaming cup of Earl Grey tea.

The setting sun lit up the sky with streaks of fuchsia, orange, and gold, casting a rosy glow over the gardens that ran along the edge of the woods. At any other time, Emma would be filled with the usual contentedness that Juliette's amazing garden instilled. But tonight all she felt was a nagging sense of unease.

"I don't know, Jules. I'm all conflicted inside. Everything Hunter has been doing for the waterfront businesses has been helpful. Why does he have to be so . . . great? And here we are, two weeks away from the festival. His new restaurant is looking so perfect and chic, and the menu items were posted on the door outside. Everything looks divine. His shop will be the death of me. I know this, yet I can't seem to stop wanting to be with him."

Juliette gave her a sympathetic look. "Okay, I understand how you feel, but can I just say one thing? When you're not stressing about the upcoming festival, you positively glow. Being with him has made you happy again—I can tell. And I know it's going to be hard for you to send him away, so . . ." She trailed off and gave Emma a pointed look.

"So?"

Juliette shrugged. "What if we don't send him away? What if you try to somehow make things work between the two of you? We could try to find another way to save the house."

Emma sighed. "I wish. But I can't think of any other way to come up with the money I need to pay my overdue mortgage. This festival is usually the big moneymaker that allows me to stay afloat." She took another sip of tea, leaning her head back against the wicker princess chair that sat out under Juliette's rose trellis. "In a perfect world, there'd be no overdue bills and no falling-apart house and no empty bank account. Everything would just be roses."

"And Hunter Kane," Juliette added.

Emma sighed and plucked a rose from the trellis behind her, breathing it in. Yes. In a perfect world, he would fit into her life. But the world wasn't perfect. She knew that better than anyone.

So what now?

Emma poured food into Buddy's dish in the kitchen, surprised when he didn't come running. He was snuffling around near his favorite corner of the kitchen cabinet, as usual. For the past several days, the puppy had been scratching near a crack in the woodwork, where Emma assumed he'd seen a mouse.

"What's so exciting about this corner?" She bent down to stroke his soft fur. "I just fed you and the food is that way." She pointed to his red dish.

Buddy didn't go for it; instead he began pawing at the crack in the wall. He suddenly let out a yip of excitement and scratched the cabinet with both paws, tail wagging furiously.

Emma frowned and peered closer to the crack in the woodwork. A tiny corner of parchment stuck out from between the cabinet and wall. She leaned down and gripped the corner with her thumb and forefinger, slowly pulling to reveal a single sheet of weathered paper. The handwriting was so faded, it was barely recognizable, but Emma could tell it was a recipe. The words were scrawled across the top in loopy, formal letters.

She stood, blinking down at the ancient piece of paper. How long had it been stuck back there? The page was yellowed from age and covered in dust. As she blew on it, the dust scattered to reveal the words "Bliss Day" at the top of the page. It looked even older than Emma's grandmother's recipes. She flipped through her book and noticed several other recipes—the oldest ones—written in the same hand.

"Wow." Emma blew out a breath. "Buddy, I think you found a recipe from one of my ancestors." It wasn't that unusual to have recipes written on loose leaves of paper. The entire book was filled with handwritten notes tucked here and there. It never ceased to amaze Emma how often she would come across a note or amendment to a recipe that she had never noticed before. It was as if the book held secret chambers and there was always something new to discover.

Emma flipped to her grandmother's least favorite recipe, "Day of Bliss," and compared them. The ingredients were exactly the same, until the very last one. Where her grandmother had written over the smudged ink "lavender," the last ingredient in the older recipe called for "lilac."

Emma gasped. Was it possible that the recipe never worked for her grandmother because, over the years, one of the ingredients had been accidentally misinterpreted? She scanned the recipes again, matching the ingredients. The only difference was the lavender and lilac.

A soft breeze tickled the hair at her temples and she smiled. "It's still not going to happen, house. You know I don't mess with any old spells that call for a 'dollop' of this or a 'shake' of that. It's too vague." She tucked the ancient leaf of paper back into the book and shut it firmly. "Nice touch, by the way, using Buddy. That's a new tactic."

Emma walked over to Buddy, who was now joyously scarfing down his puppy chow. She stroked the back of his little head. As alluring as the "Bliss Day" spell seemed, she wasn't going to risk it. Not only were the ingredients imprecise, her own grandmother had said it only caused heartache. Even if the spell didn't work because the last ingredient was wrong, there were still so many ways to mess it up, and Emma had enough to worry about without the possibility of another magical mishap.

She thought about the upcoming festival and the plan to mix strong magic with Juliette on summer solstice. It was so unlike her to do anything that crazy, but what other option was there? An unsettling feeling of guilt washed over her and she crossed her arms, hugging herself. The recent picnic with Hunter had been one of the happiest moments she could remember in a very long time. He made her feel things, and it wasn't just the wild sex they were having, although thinking of that made her skin flush with desire for the umpteenth time that day.

No, it wasn't only the physical connection. With Hunter, she could be herself. She could tell him things about her childhood and show him who she really was, and he didn't judge her for it. He listened and accepted. Emma had never had that with another man. But maybe the reason she had it now was because she didn't feel the need to guard herself. He was leaving soon, anyway. Maybe that's why she was being so free with her emotions.

But she couldn't deny that lately, she just wanted to be around him. And the more she accepted how strong her feelings were, the worse she felt.

He wasn't hers to lose, she had to remember that. When he left and took his business with him, everything would go back to normal. Everything was going to be okay.

"It's just a fling," she said out loud.

The teapot on the stove let off a sudden burst of steam. Clearly, the house did not agree.

"It is," Emma insisted. Maybe if she said it enough times, she'd keep believing it.

Chapter Twenty-Three

Hunter made his way up the stairs of the B&B, glad it would be the last time he had to spend the night with the chintz and ruffles. He couldn't wait to pack up and move into the furnished rental house the next morning.

Bethany had become increasingly clingy, which was getting to be a real pain in the ass. Just that morning she had been waiting for him in the lobby downstairs. Again. He remembered the shocked look on her face when he told her he was moving. She wasn't happy, which just made him more eager to get out of the place.

He unlocked the door to his room and stepped inside, tossing his keys on the table near the entrance. The curtains were drawn but he walked to the window, peeking out at the waterfront. Not for the first time that day, his mind strayed to a pair of smoky gray eyes and a smile so warm and genuine, it could melt ice in Alaska. Just thinking about Emma made his blood stir and his hands tingle with the desire to touch her. He was beginning to think he couldn't stay away from her anymore, even if he wanted to.

"I've been waiting for you," a sultry voice said behind him.

Hunter spun around, startled. Bethany Andrews

was draped across his bed in what appeared to be some sort of gauzy black negligee. She looked hard-edged and sexy, her impressive breasts straining under the flimsy fabric. Everything was where it was supposed to be: the curves, the artfully arranged hair, the bedroom eyes and red lipstick. The actress had set the stage, but he didn't care to see the show.

"What are you doing in here?" he demanded.

Bethany smiled like a cat licking cream. "I know you're moving tomorrow so I thought I'd give you a proper good-bye." She parted the sash on her robe and it fell over her shoulders, revealing a perfect tan and perfect curves. "Maybe I can give you some incentive to stay in touch."

Hunter glanced at the wall, annoyed. The woman knew she looked good and had no problems flaunting it, but he felt nothing for her. At another point in his life, he might have taken her up on the offer, but not anymore. Things were different now. Emma represented everything honest and true. It brought into stark relief the desperation of someone like Bethany. If he felt anything at all for her, it was pity. "Bethany, you need to leave. I'm in no mood for this."

She laughed, low and throaty. Apparently, she didn't believe him.

Out of the corner of his eye, he saw her stretch and sit up slowly. She leaned back on her hands. "I bet I could get you in the mood."

He didn't want to hurt her, but he had to shut her down, fast. "You need to go. I'm flattered, but I'm not interested."

She slid off the bed and started walking toward him.

"Stop," he said more harshly than he meant to. "I don't want you. Do you understand what I'm saying? I'm seeing someone else."

Bethany's smile slid off her face and she narrowed her eyes. "Who?"

"That's not your concern." Hunter grabbed a bathrobe off the hook on the door and held it out.

"Who is it?" she persisted. "Is it Emma Holloway?"

He said nothing.

"It is, isn't it?" Bethany demanded.

"Put the robe on, Bethany, and go." Frustration mounting by the second, he clenched his jaw and waited for her to cover herself. He'd been very clear that he wasn't interested in her, even back before he had started getting involved with Emma.

Bethany yanked the robe from his hands, shoving her arms through the oversize sleeves. "You know the Holloways are all crazy, don't you? Her mom was the town slut. Slept with anyone who looked at her twice."

Hunter refrained from pointing out that Bethany wasn't exactly Mother Teresa, standing half-naked, uninvited, in his room. He waited until she was fully covered before turning to face her. "Don't talk about things you don't understand. Emma and I are none of your business."

Bethany gave a harsh laugh. The throaty purr was gone from her voice and now she just sounded catty. "So it is Emma."

Hunter said nothing.

She tossed her hair and shrugged. "Well, you might want to ask yourself what happens to all the men who get together with Holloways. Think about that. None of them are still around, you know. It always ends badly. Someone either gets hurt"—she cinched the bathrobe sash around her waist—"or worse."

Enough. Hunter pointed to the door. "Get. Out."

She gave him a mean little smile and jerked it open. "Good luck. You're going to need it." Then she stormed down the hall and was gone.

Hunter shut the door and locked it, drawing the deadbolt home. He shook his head and let out a silent curse. What the hell had that woman been thinking? Of all the men she could try to entice, he was her least likely victory.

He grabbed a beer from the tiny fridge in the corner of the room, flopping back on the chair near the window. There was a time not long ago where he'd have gone for it. And why not? A woman like Bethany knew exactly what she was doing. She was hardwired to play the game. He cracked open the beer and leaned his head back against the wall. He had been hardwired to play once, too, but not anymore.

All thoughts strayed to Emma. Soft gray eyes filled with mischief, laughter that made him want to kiss her until that same laughter flowed inside him, filling up the empty places. He took a sip of beer and closed his eyes. What was happening to him? He couldn't get her out of his head and it didn't even bother him anymore. When he wasn't with her, he thought about her. When he was with her, he felt like everything else just faded in the background and he was exactly where he was supposed to be. Emma was feisty and generous and kind and caring. She was giving and honest and . . . impossible.

Hunter shook his head. It was all just so impossible. *Magic?* The whole idea was illogical and ridiculous, but he just didn't give a damn anymore. He was going to accept her for what she was—a delicious, glorious, fascinating mystery. The barest hint of a smile ghosted across his face as he pictured her mixing up cupcakes in her kitchen. She was so open with her feelings. He hadn't expected to share so much of his past with her, but it had all tumbled out as easy as breathing. Because of her, his past troubles in Seattle were just a faded memory. She was the closest thing he had ever felt to . . . what?

Hunter stood and began pacing the room. Best

not to think too hard on it. He cared deeply for her and he had grown to trust her; that's all that mattered. And now that Sam had finally given him the news he'd been waiting for, it was time to let Emma know.

A thrill of anticipation shot through him. All she did was help other people. Her very calling in life was to inspire happiness in others. In the short few weeks that he had known her, she had made a positive impact on him in ways he hadn't believed possible. Now he had a chance to help her attain everything she needed, and he couldn't wait to give her a little bit of happiness back.

Chapter Twenty-Four

The next day flew by in a blur of activity. Emma met with Hunter to oversee the final waterfront preparations. All the picket fences were bright, sparkling white. Storefront signs had been repainted and spruced up, and there were baskets with profusions of brightly colored flowers hanging on every streetlamp. The terra-cotta pots from Juliette's planting party also lined the sidewalks at intervals, and everything looked like a page from a gorgeous storybook. It was hard to admit, but Hunter had been right about the changes. The nostalgic, vintage feel was still present, but just brighter and cleaner. It was perfect.

Hunter was immersed in readying his place for its grand opening, and even though Emma felt a slight trepidation every time she saw the sleek new place, she also felt a surge of hope. Maybe his coming here was a good thing, after all. Whatever happened, she would figure out a way to survive. She no longer wanted to get rid of Hunter.

She wanted to keep him.

The revelation had literally knocked her off her feet that morning. She was in the shower, remembering the last time he visited and they had ended up "showering" so long the water went cold. She smiled at the memory, imagining how it would be to have him in her life permanently. Then it hit her, and she slipped. The jarring sensation of landing on her butt on the bathroom tiles was nothing compared to the crazy realization that she wanted him to stay for good. It was unreasonable. It put her livelihood in jeopardy. But there it was.

On Friday evening, Emma drove home with renewed determination. She was going to find a way to make things work with Hunter.

Like a bad omen, Rodney stood in the front yard, leaning against the porch railing. Shirtless and tanned, he looked like the boy she once believed was Mr. Right. Except now he was Mr. Not-in-a-Million-Years. He smiled, and pushed off the railing, his six-pack abs flexing. Rodney knew he still looked good, but it did nothing for Emma.

"I fixed your porch step," he drawled. "I thought you might like it." He looked so smug, so certain of himself. Emma wanted to slap the lazy grin off his face.

"I never asked you to fix it, Rodney. What are you doing here? I know it's not to actually help me."

"But I do want to help you. Look, I'm sorry for the past, but can't we put that behind us?" He almost pulled off the genuine, wounded boy routine. Almost. But there was a slight whiny edge to his words that made Emma certain she was dealing with the same old Rodney.

"There is no 'us,' Rodney. How many times do I have to tell you I'm done? All I want is for you to leave me alone. Can you help me with *that?*"

He stepped closer, his eyes narrowed. "You've really changed, you know that? You used to be so sweet. Now you're—"

"—Be really careful what you say right now. I'm not in the mood."

He bristled, a vein pulsing in his temple. "What the hell has gotten into you? I've never seen you like this. Not when we were in school. Not even when your grandmother was sick. It's like Juliette's rubbed off on you and now you're all bitchy."

"No one has rubbed off on me." Emma clenched her fists against her sides, enunciating each word carefully. "This *is* me. This is me, choosing to no longer be manipulated by you. I'm going to tell you one last time. Leave me alone, Rodney."

Rodney's lips curled into a sneer. "Well, forgive me for trying to help you. Trying to make your life easier." He flung the hammer he had been using on the front porch step and glared at her. "So I do you a favor and this is how you treat me? It's not like I asked for payment for that," he said, jerking his chin toward the porch.

Emma gaped. "I wouldn't pay you one penny,

even if I had the money. The whole reason my house is falling apart is because you stole my savings and left me when I was at my lowest. I haven't had the funds to make the necessary repairs."

"I told you I was sorry," he spat. "But now I'm not so sure. It's not my fault your house has gone to shit. I couldn't stand to be around you anymore, did you ever think of that? I mean, think about how I must have felt. You were crying all the time. Always going on and on about your grandmother's cancer. Never thinking for one moment about how it was affecting my life. We were supposed to be engaged. Except it felt more like being trapped. You were awful to be with back then, and you're just too stubborn to admit it."

Anger flared so hotly that she had to fight to control her shaking limbs. She would not punch him. Or kick him in the face. She would not. "It was always about you, Rodney, wasn't it? And it still is. You could never think of anyone but yourself. I used to try to make you happy, but I was never good enough at it. Maybe that's why you kept me around. Poor little Emma Holloway. So grateful to be wanted. Always willing to bend over backward. Well that's not me anymore. I don't care what you think, or what you feel. I only care that you *leave*." She pointed at his pickup truck. "If you ever step foot on my property again, I will file a restraining order. Or maybe I'll go ahead and do it now, anyway."

Rodney stiffened as though he were struck by lightning. His mouth pressed into a cruel line and he stepped so close she could smell the whiskey and cigarettes on his breath. *"Bitch."*

She trembled, but stood her ground. "Don't ever come back here again."

He shook with anger, and for one fraction of a moment Emma wondered if he would hit her. The wildness in his eyes was sharper than she had ever seen.

"You're going to regret turning me away. You think you can survive on your own, with your creepy house and your stupid bakery? Think again, Emma. You're *nothing,* do you hear me? You never were. I thought you were different once, but I was wrong. You really are just a crazy Holloway freak."

He cursed, then grabbed his tools and threw them in the back of the pickup. The wheels of the truck spewed gravel as he tore off down the lane toward the highway.

Emma walked into her house and the door locked gently behind her. She leaned against the wall and tried to ignore the tears leaking from her eyes. Rodney had always hit every insecure nerve inside her, and even though years had passed, that hadn't changed. When she was younger, she had tried so hard to be loved. She wanted to belong and to be surrounded by people who accepted her. For a while, being in Rodney's limelight had felt like she achieved it. But it wasn't real. It never had been. She was living his life, pretending she belonged.

Now after sending him away, he still managed to bring back all her old insecurities. But something fundamental had changed in her. She was no longer that insecure little girl she used to be.

Ever since Hunter had come into the picture, she knew what it felt like to be genuinely accepted for who she really was. She knew how important it was not to sell herself short; not to settle for someone else's life when she could live her own.

Emma gasped. It was like she was coming up out of the ocean after being underwater for too long. She suddenly recognized the truth for what it was.

She loved Hunter Kane.

It was as simple and as complicated as that. It wasn't what she had planned, and it wasn't what she had initially wanted, but there it was. She *loved* him. And no matter what the future held, maybe it was time to let him know.

Hunter spent the evening overseeing the last finishing touches at Haven. The glass light fixtures had finally been installed, the counters were polished, and the seating looked perfect.

They were waiting on the bakery oven installation—there had been a last-minute hiccup, but it wasn't going to be a problem. The rest of the kitchen equipment was primed and ready, and the ovens in the bakery would be ready the day before the festival, at the very latest. For opening day he was shipping in pastries from a warehouse bakery supplier in Seattle. Emma had advised him against it, saying it would be better for his business to connect with people using Haven's own products. She said it was more personal that way, but he knew what he was doing. It would be less hassle, and until he had that portion of his staff cemented, this was the least problematic way to go.

He watched the contractors leave for the evening, feeling a fierce sense of anticipation as he surveyed the gleaming surfaces, the warm leather booths, the Chihuly glass art fixtures. Everything was falling into place, exactly as he had anticipated. After weeks of talking to Sam Norton, the old man had finally agreed to sell Hunter the waterfront. It had been an odd conversation. One that had more to do with Sam's reasons for loving the island and wanting to preserve its culture, but it all made sense now, to Hunter. He had only been on Pine Cove Island a short time, but knowing Emma had changed him in ways he wouldn't have believed when he had first arrived.

Tomorrow he was going to ask her a very important question. A question that would change her life in amazing ways, he hoped. He'd been looking for a person to manage his bakery and she was more qualified than anyone he knew. Of course, he'd offer her a top chef's salary; enough money to solve all her financial problems and give her the freedom she deserved. He smiled as he turned out the lights and locked the door. Everything was going to be perfect.

Chapter Twenty-Five

It was a beautiful Monday afternoon. The most perfect day Emma could remember in the history of all Mondays she had ever witnessed. It could have been the calm ocean, the cotton candy clouds in the sky, or the soothing summer breeze. It could have been the boat trip Hunter had surprised her with that afternoon after he called and told her he wanted to see her. But as she sat across from him on the deck of the boat, letting the rhythmic waves lull her into a sense of deep contentment, she knew that her happiness was because of him.

She *loved* him. At some point today, she planned to tell him.

"I'm glad you came out with me," he said.

Reclining on the cushioned seat, Emma tipped her head back, letting the warmth of the sun seep into her skin. "Me too."

He joined her on the cushioned sofa that ran the length of the back of the boat. Emma leaned her head on his shoulder as he handed her a wineglass.

"I have something I want to say." His voice was serious, full of intent.

A jolt of excitement shot through Emma's

entire body. Oh my God, what was this? It had to be something big. Maybe he was going to tell her he loved her. Maybe she wouldn't have to be the first one to say it.

"What is it?" she whispered.

Hunter draped an arm over her shoulders and pulled her closer. "Emma, you know how I feel about you. At least, I hope you know by now."

She couldn't help the tiny smile that lifted the corner of her mouth. He seemed so nervous. "I think so," she said.

"I want you to know I think you are the most amazing, talented, beautiful person I've met in . . . well, in as long as I can remember. You've been a great help to me with the upcoming festival, and I know things have been hard for you these past couple of years." Hunter put his wineglass down, then took hers and did the same.

He held her hands, and stared down at their clasped fingers for a moment. "Emma," he began.

She couldn't breathe. *Don't faint!* He was going to say something wonderful. This was big. She could feel it. "Yes?" She sat up straighter. Was her hair frizzing? Never mind, who cared. This was way more important. This could be the moment when her entire life changed. He would tell her he loved her. And she'd say she loved him. And then they'd go on, happily together. Maybe even "ever after."

He smiled into her eyes.

She grinned back, feeling like one big gooey ball of joy.

"Will you be my bakery manager?"

Crickets . . . Crickets . . .

Blank. Her mind went completely blank. Then something that felt like a metal anvil dropped from the inside of her skull to the bottom of her feet. "Wh-what?"

He nodded encouragingly, a gleam of excitement in his eyes. "I've been thinking for a long time about this, and I have some important news."

"News?" She tried to swallow, but her throat seemed to have closed off. What the hell was happening here?

"I've been negotiating with Sam Norton to buy up all the properties on the wharf, and I've been lining up investors for the past couple of months. Last week he finally accepted my offer." He let go of her hands and smiled triumphantly at her. "I'm now the sole owner of the entire waterfront."

The anvil that had lodged in her feet rose up and dropped again, resonating through her bones with a jarring *clang!* "What do you mean, sole owner?"

"I mean, I own all of it. The buildings, the shops. Even yours."

Emma could almost hear the gears in her head grind to a halt, then scream slowly back into action as she tried to make sense of what Hunter was saying. "Why would Sam do that? His family has owned the wharf for decades. Why would he sell it?"

"Sam recognizes that change is necessary in order for the waterfront to thrive. He's been considering other offers for the past few years, but he hadn't found a buyer he felt right about. We talked a lot about my vision for the waterfront, and my dedication to the businesses. He's been wanting to sell for a long time, says he's getting too old to hold it all together. But he couldn't find anyone he felt would do the right thing, until now. He also agreed to sell because of you."

Emma scowled. None of it made any sense. She felt like she was spinning end over end with no gravity and nothing to grab on to. "What would I have to do with his decision?"

"My agent has been negotiating with Sam for a while now, but Sam was reluctant to sell because he thought I was going to modernize everything and not preserve the integrity of the island. But he's been watching all the upgrades I've implemented, and he saw how much better the waterfront looked. He also saw us together and—" Hunter glanced down at his hands, pausing. "He said you were the heart and soul of Pine Cove Island, just like your grandmother before you, and that you deserved to be happy.

He hoped my new plans would give you what you needed."

A wave of mixed emotions washed over Emma. She couldn't believe Sam would sell the property his family had owned for so many years, just to make her happy. Why would he bother? "I don't understand. Why would Sam do that for me?"

"I don't know the specifics, but I believe there's a story between him and your family. The important part is that he wants Pine Cove Island to be the best it can be, and so do I. I want to make the waterfront a huge success. Not only that, Emma, I want you to be a part of that success. I've been thinking about your financial troubles, and your current business model."

He kept talking. So much talking, and yet Emma couldn't register any of the details. Then she heard something that flash-froze her heart, in spite of the warm sunshine. "Wait," she said sharply. "What did you say about absorbing my shop?"

He nodded encouragingly. "I was thinking about how your business could improve, and I know its close proximity to my building isn't the best location. Anyway, I've done the research, and think it would be an excellent move on your part if you let your shop go and came to work at Haven. I would pay you the highest salary— more money than you could ever make running your own place. You could still make your baked goods, and sell them at the café. Think about it."

A tiny fissure formed along the edge of her frozen heart.

"You would have all your debts paid," he continued. "And you could afford to make the necessary repairs to your house. You wouldn't have to worry about running your shop anymore, because you'd have a whole staff under you at my café."

"You want me to give up my shop?"

"Just think about how much easier your life could be," he urged. "I can help you, Emma. And this arrangement would be perfect for both of us. You know I'm crazy about you and I want to continue seeing you. I won't be able to live here permanently, of course. I have too many business obligations to oversee in Seattle and I'm planning to expand onto other islands, once this place is settled. But I would come back to visit you all the time. What do you think?"

He smiled, then. It was the warm, melted caramel smile that always made everything seem to glow around the edges. Only this time the heat was too much to bear. Her icy heart cracked down the center, shattering into painful pieces. What the hell had just happened?

"You—" She drew a jagged breath. "You want me to *give up my shop?*"

Doubt flickered across his face, as though he

was starting to catch on that something wasn't right.

Emma scooted away to put some distance between them. The entire world seemed to tilt on its axis and she steadied herself on the edge of the boat. He really didn't understand her at all, did he?

Hunter looked lost. "I thought you'd be happy. I was keeping my acquisition a secret so I could surprise you. Don't you want a bigger salary? Enough to fix your house?"

"That's what it's all about for you, isn't it? The money. It never occurred to you that what I do, how I live, is my choice? That shop is a part of me. It's who I am, Hunter. I thought you understood that. It's my legacy. Fairy Cakes is all that I have left. You can't tear it down and expect me to be grateful."

"No," he said irritably. "Of course not. I see how you care for this town and the people. I know you enjoy what you do. But the shop isn't all you have left. You have better opportunities now. If you work in my café, you can still do what you've always done, plus save your home and make more profits."

"But I'd be doing it in *your* restaurant," she ground out. "I'd be shoehorning myself into *your* life."

"Emma," Hunter tried reasoning with her. "It just makes more sense."

"Why? Because my shop is too old and shabby to fit into your vision, right? Because who would ever want to keep something like that? Because your place is chic and fancy and new." Humiliation and anger swept through her. There was a loud roaring in her ears and she had to blink against tears that threatened to fall. She would *not* cry in front of him. She would not give him that.

She needed to get away. "I want to leave. Take me back to shore right now."

"Emma," he began.

"Right now!" She clenched her jaw and hugged herself, staring out at the clear blue water. The endless ocean that had seemed so gorgeous just a few moments ago now seemed cold and unfeeling. The breeze ruffled the hair on her heated neck and she felt almost nauseated. A painful lump had formed in the back of her throat and no matter how hard she swallowed, it wouldn't go away.

The worst part wasn't even that he thought she would just give up her shop so easily. No, the worst part was what he said afterward. *I want to continue seeing you . . . I would come back to visit you . . .* She was an idiot. A complete fool. How could she have thought he was going to say he loved her? How could she have been so stupid?

Hunter started the engine and maneuvered them

toward shore. His profile was hard and bleak in the late afternoon sunshine. When the boat dock came into view, he tried again. "Emma, please. I want things to work out between us."

"Ha!" she scoffed. She could feel hot tears brimming the corners of her eyes. "You care so much for me, that you'd like to 'continue seeing' me whenever you come into town. You want me to be your booty call, right? How noble of you." She could hear the bitterness in her voice and she hated it. "How lucky for me."

If he thought for one moment that she would spend the next few years of her life waiting for whenever he decided to visit, then he was as clueless as he once believed the locals to be. Emma had spent her entire childhood wondering when her own mother would breeze into town. Wishing that her mother would love her enough to stay. And look how that had worked out. She would never willingly go there again.

"It's not like that at all. I *do* care for you," he said in obvious frustration. "Emma, I'm trying to help you fix all your problems because of how I feel for you. What more do you want from me? Is it so wrong that I want to keep seeing you? I thought we had something good here."

She shot him a look. "So did I. I thought I meant more to you. I thought we could . . ." She hugged herself tighter.

"You thought we could . . . ?"

Emma ground her teeth together. There was no way in hell she was going to say it out loud. *I thought we could love each other and stay together and maybe someday get married and have a family and be happy and all those things I never dreamed possible.*

A strange expression stole over his face, as if he had read her thoughts.

She turned away and focused on the shore. From the corner of her eye, she could see him watching her.

He was quiet for a long time, as though unable to say what hung in the air between them. He maneuvered the boat into the dock and cut the engine. "Emma, I can't . . . I'm not . . ."

Humiliation scorched a path from her neck up to her temples. "You don't have to say anything." She quickly stood and started to climb onto the dock.

He reached out and stopped her. "Please," he said quietly. "I'm not cut out for that kind of life. I wouldn't be any good at it. I wouldn't even know where to start."

Emma avoided his eyes and shrugged out of his grasp. She should walk away, now. Take the high road and all that. But the high road was so unappealing. Less oxygen up there, for one thing. She turned to face him, forcing her voice to remain steady. "Well, then I guess you should just stick to what you're good at. Go make money,

Hunter. Just don't expect me to fall neatly into one of your spreadsheets. Because maybe you don't believe in anything except money, but I do. I want more. I deserve more."

Tears pricked the corners of her eyes, threatening to spill. She gave up trying to fight it. What did it matter anymore? "And you may not believe in love and marriage and family and all that 'fairy tale' stuff. But I still do. Maybe I've never had it, and maybe I never will. But I still choose to believe in it." She spread her hands wide. "And why wouldn't I, right? I mix up magic spells. I *am* a fairy tale." She climbed onto the dock and swiped at the hot tears that now slipped down her face. "Thanks for your stellar offer, but I'm going to have to decline. I'm sure you think that's crazy, but hey. I'm just a crazy Holloway."

"I never said that, dammit." A muscle clenched in his jaw. He was angry now. *Good.* It was better this way. If he tried to be nice to her, it would only make it harder.

"I don't want to see you anymore, Hunter. I want you to leave me alone."

"Emma, don't say that." His voice was raw with emotion, but she couldn't allow herself to empathize. All she could think about was getting far enough away before she fell apart completely. She kept her head high as she strode down the pier. Every step was pain, but she forced herself to put one foot in front of the other. He called after her again, but it only made her walk faster until she was running.

Down the wooden planks that led to the grassy path.

Beyond the whitewashed picket fence that gleamed shiny and new in the sunlight.

Past the scrubbed sidewalks and freshly painted shop signs.

The sky was still an impossible shade of blue, and everything around her sparkled like diamonds in the sun. But inside, Emma was a barren wasteland. Inside, she was crumbling to dust.

Chapter Twenty-Six

The sky was so blue, it could drown a person. Hunter scowled out at the ocean, hauled one arm back, and shot a fistful of bread across the water. The seagulls scattered in a squawking mob, fighting to be the first to reach it. Idiots. Only thinking about themselves.

After a night of pacing his living room, Hunter had ended up at O'Malley's drinking beers with the locals and pretending to watch baseball on TV. For the past twenty-four hours, Emma had refused to answer her phone. Now he had nothing but a foul mood and a hangover to show for his efforts.

Everything with Emma had gone worse than he could have imagined. He had offered her a perfectly logical solution to all her problems, and she had thrown it back in his face and broken up with him. It was the last thing he had expected, and it made no sense.

He lobbed a few slices of bread onto the rocky shore, then threw the last of it into the waves, watching as the flock split, divided over who could steal bread the fastest. Make them work for it. Served them right. Leaning back against the wooden bench, he squinted against the unforgiving sunlight and scrubbed his face with both hands.

"When I said to try feeding the birds, I didn't mean bludgeoning them with bread."

Hunter glanced up at Sam Norton. He was in his usual worn-out jeans and fisherman's jacket, with a khaki hat pulled down over his wrinkled forehead. There was a twinkle in his eye and an elfish smile on his face. If he had a beard, he could almost pass for Santa.

"Mind if I sit?"

"Go ahead," Hunter said. "It's more your spot than mine."

"Oh, I don't know about that." Sam sat down slowly, in that way that older people do, as if the body had to negotiate through a series of steps before it could settle. He pulled a brown paper bag from beneath his jacket. The seagulls flocked to his feet in a frenzy of flapping wings. "I heard you talked to Emma yesterday."

Hunter clenched his jaw. Freaking small-town gossip. News traveled faster here than responders to a 911 call. He should be pissed at the islanders, but he only had himself to blame. Somewhere around his third beer last night, he remembered mentioning to James, the bartender, about Emma breaking things off. "Who else knows about it?"

Sam let out a low, gravelly laugh. "Oh, just about half the people in town, I suspect."

Hunter shook his head and stared out across the water.

Sam opened the paper sack and pulled out a slice of bread, his arthritic hands tearing equal pieces. One by one he tossed them to the birds, taking special care to throw some to the runts on the outside of the group.

"It's a good deal," Hunter blurted.

Sam glanced up, but made no reply.

"It would fix everything for her. I offered her a salary that a lead chef would be happy to take. She'd be able to fix her house, she could still bake the recipes she loves. She'd even have creative control." He ran his fingers through his hair. "I just . . . I don't get it. She threw it in my face, like it was a terrible offer. Now she won't even answer my calls."

Sam nodded and continued feeding the birds. Some of the larger gulls, having been sated from Hunter's previous feeding, began to drift away in disinterest. The frenzy had died down, once they realized there was plenty to go around.

"She was so mad," Hunter said after another long moment. "Said she didn't want to see me anymore." A hollowness unfurled inside his chest when he thought about never seeing her again. Everything was so messed up now, and he didn't know how to fix it. "She didn't like the idea of having to sell her old shop. I mean, I get that she doesn't like change, but anyone can see her shop's days are numbered. Working for me, she wouldn't have to worry about outdated equipment breaking down. She'd have all the ingredients she needs for her recipes. It would be freedom from worry. Everything would be perfect."

Sam looked sideways at Hunter. "Perfect for her, or perfect for you?"

Hunter scowled at the rocky shoreline. "Okay," he said, nodding, "sure. It would be perfect for me, too. Emma would be a great manager, any fool can see that. Her skill in the kitchen is second to none and I'd be lucky to have her on my staff. So yeah, she'd be great for my business. But that's not the only reason I want to help her. I truly care about her. Once Haven is up and running, I'd need to move back to Seattle. I have other investment plans and I'll probably start my next project, but I want to keep seeing her. I offered her everything I could . . . and she turned me down."

For a long time neither of them spoke. The only sounds were the occasional cries of the gulls and the waves lapping at the shore.

"So, let me get this straight," Sam finally said. "You offered to take her away from her own shop and let her work in yours. You'd give her a bunch of money to run your new place while you moved back to Seattle. You said you'd swing by from time to time to see her, and she wasn't interested? Huh." Sam set a piece of bread on the bench next to Hunter, then upended the paper bag and scattered the last of the breadcrumbs. "You don't say."

Hunter sat up straighter. "Look, I'm an investor. I don't have room in my life for anything else right now. I have things I need to oversee in Seattle. It's my home base."

"In my experience, home isn't a 'where,' it's a 'who.'"

Hunter opened his mouth to reply, but closed it. He leaned forward, elbows on knees. What was Seattle to him, other than a place to run his businesses? He owned a penthouse in a prime spot overlooking Puget Sound, but he had very little ties to family. Both his parents were estranged, his mother always traveling to Europe and his father living on the East Coast. They rarely spoke, even on holidays. Aside from a few business partners, there really wasn't anyone waiting for him back in Seattle.

Sam heaved a sigh and tucked the empty bag back into his jacket pocket. "You are young, yet." He nodded. "I remember what that feels like. But life is really just a bunch of these little windows of time. These collisions we have with other people who affect us in some way. And we affect them. Sometimes these tiny moments can change everything, in wonderful ways. If we allow ourselves to act on them." He stared down at his gnarled hands. "But most of the time, we don't see the moment for what it is, and we go careening off in other directions. And then one day you wake up old and you look back and say, 'Holy smokes, that was a moment! I should have done something!' But it's too late. That, my boy, is what they call regret. I know it well. Don't be like me."

They sat in silence for a while before Sam began to rise. Hunter stood up and offered his arm to steady him. Sam smiled and slapped Hunter on the shoulder. "You're gonna be all right. Just give her a bit of time. You've been hurt before, I can see that because I've been there. So you're building things, because that's what you're good at. And I get the feeling"—Sam laughed, looking back at the wharf—"that you're really good at it. Just think about what you are building for."

Hunter watched Sam go with a sinking feeling in his gut. He knew what Emma wanted. He wasn't a complete idiot. A woman like her was worthy of so much more than he could give. Dropped on her grandmother's doorstep as a child, abandoned by her mother, never knew her father. Someone like Emma thrived on her relationships with others. Connections, roots, family. All of that was as important to her as breathing. It was no wonder she had balked when he suggested they keep seeing each other after he moved back to Seattle. The fact that he was asking her to be in a long-distance relationship went against her whole nature. Her own mother had breezed in and out of her life, whenever she wanted. Of course Emma would want more than that with him. She deserved more than that.

Hunter ran his hands through his hair and groaned. He'd been a fool. He needed to talk to her. But Sam had warned him to give her some time, and maybe he should. The last thing he wanted to do was screw things up further. He took the last piece of bread Sam had left on the bench and began tearing it into small chunks, doing his best to toss them evenly to the birds.

For the next forty-eight hours, Emma threw herself into baking different cupcakes for the festival. Many of them were from her grandmother's old recipes she hadn't tried before, but there was a comfort in those pages, and focusing on all those sweet charms made the cavernous ache inside her less painful.

Hunter had called her several times over the past two days, but Emma ignored him. The last thing she needed was to hear him explain why he couldn't love her the way she wanted. It was obvious now that he would never accept her way of life. He was too entrenched in his own.

She closed her eyes as she mixed a final batch of coconut frosting. The rich scent of freshly grated coconut sweetened the air and she drew in a long breath, then let it out slowly. Again. And again. The simple task of working in her bakery soothed her soul. This shop was where she belonged. She was born to do this, and no matter how much she wished Hunter could be a part of her life, she had to admit she was on her own.

By three o'clock on the summer solstice, Emma finished washing the last of her baking pans and stood back to look at her inventory. Each shelf was filled with boxes containing dozens of cupcakes. There was "Blueberry Maple Sunday," which brought back cozy childhood memories like pancakes on lazy Sunday mornings. The "Jelly Surprise" cupcakes were filled with wild berry jam, giving a person courage to show their true feelings toward someone they love. Then there were the vanilla cupcakes with various frostings: passion fruit to inspire creativity, peanut butter and banana for a boost of energy, apple spice for soothing comfort, and chocolate marshmallow to make a stubborn person more open to possibilities. The "Lavender Bliss" cupcakes gave a person a deep sense of contentment, while the "Campfire S'mores" cupcakes inspired a person to be adventurous.

For the zillionth time in her life, Emma glanced wistfully at her creations and wished the charms worked on herself. Given her intense need to feel something other than the crushing heartache of the past forty-eight hours, she couldn't think of anyone who needed an uplifting charm more.

Sighing, Emma reached for a box of chocolates

Juliette had left her that morning, popping one of the semisweet truffles into her mouth. She closed her eyes as the rich flavors of hazelnut and cocoa melted in a delightful symphony on her tongue. They weren't magical, but they tasted pretty darn close.

Juliette had taped a note card to the inside of the box that read:

Chocolate doesn't ask silly questions.
Chocolate understands.

Her cousin's kindness was like a flicker of warmth in the icy cavity where Emma's heart now lived. She sent a silent prayer to the universe. Juliette always had the uncanny ability to understand what Emma needed most, and she loved her no matter what. They were family. If only Hunter . . .

No. Emma slapped powdered sugar off her hands and squared her shoulders. There was no use wishing for something she could never have. Daydreams and wishes were for other people, and she'd be a fool to think otherwise. If she hadn't learned it already from Rodney, then Hunter had really brought it home. Emma closed her eyes and waited for the pain in her rib cage to ease. She was ready to do her part at the festival. Her booth would be stocked like it was every year, and if she was really lucky, she'd make just enough to pay the mortgage. She would worry about the rest of her future later. Now there was only one thing left she had to do.

Her phone rang, the jarring sound bringing on a fresh wave of grief. Just the thought of Hunter calling her made everything he said on the boat come tumbling back. When Juliette's name popped up on the screen, Emma gave a shallow exhale and steadied her voice. "Hey, Jules."

"How are you holding up?" Juliette asked.

I think I might be dying inside. "I'm fine. Do you have everything ready?" Emma had called her that morning to tell her the news. She had also decided it was time to make that "Go Away" cupcake. She knew it wasn't going to solve her financial problems, because his restaurant wasn't going anywhere. He'd hire some amazing manager to run the place and it would still be a huge success. Who knows what was going to happen to her shop. She would have to worry about that later, after the festival. Right now, she couldn't allow herself to think too far ahead.

Hunter was moving back to Seattle; that had been his plan all along. If nothing else, maybe the "Go Away" cupcake could ensure that he did all his business from afar, and help with her broken heart. She hoped never to see him again when the festival was over.

"I've got all the ingredients. Are you sure you want to do this?" Juliette asked softly. Emma could hear the concern in her cousin's voice.

She gripped her phone tightly. "I'm sure. I'll see you at my house in an hour."

The evening breeze wafted through Emma's open kitchen window, swirling around the dishes and bottles, kissing the bowl of raw sugar, the tips of Emma's eyelashes, ruffling the ringlets that had escaped from her bun.

"Can you feel that?" Juliette said excitedly. "There's magic in the air. It's strong tonight."

"Yes." Emma carefully measured the clear jasmine extract from a tiny vial, adding it to her mixing bowl. "Summer solstice is upon us." She flipped the pages of her grandmother's recipe book, scribbling notes onto a loose leaf of paper she had prepared the night before.

Juliette looked over the spell. "Meh. I think we could write it better. Give it some more *oomph,* you know? It rhymes but it doesn't sound very fancy."

"It doesn't need to be fancy," Emma said firmly. "It's straightforward."

Juliette sighed. "I guess. But I feel like the spell should be all mystical and cool-sounding. I mean, we *are* making strong magic here." Juliette opened a wrapped square of cloth filled with herbs, crushed them in her hands, and scattered them into the mixing bowl.

"Exactly, which is why it's better to keep it

simple." Emma tossed in the freshly grated coconut, then a carefully measured spoonful of pineapple juice.

"I'm pretty sure it's going to be gross, no matter how much tropical fruit extract goes in it," Juliette said. "There isn't much that can drown out the taste of all those herbs I just threw in."

"He only has to take one bite. By the time it touches his tongue, the spell will take over."

"That's good." Juliette added a few shavings of crushed garlic. "Because I'm pretty sure this cupcake is going to taste craptacular."

"Ready?" Emma asked.

Juliette nodded. They both waited to the count of three. "Here goes," Emma whispered.

She spun the whisk quickly as Juliette held the bowl steady. Together they recited the spell:

"With summer's power, let this devour
any wish to stay.
    Our charms combined will make you
find, you must move far away.
    We bind your heart with deepest
yearning for tropical summer sun.
    May you only find contentment there.
In this, our will be done."

The evening breeze kicked up between them and Emma felt a spark of magic fill the air. It prickled her skin and flowed through her, between them both. They stood motionless in the center of the kitchen, linked together by the mixing bowl they held between their bodies. The air was thick with power, ebbing and flowing like a rhythmic tide. Emma could hear faint whispers in the air around them, elusive and indistinct, like a melody in a windstorm. They stayed still until the breeze died down and everything went quiet again.

Emma locked gazes with Juliette, who was smiling triumphantly.

"We rock," Juliette said. "It totally worked. I've never felt it that strong before."

Emma nodded. Their spell had been successful; she could feel it in her bones. But there was an abyss inside her she was still trying to ignore.

"He's a goner, Em," Juliette said. "One bite of this and he'll be yearning for hula girls and coconut drinks on the beach."

Emma set the bowl on the counter, doing her best to suppress her emotions.

"Hey, don't look so guilty," Juliette said. "It's not like we're giving him a deep desire to go live with the penguins in Antarctica, or something."

"I'm not feeling guilty," Emma lied. "I just feel . . ." *Devastated. Shattered. Ripped open at the seams.* "Tired. I have some things to finish up at the shop, so we should get this done." She poured the batter into a single cupcake mold, placed it into the heated oven, then washed the rest of the batter down the drain.

314

"You sure you'll be able to get him to eat it?" Juliette asked.

"I'll figure something out," Emma said. Although how, she had no idea.

"You can always just tell him you've reconsidered his offer. Then say something like, 'Let's have coffee to go over details and, oh, hey—how about a cupcake?' "

"Yeah. That'll work," Emma said glumly. She felt horrible, because she knew it *would* work. She knew she would be able to play him so easily. Because in spite of everything, she believed he really did care for her. Probably in the only way he knew how. It would be totally devious on her part, and he would never suspect her because he trusted her. The thought of it made her feel wrong on so many levels, so she pushed it out of her mind.

An hour later, she garnished the perfectly frosted cupcake of doom with a tiny slice of candied pineapple.

"Gorgeous," Juliette said. "Makes me want to take a bite."

"Don't even joke about it." Emma set the cupcake under a tiny glass-domed cake stand, and heaved a sigh. "I have to run back to the shop. It's getting late and I need to frost my last batch before I close up."

"See you tomorrow, then." Juliette gave her a hug that was much longer than normal. When she drew away, her eyes were soft with understanding. "We don't have to go through with it, you know. We can still try to find another way."

Emma lifted her chin. "There is no other way. Even if he didn't leave, he doesn't love me enough, Jules. He made that very clear. It's one thing to have to deal with the financial hardship of competing with his new café, but it would be even worse if I had to see him whenever he comes into town. In less than twenty-four hours, I won't have to worry about him ever again. I'll be totally fine."

A door shut firmly in the hall and Emma ignored what the house was clearly saying. *Liar.*

Emma was just leaving her house when Sam Norton pulled up in his old Datsun pickup. She walked out into the driveway to meet him.

"Hey, kiddo," Sam said, slowly easing his body out of the car. "Do you have a minute?"

A sinking feeling came over Emma. "Is this about the rent on my shop? I'm sorry, Sam. I know it's overdue but I'll have enough to pay you by the end of tomorrow."

Sam raised a hand. "No, no. Don't worry about that. This is about something more important."

Emma walked over to his car, noting the weariness in the old man's eyes. "What is it?"

"I know Hunter has told you by now that I've sold him the waterfront properties."

Emma nodded, trying to ignore the painful jolt at the mention of Hunter's name. "Why'd you do it, Sam? He said part of the reason you decided to sell is because of me. Why?"

Sam folded and unfolded his hands, shifting on his feet. "Did you know your grandmother and I had a history together, when we were younger?"

Emma crossed her arms and leaned against his pickup. "She said you used to be good friends."

Sam nodded and stared at the ground for several moments. "Emma, we were much more than that. We loved each other." He glanced up. "Did she ever tell you?"

Emma slowly shook her head. Her grandmother and Sam? "I never knew that."

"It was a long time ago and we both had full lives since, but I did love her." He seemed so sad and wistful. It made Emma want to comfort him, but she had no idea how. Sam was always the jovial one. She had never seen him this way.

Sam cleared his throat. "I've come to tell you this because I want you to be happy. I don't want you to make the same mistakes I did."

"What mistakes? I don't understand."

"My family didn't approve of me being with your grandmother. They said I was too young to know what was best for me and they swore they'd disinherit me if I didn't break things off with her and focus on the family businesses." He shook his head. "I listened to my parents because I was too cowardly to take a chance on the unknown. I was too afraid to embrace change and go my own way."

Sam's face was etched with regret and Emma felt her heart constrict. "I'm so sorry, Sam. Grams never told me."

He nodded absently, his eyes staring off into the distance, a million miles away. "Your grandmother was . . . she was special to me." He swallowed visibly and his eyes misted with tears. "Did you know I almost got up the courage to ask her to marry me once? We were on a picnic over by the old lighthouse." A grin ghosted across his face at the memory. "She baked something special for the occasion and I brought champagne I stole from my parents' wine cellar. I can still see her sitting on that picnic blanket with the purple cupcake, smiling as if she had swallowed the sun. I had never seen anyone so bright and beautiful." He seemed to catch himself and shook his head. "But it didn't go well. I told her what my parents wanted for me and we fought. I never did get the chance to ask her, and after a few days things just weren't the same."

Emma placed a hand on the old man's shoulder. "I never knew, Sam."

"Well, now you do. And I'm here to ask you to give Hunter a chance. He has good ideas, Emma. And they might not be things you are comfortable with, but I truly believe he wants what's best for the waterfront. He can take much better care of those properties than I ever did. And I also believe he loves you. I've been around long enough to know it when I see it."

Emma wrapped her arms around herself and pressed her lips together, crushed under the grief that welled up inside her. He was wrong. If Hunter loved her enough, he wouldn't leave. "Sam, I can't do what he wants. I can't give up my shop and go work for him."

"I understand that, and I agree with you," Sam said. "But I only ask that you try to find a way to work things out. The only reason I agreed to sell to him is because it became clear how much he cares about you. Whenever he talked to me about his plans, they were all centered around how he could help you save your home and business. I know his ideas are different, but at least try to find a way. If you truly care for each other, there has to be a way. I don't want you to regret not taking the leap of faith later. It will always haunt you if you don't at least try, believe me. I'm living proof of that."

"Thank you for telling me, Sam," Emma said. "But it's not going to work out." She swallowed past the pain in her throat. "He doesn't actually love me. He asked me to be his bakery manager because he's moving back to Seattle. That's his plan."

"And it's a ridiculous plan," Sam agreed. "The

man doesn't know how to change, either. You have to make the first step. You're strong, Emma. You have to find a way."

"I'm afraid it's too late for that," she said.

Sam heaved a sigh. "I hope you're wrong, my dear." He patted her on the shoulder and turned to go. At his car, he paused. "You know, back when I was just nineteen, my whole future was laid out for me. The Norton family properties were passed on from my grandfather to my father, and they were soon going to be mine. I never had to worry about bills or mortgage payments, or anything like that. Life was pretty easy and I believed that the path my family chose for me was the right one. But Emma, if I had it to do over"— he shook his head and smiled sadly—"I'd have taken the leap. I'd have listened to what was in my heart and tried harder to make it work with your grandmother. Maybe I'd have failed, but at least I could stand here, knowing I gave it my best shot."

Emma watched Sam drive off toward the highway. She felt as though her entire future were just a hazy fog. It would be so much easier to take a leap of faith if she could just see through it to the other side, but she couldn't. And Hunter didn't love her the way she loved him. He had made that very clear, and as painful as it was, she couldn't change that.

Chapter Twenty-Seven

The red and blue lights of two police cars flashed like a bad omen when Emma pulled into the parking lot behind her shop. Mrs. Mooney was talking excitedly to one of the policemen, while Bonbon yipped at her heels. Something was very wrong.

"Oh, Emma! You're finally here," Mrs. Mooney cried. "We called you twenty minutes ago, did you know? Your shop has been *vandalized!*"

Emma's heart stutter-stepped in her chest. She slammed her car door shut. "What? When?" Her phone had been on silent mode all evening, because she couldn't stand the grief that spiked inside her whenever it rang.

"Less than an hour ago, Ms. Holloway." A tall, gray-haired police officer stepped forward. He had a kind, Pillsbury Doughboy face that should be offering after-school cookies, not news of vandalism. "Mrs. Mooney here saw the perpetrator and called us."

Mrs. Mooney, now clutching Bonbon in her arms, nodded her head vigorously. One side of her shellacked pouf had fallen like melted ice cream. "Oh, I saw him all right. It was Rodney Winters, I tell you. I've known that little hooligan his whole life and there's no mistaking it. He was weaving down the street, coming out of O'Malley's, which made me suspicious because it was clear he'd been drinking. And the next thing you know he was breaking the glass on Emma's front door. That's when I called the police." Mrs. Mooney gave the officer a huge smile and batted her eyes.

The officer glanced away uneasily. "I'm sorry, Ms. Holloway. There's been considerable damage and we'll need a statement."

Emma barely heard him over the whooshing sound in her ears as her adrenaline took over. *Her shop.* She started running for the back door, then stopped at the threshold.

It looked like a war zone inside. Her kitchen supplies were scattered all over the floor, covered in flour and sugar and broken dishes. Ruined bits of cake and frosting littered every surface. All the carefully prepared boxes were smashed and torn.

"This Rodney Winters has a criminal record, Ms. Holloway. We're going to need to ask you some questions." Emma nodded mutely, unable to take her eyes off the wreckage in front of her. She slowly walked through the kitchen, stepping over broken glass and debris.

The dragonfly wind chimes were torn from the hook above the front door, the iridescent wings cracked and scattered on the floor. The cash register lay open, and what little cash she had was now gone. But that part didn't matter. Rodney had single-handedly ruined all her inventory for the summer festival. Emma shook her head in disbelief, tears gathering in her eyes. *"Why?"*

"I'm so sorry, Emma," Mrs. Mooney said, patting her on the back. "That boy was never any good. I always said so. And he has a criminal record in Southern California and Nevada, did you know? This isn't the first time he's been in trouble with the law, but once these nice officers find him it will be his last." She continued patting Emma's back. "A real hooligan."

Emma murmured something and followed the policemen outside. They asked her a series of questions and she answered mechanically, as though her entire body and mind were on autopilot. Through the whole ordeal, all she could focus on was one blinding truth. It was all over. She was finished. First Hunter's betrayal, and now this.

She had nothing left.

Emma crossed the street to Hunter's shining new restaurant. The Haven sign glimmered in the moonlight with bits of mosaic stone and glass, a gorgeous work of art to mirror the lush interior. Hunter's car was parked outside and she sent out a silent prayer to the universe that he was still there. It would be easier to tell him straight to his face.

She drew a serrated breath and lifted her chin, determined to make it quick. This was what defeat felt like. Her face was dry, thankfully. Crying was useless.

She knocked at the back door, then wrapped her arms around her waist and waited. When Hunter opened the door, she took a tiny step back. His gaze was so intense that it brought back a flood of memories, and she forced herself to breathe evenly.

For a small space in time, he had been hers. Or at least she had thought so. It almost hurt to look at him. *This* was why she needed him to leave. There was no way she could go through the rest of her life seeing him; a constant reminder of what she would never have.

"Emma," was all he said. They stood there for a few moments and the silence roared in her ears.

She cleared her throat. There was a permanent lump that had taken up residence there over the past couple of days, but she was learning to talk around it. "I came to tell you I'm unable to fulfill my obligation at the summer festival. I won't be there tomorrow."

Confusion creased his brow. "Why not?"

She fought to keep her voice steady, but she couldn't help the needle-thin tremor that stitched each word together. "My shop—everything. It's all been ruined." Emma plunged ahead, filling him in on what had happened. As she spoke, Hunter's expression grew darker, his eyes glittering with suppressed anger.

"I'm just here to let you know that you'll be solely in charge of the catering tomorrow, since I have nothing to sell. Also," she said, and swallowed hard. "Also, I probably won't be able to make rent on my shop, so it looks like you can go ahead and do what you want with it. Or maybe you were planning on doing that anyway. I don't know." She couldn't look at him. She looked at the doorframe, the floor. "So that's all."

Hunter said nothing and for a moment Emma wished she could just disappear. She wished she could collapse in on herself like a dying star until nothing was left but a blank space. Then maybe she wouldn't have to feel.

He placed his hand on her shoulder and pulled her into his warm embrace. "I'm so sorry," he whispered.

She wasn't going to cry. She wasn't. Except her face was wet all over again and he smelled so familiar and felt so warm and wonderful. He was the enemy, but she wanted his comfort anyway. Everything was so messed up.

"Emma," he murmured into her hair. "We can fix it."

She was shaking her head. "No, we can't. We can't. Everything's ruined, don't you get that?"

"Not ruined," he said forcefully. He drew back and held her face between his big, warm hands. "That's what I've been trying to tell you, but you wouldn't answer your phone or see me. Sam said you needed time, but it's been damn hard to stay away. I don't want to lose you like this. I'm so sorry I asked you to leave your shop and come work for me. That was"—he grimaced—"that was asinine of me. I was an idiot to think you'd just walk away from everything you love. Emma, please," he said, and hugged her again, so tight she felt the air *whoosh* out of her. "Please don't give up on us. We can fix this. I already have. I'm not ever going to tear down Fairy Cakes, not if you want to keep it. I understand that it's as much a part of you as this island. It's part of what you call home. I'm not ever going to take that away from you."

She was afraid to believe what he had just said. He wanted her to keep her shop? "But it's been vandalized. Half of my equipment is ruined beyond repair, and I'll never make my financial quota for the festival tomorrow. Everything's over for me. I won't be able to stay afloat, anyway."

"Yes, you will. You'll think of something because you are an amazing, brilliant, talented woman. I'll help you. I want to help you. If you'll let me." He stroked her face with one hand. "Please don't push me away. I—" Hunter stared down at the ground for a moment.

Emma held her breath, though she didn't know why. The wind swirled around them suddenly, and Emma could almost hear that whispering melody she had heard earlier in her kitchen.

Hunter clenched his jaw and lifted his head. "Emma, I don't want to lose you. I'll do whatever you want. You're too precious to me."

Her mouth opened on a tiny inhale. "Oh." Then he was kissing her, and she was kissing him back, and everything else and all the problems and all the worries fell away, and the world was just the two of them, standing there in the moonlight. A little while later, he leaned against the doorframe and smiled down at her. She could feel a silly grin splitting her face.

"Everything's such a mess, though," she said, swiping at her tears.

He nodded, then took her hand. "You don't know the half of it. Come here, I have something to show you." Emma followed, dazed, as he led her into the huge industrial kitchen. Everything was state-of-the-art gorgeous, bringing into stark relief the contrast of her tiny, ruined shop. The new equipment and ovens gleamed and there was enough space for an army of cooks. On the kitchen island, sealed boxes of pastries were stacked halfway to the ceiling. Hunter opened a box of croissants, and held one out to her.

"Taste this," he commanded.

Emma frowned at him, then looked at the croissant. "I'm not very hungry."

"Just taste it. Please?" He held it out.

Emma took the croissant and bit a small corner,

chewing carefully. She coughed, then swallowed. "It's—"

"—Stale," he finished. "They all are. I ordered this shipment last week from Seattle. My kitchen staff was so busy working on the new menu for the grand opening tomorrow, that I thought it would be easier to ship the pastries in from the mainland. And now, I'm stuck with all these boxes and they're useless." He turned toward her and gripped her shoulders softly. "You see, Emma? I'm an idiot. All this time you've been trying to tell me to pay attention to what's important, and I was too busy with the finances and investments. I wasn't looking at the details. The bakery that made these stocks some of the hotel chains in Seattle, so I just assumed everything would go according to my plans. But I didn't check the quality and now, I'm screwed."

Emma slowly walked around the kitchen island. It was big enough for ten people to sunbathe on. She peered into the boxes of croissants, muffins, and cookies. "Are you sure they're all stale?"

"I checked. They're garbage."

"So without your catering, or mine, there won't be much in the way of vendor food at the festival tomorrow."

Hunter placed his hands on his hips and stared at her intently. She had come to recognize that gleam in his eyes. He had a plan. "Unless we do it together."

"What do you mean? My shop is ruined. It will take me days to clean up and repair the damage."

"We have my place. The kitchens, the ovens. It's all ready to go."

Emma glanced around at the industrial-size ovens. The sleek pantry shelves, stacked with everything she could ever need. It was a baker's dream come true. And it could work, she realized. There was so much space, they could work through the night and have more than enough inventory.

"You want me to work here? Tonight?"

Hunter shook his head. "No, I don't want you to work here. I want you to help me, because I need you. But only if you want to. And I want you to let me help you. We could do it together."

Emma ran her hands along the shelves. She walked over to the brand-new ovens, taking in the diamond-bright appliances. Her limbs began to buzz with brightly coiled energy. They could do this. They could make it work. "We don't have much time."

"No, we don't. But I bet if we worked together, we could do it." Several moments of silence passed between them.

"But this is your inventory. These are your supplies. All mine are gone."

"We'll share the profits," he said decisively. "Though you'll get more, because I'm just supplying the raw ingredients. That's nothing compared to what you do."

"No, we have to split it evenly," she insisted.

"We can argue about that later. Tell me you're in." He placed his hands on her shoulders and kissed her, a mischievous glint in his eyes. It was the same look he had when he recounted the tale of his GI Joes waging battle on his mother's tulip garden. "Are you in?"

"This is crazy," Emma said, unable to stop the grin that stretched across her face.

"Yes." He rested his forehead on hers. "That's how I know it's right."

They worked together in perfect synthesis. Hunter had no idea how to bake, but he made an excellent understudy. Emma pulled out all the recipes from memory that would be the easiest to create in bulk. Chocolate and vanilla cupcake batters, with several different frostings to distinguish them. She should have been worried that she didn't have her grandmother's recipe book with her, but she felt nothing but exhilaration.

An hour into baking, Emma rummaged in her tote bag for her phone. She dialed Juliette and explained where she was.

"Are you kidding me right now?" Juliette asked. "You're really in Hunter's kitchen with him. Baking."

"That's right," Emma said. "We're going to be here pretty late, so can you take Buddy until tomorrow?"

Juliette agreed, then added, "Be careful."

"Why?" Emma asked.

"Oh just, you know. It seems like whenever you and Hunter find yourselves alone in a kitchen . . ."

"Right," Emma said, glancing at Hunter. He had rolled his shirtsleeves up to his elbows, revealing tanned, muscled forearms, and he was licking chocolate frosting from a spoon. It was far more distracting than she wanted to admit. "We'll be fine."

When Emma said good-bye and tossed her phone back into her tote, a single leaf of paper slid out and fluttered to the floor. She knew what it was before she even picked it up. Emma cradled the ancient recipe in her hands, a twinge of nervous excitement settling in her stomach. It was "Bliss Day," the recipe her grandmother had said was nothing but discord and heartache. Somehow it had made its way into her purse. She tilted her head to the ceiling and wanted to laugh. The house was nothing if not persistent.

Emma was about to tuck the paper back into her bag, when she stopped, stunned.

"What is it?" Hunter asked, eyeing her as he washed utensils in the sink.

"It's just . . . this recipe," Emma murmured.

The recipe never worked for her grandmother,

331

but that's because she had the last ingredient wrong. With diamond clarity, Emma suddenly understood why her grandmother hated that recipe. It was the one she must have used for her picnic all those years ago with Sam. The purple cupcake. Her grandmother had been trying to create a day of bliss for herself. The thought flooded Emma with a sudden heartache for her grandmother. If only she had used the correct recipe. Would it have worked as it was supposed to? Would her grandmother have married Sam? Would Emma have ever been born?

She sighed and brushed her fingers lightly over the aged paper. She would never know the answer to that, but she ached for her grandmother's loss. Life was so unpredictable, and sometimes seemed too fragile to bear. But what could be done about it? The best anyone could do was to be brave and hold on, and try to love each other no matter what. In the end, that was the only thing that mattered. It was the only thing you carried with you.

Emma now knew she held the true recipe for "Bliss Day" in her hands. What if she let herself be brave? What if she threw caution to the wind and just tried it? It was rumored to create the happiest of days to all who tasted it, even a Holloway. God only knew she could use a little bit of bliss.

Turning to Hunter, she laid the recipe on the

counter. "This is an ancient recipe from my grandmother's book."

"I can see that." He peered down at the faded leaf of paper.

"It's rumored to bring about a day of bliss for everyone, including Holloways."

Hunter glanced up at her and shrugged. "We'd better get to work, then."

Emma wanted to laugh. He made everything seem so simple. Maybe it was.

A sense of carefree happiness rolled softly over her skin as she glanced at the recipe. The ingredients were simple enough, but the measurements weren't precise. She would have to go with her instincts this time, just like her grandmother had always urged her to do. Emma closed her eyes and found that for the first time, she wasn't afraid. She was . . . excited. She felt stronger than she had ever felt before. A soft breeze floated into the kitchen and Emma heard the faint whispering on the wind as it surrounded her, lifting the curls around her temples. This was her calling, and she had the power. She could do this.

"Hunter, could you do me a favor?" she asked.

He leaned against the edge of the kitchen counter, crossing his arms. A soft smile played about his lips. "Anything. You're in charge here."

"Remember that lilac tree in my secret lunch spot? The one you were beating with that stick?"

He cocked his head to one side and gave her a sheepish grin. "I do."

"Can you go and grab me a few sprigs of lilac?" The recipe called for lilac petals, not lavender, and what better place to get lilac than the bushes she and Juliette had planted when they were little girls? Emma had always loved those lilac trees. It seemed right that they should be a key ingredient in this ancient recipe. For the first time in her life, Emma was going to listen to her instincts and "go with the flow." After all that had happened, it was the only thing left she could do.

Hunter brought the lilac petals as Emma mixed up the ingredients. He proved to be a very attentive understudy, placing and pulling trays from the ovens, watching the timers, washing dishes as she started on the next batch. Throughout the night, Emma used the huge mixers to throw together basic cookie dough, adding different ingredients to different batches, based on her instincts. Chocolate chips, cranberries, toasted almonds, crushed toffee bars. Her skills didn't only translate to cupcakes, and there was freedom in allowing herself to try other recipes. She was filled with a carefree sense of abandon, a sort of reckless joy she had never experienced before. A soft smile kissed the corners of her mouth as she worked. She was having the time of her life.

The "Bliss Day" cupcakes proved to be

gorgeous, each one of them a perfect vanilla concoction with the faintest of lilac frosting. Emma knew without a doubt that they were going to work, and she felt a wild rush of happiness at what she had just accomplished. For the first time in her life, she had embraced her gift completely and used her instincts. This was what her grandmother had wanted her to do. This was what she was born to do.

Somewhere before dawn, Hunter pulled the last tray out of the oven. The sweet scents of chocolate and cinnamon enveloped the entire kitchen. He set the tray on the counter and they stared at each other in companionable silence. The energy flowing back and forth between them permeated the whole room with passion and joy. She scanned the neatly wrapped boxes of cupcakes and freshly baked cookies with deep satisfaction. Without a doubt, these would be the most uplifting charms she had ever created.

They were both exhausted, but the air still crackled with possibilities.

"Do you want some coffee?" Hunter asked, nudging her with his shoulder.

"Mmm." Emma yawned and stretched her aching muscles. "What time is it?"

"Just past four o'clock. Almost time to wake up and set up the stalls." They had to set up their tents by seven o'clock to begin prepping for the crowds.

"We are going to be dead on our feet today," she laughed.

He gathered her up and murmured into her ear. "But we did it." He kissed her cheek. "*You* did it."

"You helped," she said, swiping flour from his hair. "I would have had a hard time doing this alone."

"I would have had an *impossible* time doing this alone. It's all because of you." He kissed her again, nuzzling into the sensitive hollow of her neck. Emma's body flooded with warmth and yearning.

"So about that coffee," she said.

"Forget coffee." He lifted her up and carried her to the door. "Come home with me. To bed."

"We have to start setting up in three hours," Emma laughed.

He placed tiny kisses along her collarbone. "Not nearly enough time, but I'm game if you are."

"You're crazy," she whispered.

"Yes," he said wickedly. "Are you in?"

She was.

Chapter Twenty-Eight

Emma didn't even care that her clothes were the same things she wore yesterday, hastily laundered in Hunter's machine when they had arrived at his house several hours earlier. She smoothed her T-shirt over her jeans and blushed at the memory of them stumbling through his front door in a heated rush. They had been so consumed with each other, it was a wonder she had remembered to throw her clothes in the wash at all. But now, with the summer festival in full swing and her hair tied back in a ponytail, she had never felt more beautiful.

She spotted him walking toward Haven on the other side of the wharf. He glanced back and smiled at her, and she could feel his warm gaze all the way to her toes. Hunter's grand opening had been advertised in Seattle and the surrounding Puget Sound areas, and more tourists were visiting than ever before.

They had set up their vending tents side by side, on one corner of the square. Molly and three of Hunter's staff were busy selling the cookies and cupcakes they had painstakingly created through the night.

James Sullivan had been checking in with Molly throughout the day, buying cookies for some of his nephews or coffee for himself. From the number of cups he had purchased, and the way he was flirting with her, it was pretty clear he was smitten. Molly seemed pleased by his attention, even though she pretended to ignore him.

Emma smiled secretly to herself. Today was turning out so much better than she expected. No doubt her hasty breakfast of a "Bliss Day" cupcake and coffee had something to do with it. A day of bliss, indeed.

Mrs. Mooney sidled up to the cupcake stand with a triumphant smile. Today she wore a batik caftan with purple eyeshadow and a matching purple flower pinned in her hair. Poor Bonbon was clutched under her arm like a designer bag reject, his claws painted lilac.

"Well, what an amazing success you've had today," Mrs. Mooney burbled. "And my dear, I have even better news." She turned and waved over a young couple. "This is Tom and Betsy."

The man carried a little boy on his shoulders and the woman was holding a baby. The adorable baby gave her a gummy grin.

Mrs. Mooney beamed. "They're looking to adopt a puppy, and I told them about Buddy needing a home!"

Emma's smile faltered. "Oh." She stared out across the field where Juliette was taking Buddy on a walk through the festival. He scampered around on his leash, sniffing joyfully at everything he encountered. Emma had grown so fond of having him in her life, she hadn't realized how much she needed him until she was faced with the prospect of losing him.

The woman named Betsy smiled warmly and shifted her baby to the other hip. "Now that our son will be starting kindergarten, we wanted to add a puppy to the family. Yesterday we met Mrs. Mooney in her shop. She mentioned you had a puppy who needed a home."

Emma tried to nod, but failed. Instead, she found herself shaking her head. She just couldn't give him up. That day Juliette had shown up with him at her house seemed like a million years ago. He belonged with her and the house now. They were family. It might not be the typical family with parents and kids, but it was still real. "I'm so sorry, but I've decided to keep him. I've found I just can't live without him."

The woman nodded her understanding. After they said good-bye, Emma turned to Mrs. Mooney. "Thank you for trying. They really seemed like the perfect family. I'm sorry I had to say no."

"Sorry?" Mrs. Mooney cackled. "I'm thrilled you're keeping him. I didn't want to sway your decision but Bonbon would have been so heartbroken to lose his friend."

In a rush of gratitude, Emma gave Mrs. Mooney

a hug. As she squeezed the woman tight, Bonbon licked her cheek.

Emma pulled back and stared wide-eyed at the little dog.

He snarled politely.

Emma blinked. Maybe it wasn't an actual snarl. She tilted her head and squinted her eyes.

His gums lifted around the edges to reveal snaggled teeth. To Emma, it almost looked like the dog version of a smile.

She reached out and patted his head. "Thanks for the kiss, Bonbon."

Mrs. Mooney nodded her approval. "That's my good boy. He's always had impeccable manners, did you know?"

"Mmm." Emma gave them free cupcakes and waved as Mrs. Mooney wandered away, her purple caftan billowing behind her.

"Coffee?" murmured a voice behind her. Emma smiled and turned to find Hunter standing there.

"Definitely." She took the cup he offered, and felt another swell of the giddiness that had permeated her brain all day. They had spent two blissful hours at his place early that morning. Who knew what would happen next? All she knew was she'd finally be able to pay her mortgage, her shop wasn't going to be torn down, and he wanted to be with her. It wasn't perfect, she knew that. But what was?

He wrapped an arm around her waist and smiled

340

down at her. Maybe the truth was, there was no such thing as "perfect." Maybe you just hoped for the best and held on and weathered whatever came next. Maybe the answer was that life would always be uncertain, but it was so much sweeter when shared with someone you love.

And she really loved him. Emma knew it with a certainty that eclipsed every other emotion. Even if he didn't love her back, she had to be honest with herself. No matter what happened next, she deserved that.

She leaned her head against him and sighed. "I think I've met my quota ten times over today. And I've got some catering contracts lined up for the rest of the summer. Things are definitely looking up."

"Yes." He bent closer and murmured, "When this is over, I say you come home with me so we can celebrate."

Emma laughed. "Aren't you exhausted? It's five o'clock and I'm about to keel over."

Hunter had spent the day back and forth between their vendor booths and his restaurant. The floor manager had assured him everything was going smoothly, aside from the low variety of baked goods and desserts, but the stellar lunch menu made up for that. All in all, things were going better than he had thought possible.

"Sure I'm tired." He winked. "But some things are more important than sleep."

Emma stared at his mouth. Sleep? Pshaw. Who needed sleep? It was totally overrated. Then she remembered Buddy. "I want to, but I have to go home. Juliette's been taking care of Buddy, but I need to feed him." She gestured to the till as Molly handed a tourist a bag of cookies and made change. "I also have to take the money home. But you can come with me. I mean, if you want?"

She felt shy all of a sudden, and worried he might say no. As much as she vowed to embrace whatever came her way, the little girl inside her still wanted assurances that everything was going to be okay. That same little girl wished so much that she could just skip to the end of the story to make sure.

"I want that very much," he said.

Warmth radiated through her body. Elation. That was the feeling. Emma wanted to kiss him right there, in front of everyone, but she didn't get the chance, because he kissed her first. Hunter brushed his lips against hers, and everything around them fell away.

Molly giggled.

James clapped.

Gertie and Walter hooted from across the field.

Emma smiled against Hunter's mouth. "I think we have an audience."

"Then we better make it good." He kissed her again, slowly, softly, thoroughly, and she melted against him. For one perfect moment, the pages of her story seemed to flip to the end and Emma glimpsed nothing but happiness.

Looking back, she often wondered if she could have stopped what came next. If only she could have done something different that day. If only she had known.

Chapter Twenty-Nine

Later that evening, Hunter parked his car in Emma's driveway. The day had been successful, but it wasn't over yet. There were things he needed to say to Emma, and he wasn't going to wait until tomorrow. He had waited long enough, and he knew now, more than ever, what he truly wanted.

She yawned as they walked toward the house. "I say we feed Buddy, then jump into bed and sleep for the next forty-eight hours."

He settled an arm around her waist and breathed in the honeysuckle and vanilla scent of her hair as they approached the front porch. "Sounds like a solid plan, but you're missing a very important step."

"What step?"

"The one that goes after 'jumping in bed' and before 'sleep.'"

Emma grinned and began to comment, but the porch light flickered a warning.

The hair on the back of Hunter's neck stood on end. Something was wrong.

Emma gave a choked gasp. "The window."

The narrow glass window that ran parallel to the front door was smashed. A surge of adrenaline shot through him and he stepped in front of her.

"Wait here," he commanded.

Emma shot him an incredulous look. "No freaking way."

Of course she wouldn't wait. This was Emma he was dealing with.

She ignored his scowl and set Buddy in the grass to roam the yard, where he'd be safe.

"At least let me go first," he said.

Emma looked like she was going to protest, but—thank God for small mercies—she stepped aside and let him lead. A crash came from the kitchen, and when they reached the porch, the door swung silently open for them.

"Thanks, house," Hunter whispered. So, yeah. He talked to houses now. What of it? They crept toward the kitchen, then stopped in the doorway and stared.

Rodney Winters was rifling through the cupboards, flinging dishes behind him and cursing as they crashed to the floor. He was stupid drunk; that much was clear. The scent of unwashed male, whiskey, and cigarettes permeated the air.

Hunter drew his phone and dailed 911, reflexively stepping in front of Emma to keep her safe.

One of the kitchen drawers flew open, clipping Rodney's hip. He turned and ripped the drawer out, tossing it across the tiled floor. "Damned haunted house," he muttered, then yelled, "Where's the money?"

He yanked another drawer out and flung it across the tiles. The curtains in the kitchen window rustled and doors slammed throughout the house.

"Rodney, stop!" Emma pushed her way past Hunter.

Adrenaline spiked and Hunter reached for her, dropping the phone before he could answer the operator. He didn't want Emma anywhere near the man. Over the years, Hunter had seen his fair share of people who had drunk too much and gone off the deep end. In this state, Rodney was dangerous.

Emma wiggled out of Hunter's grasp as Rodney turned bloodshot eyes on them. His face contorted into a sneer, then darkened into something sharp and menacing. "Where's the money, Emma? There's nothing in the tin and I know you have some. You always have a stash." His gaze darted around, jerking from her to Hunter and back again.

Hunter studied Rodney, noting the twitching limbs, the dilated eyes. He had to be on something stronger than just alcohol.

"I see you've brought your *friend* home with you," Rodney sneered. "I had her first, asshole. Back when she used to be sweet. Isn't that right, Angel? Tell him how good you used to be for me."

Hunter felt his vision go dark around the

edges. He took a step closer, hands clenched into fists.

"Shut up, Rodney," Emma said.

"Where's the money?" Rodney spat. He lurched forward, grabbing Emma roughly by the arms, shaking her.

She cried out.

A white-hot fury sliced through Hunter. He launched himself at Rodney, backing him against the kitchen cabinets. "Don't touch her," he said flatly. *"Ever."*

Rodney shoved at him, but Hunter didn't budge. He knew he had the upper hand, but he couldn't afford to let his guard down. Rodney was a weaker man, but drugs made a person unpredictable. Hunter wrestled against Rodney's flailing arms, pinning him to the counter.

With a frantic twist, Rodney whipped his arm out, catching Hunter on the side of the head with a plate.

A sharp pain seared across the side of Hunter's head. He reeled backward as shattered porcelain rained over the kitchen floor.

"No!" Emma cried.

Rodney laughed, dropping the broken dish he had used as a weapon.

Hunter caught himself against the edge of the kitchen island as blood spilled from the gash on his head, filling his eyes.

Rodney yanked something from an upended

drawer. The butcher knife flashed sharp and silver in his hand, then he launched himself at Hunter.

Hunter twisted sideways, but a hot, excruciating pain spiked through the side of his rib cage as Rodney shoved forward, slamming Hunter back against the countertop.

Emma screamed.

Hunter blindly reached for something to use as a weapon. Anything. A small glass dome with a single cupcake on it. It was the only thing within reach. He grappled, knocking the lid to the floor in a shower of broken glass. His hand made contact with the platter, and he hurled it at Rodney with all the strength he had left.

The glass platter hit Rodney's face with a solid *crack*.

Rodney roared and dropped the knife. He grabbed his nose, blood spurting between his fingers. "You broke my nose," he bellowed in a hoarse voice that hitched on a gurgle. "I'll kill you for that."

Hunter kicked the knife across the tiles, just as the room tilted sideways and he slumped onto the floor. He was vaguely aware of Emma throwing herself over him. He wanted to shield her, to protect her, but his limbs were too heavy and he couldn't get up.

"Don't try to move," Emma cried.

Through slitted eyes, Hunter watched Rodney

wiping bits of frosting and cake from his face and mouth.

"This thing tastes like shit," Rodney spat. "No wonder your business is going under."

"Get out of my house." Emma slowly stood, her voice shaking with the fury of a thousand storms. A swirling wind blew in through the open window and Hunter thought he heard whispers joining with the sound of Emma's voice. "Leave and never return," she said. "In this, my will be done."

The wind grew louder and more frenzied until it seemed to spin around the kitchen like a vortex. Broken bits of dishes scattered on the floor and Hunter could feel the force of it as it swept through the room.

The sound of police cars pierced through the night outside.

Rodney didn't try to run. He stayed frozen in place, licking at the bits of frosting and cake clinging to his mouth. He had a confused, stunned look on his face.

Hunter's vision began to blur and everything grew colder. He blinked, focusing on Emma's face above him. She was crying. He lifted one hand and tried to touch her hair.

"It's going to be okay," he whispered. His eyelids felt heavy. He wanted to tell her so many things, but he couldn't focus.

Police officers poured into the kitchen.

Someone was reading Rodney his rights. The last thing Hunter saw was Emma's face. She was leaning over him saying something over and over. He wanted to reply, but the room grew dark around the edges and then there was silence.

Chapter Thirty

Hunter floated in the space between wakefulness and sleep. Milestones of his life ebbed and flowed around him; snippets of faded memories. The scent of lemon oil on the polished hardwood floors of his house when he was very young. His father's impatient smile as Hunter showed him he had learned to ride a bike. The nanny teaching him table manners. His mother's pearls, yanked off in a drunken argument with his father, the white beads scattering and bouncing off the floor. The strawberry bubblegum taste of his first kiss in middle school and the squeaky sound of tennis shoes on the gymnasium floor.

Then there were other memories from when he grew older; the suntan lotion scent of a college girlfriend on a trip to the beach. The noisy, colorful jumble of patrons in pubs and restaurants. The sleek, floor-to-ceiling windows overlooking the Puget Sound, and a woman standing in front of them, her lips pursed in judgment. Melinda, his ex-girlfriend. There was nothing warm or comforting about her. She had always been calculating, and cold. Hunter wondered how he had ever thought her desirable.

He struggled through the haze to the only memory that mattered: Emma.

Latching on to the thought of her, he willed her face to appear in his mind. Clear gray eyes, soft skin, a riot of golden hair. A smile so genuine and true that everything else faded away. She was the only thing that mattered. When he saw Rodney grab and shake her, he had wanted to tear the man apart. The force of his emotions should have alarmed him, but it didn't. Hunter realized in that moment what he should have admitted to himself sooner: He loved Emma Holloway. He hadn't realized how much until the moment he thought he could truly lose her. And no matter what came next, he needed to let her know.

Hunter shifted on the bed, slowly becoming aware of his surroundings. He could hear the soft whir of a machine near his head, and the rhythmic footsteps of someone pacing the room. With infuriating slowness, he focused on the light behind his eyelids, and willed himself to wake up.

Emma paced the tiny hospital room, glancing at Hunter as he lay sleeping on the bed. It had been a heart-wrenching several hours, but the doctor had assured her he was going to be okay. The knife had gone through his left side. He had lost a lot of blood, but thankfully, no serious damage to vital organs. She took the seat next to his hospital bed and softly stroked his forearm.

The news that Hunter was going to be okay

made her cry all over again. She now knew there was no amount of magic that could ever make her stop feeling what she felt for him. Even if the stupid cupcake had succeeded, she would never love another person the way she loved him. Though the magic spell hadn't worked out the way she planned, it did work to her advantage in the end. Rodney had been hauled off by the police, and he was being transferred to prison where he'd stay locked up for a very long time.

A nurse poked her head in the doorway. "Ms. Holloway? There's someone here to see you."

"Me?" Emma asked. Who would come to see her? Juliette, Gertie, and Molly had already visited with flowers and kisses and hugs of reassurance. There was no one else Emma knew who would come to the hospital. Hunter's mother had been contacted, but she was somewhere in Europe, and his father hadn't been available.

Emma glanced up as Bethany Andrews stepped into the room.

"Bethany." Emma could barely hide her shock at seeing the other woman. "What are you doing here?"

Bethany jerked out her hand. She was holding a bouquet of carnations from the hospital gift shop downstairs. The tag was still on it but she had made an effort, which was mind-boggling.

Emma reached out and took them.

"I just came to say something, and then I'll go,"

Bethany said. She straightened the hem of her fuchsia top, yanking it down over her painted-on jeggings. "I came to apologize."

Emma eyed her warily. A pig may have just flown past the window. "What?"

Bethany crossed her arms, her wrists jangling with charm bracelets. "I said some things to Rodney when we were drinking at O'Malley's Pub the other night. It was the night he vandalized your shop. I think it may have been my fault."

Emma shook her head, confused. "How was that your fault?"

Bethany pressed her lips together, then rushed on. "Look. I was angry because I wanted Hunter but he wasn't interested, all right? Apparently, he wants"—her perfect forehead creased as she swept Emma up and down, clearly baffled—*"you."*

Emma had no idea what to say. "I don't understand."

Bethany heaved a sigh. "Listen. I was at O'Malley's that night, and Rodney showed up. We hung out and talked for a couple of hours, and we were drinking. Drinking a lot, okay?" She glared at Emma as if she wanted to make that part very clear. "Anyway, I said some things, and he said some things. And I mentioned something about how you put all your money into your stupid cupcake shop."

Emma crossed her arms. If Bethany came to

apologize, she was doing a crap job of it.

"I only meant that it was all you had," Bethany rushed to add. "And you didn't have much else going for you." She didn't seem to realize her explanation wasn't helping.

"What are you getting at, Bethany? Just spit it out."

Bethany looked taken aback by Emma's tone. She scowled and tossed a lock of hair from her shoulders. "I'm trying to say I think I may have planted the idea in Rodney's head. The idea that you kept all your money in your cupcake shop, or something. I never thought he'd go breaking in and ruining the place. And then what he did to Hunter after the festival . . ." She gestured to Hunter sleeping in the bed. "I'm just sorry it happened. And I wanted you to know I didn't mean to say things that would make Rodney go and do that."

Clearly, Bethany wasn't used to apologizing. She was glaring and tapping her foot, as if she was annoyed with herself for stooping so low as to apologize to a Holloway.

Emma had to hand it to the woman. At least she was trying. "Rodney is responsible for his own actions. It wasn't your fault."

"I didn't really think it was," Bethany assured her. She cocked a hip and placed a manicured hand on her waist. "Anyway, there's the flowers." She pointed to the bouquet Emma was holding.

"Thanks," Emma said. "I'll make sure Hunter gets them."

Bethany rolled her eyes again and gave her a look that said she was dumber than dirt. "They're not for him."

Emma's mouth opened in a surprise.

Bethany glanced around the room, avoiding Emma's gaze. "I just thought, you know. I'm sorry about what Rodney did, and what happened to Hunter. Anyway, I'm glad he's going to be okay and I hope you guys are . . . happy." She grimaced. "Or, whatever." She let out a frustrated breath. "Look, I have to go. Enjoy the flowers, all right?" She turned to leave.

"Wait," Emma said.

Bethany spun around, scowling. *"What?"*

Yeah, they weren't going to be BFFs anytime soon. "Thank you for letting me know," Emma said quietly. "And none of it was your fault."

After Bethany left, Emma walked over to the bed and glanced down at Hunter.

The sight of him, so vulnerable with the IV tube in his arm, made the reality of what had happened come crashing back. She swiped at her eyes with the back of her hand. Whatever happened next didn't matter. All that mattered was he was alive.

Her head throbbed and her eyes felt raw from crying. There was no getting around it. She loved him so much, it hurt. Seeing him lying on her kitchen floor, his torso covered in blood, had been the most terrifying thing she had ever witnessed. The thought of losing him made it hard to breathe. It wasn't right. No one should have this much power over a person, but he had it over her. He mattered more to her than anything else in the world. And she had almost lost him.

"When you wake up," she said shakily, "I'm going to kill you."

A choked cough.

Startled, Emma's gaze flew to his face. Bright green eyes were fixed on her, and he was laughing.

Emma jumped up from the chair and leaned over him.

"This is what I have to look forward to?" he wheezed.

She bent and kissed his face. Kissed it again. "You scared me to death. I thought you weren't going to make it."

He reached a hand up and settled it lightly on her head. "I'm okay," he whispered. "I'm still here."

A tidal wave of guilt washed over her. "But you almost died. You could have! And it would have all been my fault."

"How is any of this your fault?" He softly stroked her head.

Emma took a shaky breath. "Listen to me. There's something you need to know. I haven't been honest with you. Juliette and I combined our magic to create that chocolate cupcake you smashed into Rodney's face. It was meant for you. It was supposed to make you leave town and never come back. Because I never meant . . ." Emma pulled away from him, wringing her hands. She had to tell him the truth. "I never meant to fall in love with you."

She couldn't look at him, too afraid to see disappointment or anger or indifference on his face. Instead, she stared at the wall on the other side of his bed. "I was hurt when you asked me to manage your bakery. And then when you said you were going to live in Seattle, and visit occasionally, I realized you didn't feel the same about me. And that's okay," she rushed to add. "It's totally fair. You never promised anything and I never thought I would want more. But I did."

Emma hugged herself and continued. She still couldn't look at him. "So I planned to make you go away forever, so I'd never have to see you again. I thought if you were out of sight, it would hurt less. But that's where I was so wrong. It wouldn't matter where you went. My feelings for you wouldn't change. Not in this world, or the next." She finally dared to glance at him, expecting condemnation in his eyes.

Instead she saw what looked like . . . resolve. What was he thinking? She went back to the chair next to his bed and sat down. "I'm so, so sorry. I will never try to spell you again. Your choices are your own, and I was wrong to try to control that." She stared down at her hands, her cheeks burning. At least now she had finally told him the truth.

"Emma." He reached for her hand and squeezed it. "You *have* bespelled me. And it has nothing to do with herbs and potions. Nothing to do with your recipe book or Juliette's garden plants. I don't care about any of that. What I feel . . ." He paused as though searching for the right words. "I've never felt it before and to be perfectly honest, I never believed it was possible for me. But what I feel for you . . ."

He tried to sit up, wincing.

"Stop," she cried. "You need to lie down."

"No," he said through a clenched jaw. "This is important."

"If you don't lie down right now, Hunter Kane, I will kill you for real," Emma said.

He started laughing, though it obviously pained him. "Come here."

She carefully climbed up and lay beside him.

He lowered his forehead to hers and whispered, "I love you, dammit."

Emma sucked in air. "What?"

"You heard me. I love you. Forget all that idiotic crap I said before about not believing in it. I didn't know what it could be like, but then you made it all real."

A giddy rush of warmth flooded her limbs and her mouth fell open. She couldn't breathe. Wait, yes, she could. He *loved* her.

Hunter gripped her hand in his. "Look, I don't know how this works. I've never been here before. But I know one thing that really matters. I believe in you and I want to be wherever you are."

A tiny thrill of joy zipped along her spine. "Are you sure?" *Dumb question!*

"I've never been more sure about anything in my life," he said solemnly.

"But how do you know it's real?" Another dumb question. *What the hell, Holloway?*

He gave her a molten smile. "Because without you, nothing else matters. And even if you turn me away, I'll be like that man in the lighthouse legend. Always yearning for you. There's no one else for me, Emma. There never will be." He pulled her closer, as if he was afraid she'd disappear. "Tell me you still want to be with me. Tell me you feel the same way."

Emma took a tremulous breath.

He waited, his leaf green eyes intent on her face.

She grinned and exhaled on a "yes."

Then they were laughing and kissing and whispering to each other in a way that could only be described as dopey-in-love-struck, but Emma couldn't remember a time she had ever felt happier. Hunter told her the first thing he wanted to do was make arrangements to move to Pine Cove Island, for good. Emma admitted she might like to branch out and sell her creations in both their establishments, since she had so much success with her new recipes. There was so much to discuss, though their conversation was frequently broken up with more kissing and whispered endearments and—eventually—mingled laughter and apologies to the stern-faced nurse who checked in on her patient and found him *not* resting.

Somewhere outside, thunderclouds began rolling in from the west. The sky cast dark shadows over the sleepy island town and an icy gale blew in off the ocean, gaining momentum until the trees swayed and the grassy fields whipped in the howling wind. Mother Nature was bringing back the storm.

On that day, there was so much rain and hail that for months afterward, the people of Pine Cove Island would talk about it. But Emma and Hunter never saw it.

That day, they only saw each other.

Epilogue

Eight months later

"See, I don't get why that British vampire guy keeps trying." Hunter tossed a piece of popcorn to Buddy, who was sprawled on the sofa beside him. The dog had grown so huge, his legs dangled over the edge of the seat cushions. "I mean, it's clear the woman doesn't like him."

"You're such a newb," Juliette said from the armchair near the TV. "Buffy and Spike are meant to be. Anyone can see they're crazy about each other."

Emma turned from stoking the fire and felt a rush of warmth at the sight of everyone in her living room. Juliette, Hunter, and her dog, watching old *Buffy* reruns on a Friday night. These were her people.

Hunter gently nudged the massive dog aside to make room for Emma. He wore a rumpled T-shirt, needed a shave, and was still the most gorgeous man she had ever seen.

She settled next to him with a contented sigh. It was hard to believe he was a permanent fixture in her life now. In the past several months, so much had changed. He had moved in with her and hired managers to oversee his businesses in Seattle.

The house had a new roof, a new front porch, and fresh paint. Emma had renovated her shop and was now successfully selling her creations at both Fairy Cakes and Haven. She had even created a new recipe for dog biscuits, "Bon Bones," which tickled Mrs. Mooney to no end.

And her house and business weren't the only things that had changed. All the shops on Front Street had benefited from Hunter's ownership. New upgrades were being made, the merchants were reporting higher sales because of the increase in tourist traffic, and Hunter was now a member of the chamber of commerce alongside Sam. They were already planning a community park near the wharf for the upcoming summer.

Hunter slung an arm around Emma and placed a kiss on top of her head. He gestured to the TV as the *Buffy* theme song ended. "But I thought she liked that other guy. The angel without the wings."

Juliette let out an exasperated groan and stood, stretching. "He's not an angel."

"His name is Angel," Emma explained. "But he's not an actual angel. He's more of a demon."

Hunter propped his feet on the coffee table with a sigh. "And you guys wonder why I'm confused."

"Don't worry about it," Juliette said through a yawn. "It takes time to ramp up. You'll get there."

She gathered her patchwork bag and headed to the front entrance.

Buddy heaved himself off the couch and padded after her. The big dog's tail whipped back and forth as she bent to scratch behind his ears.

"Come visit me at the flower shop tomorrow," Juliette called, slipping her bare feet into a pair of shearling boots. "Romeo's serving mulled cider and I'm going to spike it when he's not looking."

Juliette managed Romeo's Florist Shop, and with her knowledge of plants and garden charms, business was booming. There was even a shelf in the store devoted to her handmade soaps and bath products.

She gave Buddy one last pat on the head, waved good-bye, and disappeared into the night. The house shut the door behind her, but not before an icy blast of February wind billowed into the foyer.

"I'll put another log on the fire," Hunter said.

Emma gathered the empty popcorn bowls and walked down the hall into the kitchen. She cocked her head when she heard him speaking in the other room. "What was that?"

"Nothing," he called. "I was talking to the house."

She smiled and placed the bowls in the sink. Lately, Hunter had been having a lot of covert conversations with the house. Once, she caught him muttering to it while he fixed the floor in the attic. Another time, she heard him scolding it in the kitchen, his voice lowered to a whisper. Whatever the issue was, she was grateful for how accepting they both were of each other. When Hunter moved in at the end of the summer, the house had welcomed him with open doors, like he belonged there. And now he talked to the house like it was no big deal; like they were family. The ease with which he had slipped into her life brought her more happiness than she had dared to hope for.

"You know," Emma said, walking back into the living room, "you're beginning to sound like a Holloway. People are going to start calling you eccentric."

Hunter threw her a guilty glance and shoved his hand behind his back.

She stepped closer to the sofa, avoiding Buddy, who was now dozing on the floor. "What's going on?"

He dropped his head back and sighed up at the ceiling.

The window curtains billowed out in a *huff*.

"I had a plan," he said. "But clearly, the house has a different opinion."

"It can be very stubborn like that." She settled beside him on the sofa. "What's the plan?"

He hesitated, then drew a small velvet box from behind his back. With a tentative smile, he opened it to reveal a sparkling engagement ring.

Emma's heart thumped once. Twice. A warm, giddy feeling began unfurling inside her. "It's beautiful," she whispered.

"Do you like it?" He seemed almost nervous as he held it up. "It's okay if you don't. You can pick something else, if you want."

"No." She stared down at the brilliant diamond, bracketed by two crescent-shaped sapphires. The ring was beautiful, but it signified something so precious, it wouldn't have mattered if it were a loop of string. A flood of emotion swept over her and she gave him a tremulous smile. "It's perfect."

He glanced at the ring, then back at her. "I've had it for a couple of weeks, but I was planning to take you someplace special so I could do it right. I hid it in my desk drawer, but it kept appearing in front of me, wherever I went. When I was in the attic fixing the floors last week, I pulled up a floorboard and there it was. Yesterday, I found it in the kitchen cupboard when I went to make coffee. And just now, it showed up here on the sofa. Apparently, the house thinks it's time."

The clock on the mantel chimed once, and Hunter laughed. "To hell with my plans. The house is right, anyway. I don't want to wait any longer." He took the ring from the box and fixed his emerald gaze on hers.

"Emma, will you—"

She kissed him, because she couldn't help it.

"—marry me?"

She kissed him again, because her happiness was too much to contain.

He pulled her into his arms and murmured, "I'm really hoping that's a 'yes.' "

She laughed and wiped her eyes. "Of course, yes."

When he slid the ring on her finger, a sudden breeze swirled into the room. It caressed the hair on their temples and brushed over their lips and eyelashes. Emma felt as though they were being blessed, and a fierce sense of joy rocketed through her at the rightness of it. There was powerful magic in the air, and this time she knew it was just for them. She whispered softly in Hunter's ear and he grinned, then chased her up the stairs.

The lights in the room dimmed, then winked out.

The curtains drew quietly closed.

The dog sighed happily in his sleep.

And the house settled in a satisfied *hmph*.

Books are produced in the United States using U.S.-based materials

Books are printed using a revolutionary new process called THINKtech™ that lowers energy usage by 70% and increases overall quality

Books are durable and flexible because of Smyth-sewing

Paper is sourced using environmentally responsible foresting methods and the paper is acid-free

Center Point Large Print
600 Brooks Road / PO Box 1
Thorndike, ME 04986-0001 USA

(207) 568-3717

US & Canada:
1 800 929-9108
www.centerpointlargeprint.com